BOOKS BY

FREDERIC MORTON

THE SCHATTEN AFFAIR

FREDERIC MORTON

THE
SCHATTEN
AFFAIR

NEW YORK

ATHENEUM

1965

For my wife

CONTENTS

"I suppose when you feel the absence of God as strongly as that, it's known as faith."

ROMAIN GARY, *The Ski Bum*

INITIATION

1

I STEPPED OUT of the plane, and the interesting thing is not that he noticed me. I'm sure he'd had a description. The point is that I noticed him. I knew neither him nor the fact that he existed. I was still lightheaded from my Paris bout with the flu. The propellers and the stewardesses and those efficient Berlin airport signs, chockful of cheer and of arrows, danced about me. But I knew immediately that the distant figure was waiting for me. In fact, at first I thought he was Prince Schatten, graciously coming to meet me for our appointment that afternoon. I think I stripped off my gloves to carry the pair suavely in the left hand, right hand free for an affable handshake. Then I realized that the Prince wouldn't greet anyone at the airport—much too great, too difficult, too old. Still the figure kept coming at me. It was someone in uniform, with a visored hat wedged under his armpit and a ludicrous blond goatee under a strapping chin.

"Mister Spey?"

He hardly stopped walking as he brought his heels together. And barely touching my arm, he somehow

managed to grip it. He was, of course, only a chauffeur
—a chauffeur named KarlHeinz, to judge from his
murmured introduction. But with his touch my luggage
whisked past the VIP gate of the customs, the official
there waving it through with a bow. With KarlHeinz's
touch a photographer was evoked, half kneeling as he
aimed a flashbulb at me. With that touch all the options I
might have had up to this point vanished. Up to this point
my cold could have relapsed; I could have missed my
appointment with the Prince and therefore all of Schatten; a telegram might have arrived from New York to
crush the whole thing. But KarlHeinz touched me. The
luggage zoomed, the flashbulb leaped, and I was off down
a street that was forty days long and relentlessly one-
way. KarlHeinz touched me, skimmed me past barriers,
luggage carts, loudspeaker welcomes, and deposited me in
a Mercedes "300" next to his boss, Dr. Ida Holze, head of
the Berlin Municipal Promotion Bureau.

That's how it started. And since it started, could it have
been stopped? Or is it only arrogance that makes the
important things that happen to us seem so inevitable in
retrospect? Or are we all anvils to rawest chance, all
barely unswatted flies? Or is the ultimate end of human
wisdom imprinted on the most Jewish of typewriter
keys—the question mark?

Hm?

Anyway, Dr. Holze in person. Dr. Holze of the many
letters. She turned out to be a youngish ample woman,
strapped into a lavender tailored suit and tapering into
tiny lavender pumps like a genie into a bottle.

*oo*Wonderful! to meet me! Excellent! to see me recuperated. Privilege! to open a Dowle hotel in Berlin. And fortunate! most fortunate! to have two plans for the opening.

She was extremely English-speaking. Her mouth compensated for the Teutonic *rrr*'s with exaggeratedly perfect Anglo-Saxon *w*'s. After each *w* her plump little lips remained goldfish-pursed in position, prolonging the echo of the phonetic feat.

*oo*Why was it provident! to have two openings planned? Because Dr. Holze's appointment-postponement cable to Prince Schatten had elicited but not the slightest answer. She had wanted to change the date to tomorrow, to give me a recuperation-chance from the trip. Nothing! No consideration for an influenza-convalescent person. No, Dr. Holze, always skeptical in her letters, must now propose dropment of the whole Schatten possibility.

I said I'd better drive on to Schatten just the same, thank you, right after looking at our hotel construction.

My hostess was unbendingly gracious.

"*oo*Wonderful! . . . So—so bull-by-the-horn, no? So American!"

It was the cleanness which struck me during the ride. Berlin was such a clean place. The late-afternoon light was so much clearer and crisper than the lucid Paris light I'd left. Rain had just washed the streets, shined them up for the sunset. Whole quarters of the city flashed past, spic-and-span new, neat rectangular formations of sheer sleekness, glass, concrete, bright pastels, much brighter and happier than new buildings in other cities. I looked for bombed-out ruins, but found them cleverly and prettily hemmed in by green, by weeds tamed into almost-lawns. The division of the city into East and West had also become an attraction, or at least an attractive booklet entitled "The Edge of Freedom," which Dr. Holze pressed into my hand. It featured the Western flags in the most glowing full-color reproductions I've ever seen.

Everything glowed and flickered and didn't exactly cure my post-influenza giddiness. The chauffeur plunged us into the Kurfürstendamm, Berlin's Champs-Elysées. A titanic espresso shop closed around the car: miles of café terraces, along which thousands of glinting clean cups were raised by thousands of matrons, all mutually acquainted, nodding from one end of the landscape to the other. Above these armies of coffee klatsch rose the smooth marble of cinema palaces, and above them a heroic phalanx of movie posters, a mountain range of bosoms, hips and buttocks, all freshly washed.

Dr. Holze's lavender gloves pointed left, pointed right. She *oo*wanted me to know, as a matter of amusement, that the Berlin folklore had given remarkable slang titles to some of these monuments of modern architecture. Like the Memorial Church over there. She pointed at a bomb-wrecked church tower against which a huge piece of skeletal sculpture had been fitted. Now *oo*what *oo*was the official slang name?

To a woman of Dr. Holze's enormous decision, forgetfulness was intolerable. *oo*What *oo*was this slang name? Her tiny tweezed eyebrows tortured themselves in frustrated recall. Exasperation snapped her lavender fingers. And—amazing—the chauffeur KarlHeinz snapped back his own fingers softly, as though taking up a jazz beat.

"*Sankt Pandora von der Kiste*," he said, low.

" 'Saint Pandora of the Box!' Imagine this!"

The expressionist sculpture really did suggest a box from which the remnants of the church rose weirdly, like

Pandora's spirits. We glided along, Dr. Holze energetically idiomatic, KarlHeinz jazzily informational, Berlin immensely clean, I lightheaded and polite.

KarlHeinz wasn't the only unusual resource of the limousine. It had a built-in bar, whose whiskey I declined. But it also had a little fruit basket. I took an orange because I had been unable to eat on the plane, Dr. Holze selecting another out of sociability. Then she displayed the crowning ingenuity of her car. The gadget, built into the door, looked like an ashtray with a trapdoor in the middle. Dr. Holze explained that it not only swallowed all my orange peels but destroyed them instantly by God knows what arcane Prussian efficiency, no smells, no contamination, nothing remaining. You just dropped your mess, and those spotless, gleaming nickel jaws put it away forever.

It was one spotlessness too many. It came on top of the polished metal on policemen's helmets and the glittering regiments of coffee-drinking matrons. Ascribe it, if you will, to ill humor born of fatigue; or to distemper born of being on German soil. That clean-making gleaming ashtray was too much. I felt a need to dull down Berlin's immaculate perfection. I craved a little humane garbage. So instead of putting the rest of my orange peels into the gadget, I threw them, apparently absent-minded, out the window. One by one they dropped out of the official black limousine onto the fatherland's most pridefully clean street. Say this for me, though: it was well-mannered littering. I flicked those peels elegantly, casually, as if feeding swans.

Dr. Holze watched me with an *oo*-shaped mouth on which a smile began to form. I guess she began to think that this was a very typical and therefore desirable idiom of Yankee behavior. Some chic new extreme of American informality. Dr. Holze gave a shrill little laugh, and tore her own orange peels into shreds with her strong chubby little hands, and threw them out the window, laughing, watching closely how I did it, learning fast.

"*oo*Wonderful!"

Until, suddenly, she said, "Ah . . ." She wiped her fingers clean on a napkin dispensed by the car's napkin dispenser. "Ah . . ." She put on her gloves, radiating arch expectancy. "Ah . . ." It loomed ahead, the round white shape, the silhouette Dave Dowle has made famous the world over. Fingersnap backseat, fingersnap front.

"*Das Dowle Yo-Yo*," said KarlHeinz.

"The Dowle yo-yo!" Dr. Holze beamed. "You see? Already incorporated in the Berlin folklore!"

It was a triumphant crescendo. But she knew how to quit while ahead. Would I forgive this little bit of fun, this little detour? She had wanted to show me Berlin the relaxing way, instead of troubling me right away with business. Now I would not forget my dinner appointment at Dinny's Club? And my little lunch with her tomorrow at one? KarlHeinz was standing at my disposal to drive me anywhere, including even to the Schatten estate right after this. Good luck! there. I would need it. Her respects! to my esteemed colleague, Mister Mac-Lister, the hotel architect. Her pleasure! to have met me. Her delight! Her exit! in a second official car that had followed us all along.

My Berlin initiation.

Assume that God had hired a press agent during the creation of the world; and that this man, like most, thought that he was really cut out for much better things and wrote the Book of Genesis only for a living. After finishing his handout on the eternal glory of it all, he no doubt got pretty weary of the business. The chances are that in other parts of the universe he had seen the Boss pull the same stunts before—like letting there be light, or making girls out of ribs—and that it was a bore beating still another drum about the same old transfiguration. After a while the poor bastard must have lost sight of the fact that he was truly in the presence of a miracle.

Suitably altered, this is a parable applying to Dave and me. Dave isn't God; I wasn't exactly his press agent; and the spawning of another Dowle hotel not analogous to hand-finishing a planet. The fact remains that while I was part of the Dowle operation I couldn't and wouldn't appreciate it.

It was really a remarkable caper. Once Dave decided to Dowlify a city overseas, he first sent over a platoon of specialists who wangled real-estate deals, contractors' discounts, tax advantages and travel-agency guarantees —all with a fine artistic air, as if embarked on some very daring creative vision. Next came Andy MacLister's job of designing the Oyster on Stilts, as we called the futuristic Dowle shape, stuffing it full of chandeliers, bidets, Matisse prints and the initials DD folkloristically appropriate for each country. After that, my turn. It was up to me to stage a palace-warming true to local culture, yet with all the stagecraft of a hip party *and* resounding to the four corners of the earth. At the climax, enter David Dowle—honor ribbons, gossip columnists, Bohemian vocabulary and all—calling me his genius and making the inevitable parachute jump from the Oyster roof into the swimming pool. Splash. Forever after, no art-conscious three-car family from Boston to San Diego could make a

European trip without stealing a Dadaist ashtray from their suite at the newest Dowle.

I guess Berlin was just one time too many, and German yet. The thought that I'd soon be ditching Dave helped some, but not much. Berlin was, to be exact, our ninth Dowle stint. For the ninth time Andy MacLister came out of his ninth Executive Shack on the ninth building site. More of the red had gone out of his hair into his nose and cheeks. The heavy horn-rimmed glasses were new, but they couldn't neutralize the familiar Irish face. He was, as usual, behind schedule, worried, and therefore doubly ebullient.

"Leon Spey, you Kraut!"

"How are you, Andy?"

"Hey, what're you looking so wan for? You ought to feel at home in good old Über Alles!"

"I guess they must like me," I said. "I'm one of the few they didn't burn. I see you're coming along here."

"Well, I'll show you the goddamn pad."

We walked past carpenters and painters to the elevator.

"Which way you going to wave the magic wand?" he asked.

"You mean which opening? No definite decision yet."

"Want to bet it's going to be the Volksrocket stunt? Twenty astronauts getting drunk with Salvador Dali in a dirigible! It's a Dowle natural!"

"I still like Schatten," I said. "We could use some chic nostalgia."

"Come on," Andy said. "A ninety-year-old Prince? Because he had a hanky-panky with Sarah Bernhardt or something?"

"Well, yes," I said, "he's class and he's Nazi-clean. We can use that in Berlin."

"Dave and nineteenth-century elegance!" Andy said. He roared. Andy always sounded like a hopped-up Santa Claus when he forced out his big laugh. And it always sounded spectral in the bare halls of the unborn hotels in which we met.

"Which reminds me," he said. "I thought I'd have a little fun. I wrote Dave my idea for the casino. I said we ought to put it right next to the hotel."

"Here?" I said.

"Instead of the parking jazz. Put the parking jazz underground, and on top a sort of Ionic Temple of Chance. Crazy?"

"Gee," I said.

"Oh, I haven't got a prayer, man, I know. Your pal Dave is going to give me the works. I can see the cables. 'Who's going to gamble here? Stop. Socrates?' I love to watch him blow his stack by cable. It's my kicks. It's better than getting drunk."

"Well, anyway," I said, "why don't you bring up your temple idea tonight at the dinner conference?"

It was a goof. Apparently no one had informed him of the conference.

"Tonight? Man, I cut that out. I told them, no more nightshifts for me. Too many pansies in Berlin trying to make out through these midnight suppers!" He worked up a great deal of amusement. "I got them trained now. They don't even ask me any more."

"This one's at a place called Dinny's," I said. "Come and I'll protect you from the gay boys."

"Got a little conference myself, Lenny-boy. Thirty-six, twenty-three, thirty-eight." He laughed. When he stopped, he said, "That the Dinny's of Kurfürstendamm, number forty-six or something?"

I looked it up in my appointment book, and it was.

"Wait," he said suddenly. "Watch now." We were on the top floor. He unlocked what looked like a laundry closet. Inside, a rounded fretted little cavern disclosed itself, carved in ebony wood, with shelves propped up by flying buttresses. The whole thing resembled a miniature Gothic chapel. Where an altar might have been, he had placed a fuse box, inside whose glass shield a dim bulb gave off an ecclesiastic glimmer. Andy smuggled one such antique anomaly into every supramodern Dowle hotel. In Tangier it had been a pantry; in Athens a refrigeration room. And though Dave might well love the joke, Andy never mentioned it to him. But to me he always showed it, and for some reason always stashed liquor there.

Sure enough, there was a bottle of Scotch and two glasses. "Come on," he said, "let's get some fresh air." He pushed me up the stairs onto the roof.

"One of these days," I said, "you must build me a great big MacLister cathedral with a little Dowle hotel in a closet."

"Aaah, shut up and drink up," he said. But he looked at me, glowing, whether I'd really meant it or not. And I had, for with that one crazy closet he'd put the whole glib building to shame. He laughed again, but this time with a happy, grateful ease. He no longer had to roar.

We met just about twice a year, and the fact that he was a Dowle senior vice president, with more rank and money than I, never gave him enough security. I think he always suffered from the suspicion that I was not only editor of *The Dowle Scene* and Dave's house genius but something mysteriously, treacherously more. At each meeting he first had to show me how he didn't give a damn, though he couldn't help trying to feel out, anxiously, just what it was he didn't give a damn about. But the ice was broken now. His glasses had come off. His face shone red, naked, tensely relieved. The Scotch gleamed in the glass.

"Look at those Kraut laundromats," he said, pointing down to modern Berlin. "What do you say we blow the whole place up and give it to the Russians?"

"What do *you* say?" I said, smiling.

"You Jew phony," he said. "You're a cold fish. And you're just a polite drinker, that's the worst."

I poured it down, as impolitely as I could.

"We're three weeks behind in construction," he said. "I haven't hit Dave with it yet, because I thought we could catch up."

"Well, the flu killed *my* schedule," I said. "We couldn't dream up an opening before December."

"You sonofabitch," he said warmly. "Come on, let's make a tour."

Arm around my shoulder, he walked me down to the presidential suite with its special scenic view of the Wall; and to the site of the Brazilian Terrace Restaurant, where within three months an artificial bamboo thicket would shake to the strains of the Mushroom Cloud Cha-cha-cha, or so Andy promised. Then we went to the seafood restaurant, whose floor would be one giant aquarium. Here, Andy swore, he'd suspend a hunk of horsemeat under Dave's chair on opening night, drill a hole in the glass and let a shark into the tank. We enjoyed the prospect and then agreed that a still more constructive welcome would be to pipe gin into the conduits of Mrs.

Dowle's bidet—a nice way of decalcifying a society dame from the bottom up.

So we went horselaughing through the Oyster. I had my note pad out as usual. As usual, we were busy making ourselves comfortable not only with each other but also with our jobs. We achieved such outrageous conviviality. We treated the whole Dowle operation as a prank; a multimillion-dollar glamor prank it was fun to play along with; a lark in which wits like us indulged mainly to humor good old crazy Dave and sometimes to get a rise out of him, but which we wouldn't honor by getting *personally* involved; we made light of it. But, oddly enough, this business of making light of it was something which we took, at bottom, very seriously. That's why we were so thorough about it.

Twice we walked around the D-for-Dowle-shaped pool on whose bottom a life-sized pregnant-bellied mermaid would soon start wriggling. Andy got into a great good mood. He confided that Barb, his almost ex-wife, was coming around, this separation business was getting her down too; though he'd just made out with a German proposition (a sweet kid, I must meet her) because it was psychologically dead wrong at this juncture to stay unlaid even for a moment; you had to deal with Barb from a position of strength. But that might really be *the* showdown reconciliation coming up, he'd get uncastrated and it might just change his life. In fact, he wouldn't dream of coming to Dinny's tonight to plead for his goddamn Ionic temple. He was through with castrating things like that. Instead, he'd hide an Ionic little lavatory someplace in the Swedish Dowle! How about that? With a little statue of the Discus Thrower, a regular Praxiteles, but with no balls and a face looking like Dave!

He pushed me out of the elevator, laughing, sweating, full of strenuous wisecracks and introspections, and walked me along the half-finished drive to where my car was waiting. We clapped each other on the shoulder and yelled final loving insults at each other through the rolled-down window, and then I was taken away to the Prince.

2

As a rule I can drop off instantly, anywhere, and I had been counting on a nap in the car. All that joviality had been exhausting. But I couldn't manage to keep my eyes closed. My lightheadedness returned as soon as I let my lids drop. The strange new city made me restless.

My chief disturbance, though, was KarlHeinz, the chauffeur. Right here I got my first dose of him. A tall barrel-shouldered type, with the kind of relentless handsomeness you find in Germany—classic nose continuing the line of a classic forehead—and a somehow relentless uniform, all black and buttoned and visored. But the blond tuft of a very small goatee sat under his chin like an absurd jazz note. It gave the massiveness of the man a rather comic and innocuous flavor. That wasn't the only odd thing. After a while I sniffed a vague odor coming from the driver's seat. Just as I began to puzzle about it, he began to talk.

"Suhr." A pause. "Excuse me. Everyone says they are wonderful, the hotel premières you make."

"Thank you," I said.

"I understand it is like an opera, suhr. I am looking forward to it here."

"Where did you learn your English?"

"Camp Balmouth, Alabama, suhr. PW, suhr."

That accounted for the combination of guttural German accent and Southern inflection made still more preposterous by his deep voice. And he spoke with the impassive simper of the professional inferior, like a Negro porter far south of the Mason-Dixon line. Not the sort of thing I cared for, particularly in a Prussian chauffeur.

"Suhr? I read about your fine Paris opening. About the Louis the Fourteenth—"

"Thanks."

I rather pointedly cut him off and looked out the window. But underneath the simper lived a definite will.

"Pardon, suhr, in the newsreels, I remember your Madrid show, Don Quixote. And Tangier, Thousand and One Nights—"

"One does one's best," I said. I let my head fall, with finality, into dozing position. He ducked forward, concentrating on some obstacle in the street, and then the simper floated back again into the rear-view mirror.

"Always such wonderful spectacles, suhr. I am sure it will be wonderful in our Berlin."

"Well, I'm trying to think up something, if you'll give me half a chance."

The simper came at me, undaunted, unfazed, until he ducked forward once more. All of a sudden I knew. It explained the odor. He was smoking.

Now, I've always been an expert on chauffeurs. There's that avid, peeping-tom expertise you apply to what is yours only by other people's courtesy. I know about chauffeurs the way some people know about extremely expensive wines. Chauffeurs come in subtle but distinct vintages. A number palm a cigarette as they wait beside their cars. On a higher plane are those who can sneak a smoke while seated inside a parked car; they let the cigarette-holding hand trail out the street-side window, so that it can't be seen from the curb.

My KarlHeinz was far beyond such middling tricks. He managed to smoke while both his hands chased the huge Mercedes through the city. The cigarette lay hidden somewhere amid the dashboard glows; silently, swiftly, it would rise, camouflaged under his white-gloved fingers. And when his hand, turning the wheel around a curve, reached a position close to his mouth, he hunched forward as if intent on traffic, consummated the deception with a small swift puff and leaned back, dispersing the smoke among the vowels and diphthongs of an Alabama Kraut. The side vents of the front windows were arranged for maximum ventilation.

It was a schoolboy fraud heightened to virtuosity. I should have been amused. But the deadpan simper riled me. And I was dead tired. And the man would not give peace.

"Suhr? Excuse me. You will open the Berlin hotel with something from Schatten?"

"Possibly."

"A wonderful idea, suhr. Wonderful. Once upon a time they called Schatten 'The Appendicitis Palace.' "

"What?" I said, despite myself.

" 'The Appendicitis Palace,' suhr."

"Why?"

"Well, former days, suhr, it was the most famous palace here. When the Nazis confiscated it, all the high

officers went there for a rest after they had their appendix
out." In the rear-view mirror the simper broadened
without gaining an iota of expressiveness. "They always
rested with their girl friends."

"I see."

"Yes, suhr. My uncle who is dead now, he worked at
Schatten. He used to tell me things." He bent forward
and sneaked a puff.

"Your uncle was a mine of information," I said.

"Yes, suhr. And I read things in the illustrateds too.
There was a story, when the Austrian Empress came to
Berlin she visited only the Prince and didn't even see the
Kaiser. Wonderful the Prince is still alive today."

"You've done tremendous research, my friend."

"Yes, suhr. One does one's best, suhr."

With that he shut up and let the car zoom. "One does
one's best." Was the joker getting back at me for my own
reply to him a few minutes ago? Was he putting me on?
And who cared? We had arrived.

I disembarked amid great loud ceremonies by my
devoted driver; such running around the car, such opening the door and slamming it behind me. After all that
fuss he merely pointed in the direction I was to go and
stood at attention by the front fender.

I remember the sudden hesitation in me. I was to go
across an arched marble bridge you'd associate with a
Venetian canal. Underneath that bridge, though, there
was no water, only an empty highway. And in the middle
of the highway, flagged in red, stood a sentry box. My
briefing had defined the Schatten estate as a Western
peninsula jutting into East Germany. The deserted road
looked like a boundary line, and the somewhat hunchbacked soldier who sat on a chair beside the box wore the

East German uniform. KarlHeinz waited by the fender. I walked straight ahead.

On the other side of the highway nothing was visible but a huge green hedge. It turned out to be matted ivy clinging to a tall grillwork fence. At first I couldn't see inside. Then I found the high-arched gate from which all the green had been cut away. Bang, the estate lay before me.

My first impression was a kind of rich unreality. It just had no relation to the rest of the landscape, to Berlin or even to the twentieth century. Inside the fence paraded a formal French garden, mazed with yew and graveled walks. Beyond that, grass grew freely, full of wild flowers. Willows bent into a pond. A pavilion, overgrown with green, stood between two vine-matted stone benches. In the background the big manor surged up, with all sorts of baroque unorthodoxies and waywardly weathered bricks. Four semi-oriental onion spires, many oriels and gargoyles and a playful little tower with several roofs, reminiscent of a pagoda—it was all held together by an antique improbable jollity. Four immense poplars reared to the left and right like rigid sentinels guarding a bacchanale. The gardens were dotted with gas lamps. And as if that weren't enough, there, right before me, two doves were mating in a lazy white blur of wings.

I pushed down the huge cast-iron lever. Two things happened. The gate yielded slightly, slowly. And a woman appeared from the pavilion and walked toward me. For a moment I had the uncanny notion that my touch against the gate had produced the figure in the distance.

It was merely that she had seen me, of course. Yet

the whole estate seemed so peculiar; so different from the photograph in Dave's office and from some of the other eccentric chateaus of my experience. The others appeared always somewhat at bay among the highways, under the jet streaks. This one was such a sly and fierce grotesque. It put the rest of the world, including me, on the defensive.

I glanced back and saw KarlHeinz beyond the empty highway, still standing at attention, seeming to nod encouragingly. A wild idea popped into my mind: this might be some sort of elaborate practical joke. The thing smacked of Andy's cathedral closets. I turned again. The woman stood in front of me.

She looked like a tall shapely nun. Her dress was light gray, quite long, dimly like a nurse's. The linen covering her hair could have been a Sister's coif. Actually it was a beach hat, with a wide white brim bent forward to cover her hair and forehead. In the evening light I could make out only a chin and nose, both small and well-shaped. Pruning shears glinted in her hand.

"Herr Spey?"

"Yes," I said. "Good evening."

"There's a message for you from Dr. Ahn, the physician in charge here."

"Oh," I said. "I have an appointment with—"

"My father wants me to tell you that the Prince isn't well. He is sorry you can't see him."

"Wait a moment," I said. "I was told to be here at half past six. I came straight from the airport—"

"We couldn't call. There's no telephone here."

"But I came here specially—didn't you get a cable?"

"They're not always delivered here." She shook her head slightly. "I am sorry."

We confronted each other through the gate. Its dusk-filled meshes printed on her dress an ornate design. She was the first person in Berlin to speak German to me, quite as though she knew it was my mother tongue. Her slightly hoarse voice had an abstracted rhythm, the same rhythm with which the pruning shears tapped softly against her palm.

"I am sorry, too," I said. I knew I should be angry. Instead I was embarrassed to hear my hand rattle faintly against the gate. She looked at my rattling.

"We are still open," she said, "but only for a few more minutes."

"Open?"

"The East Germans lock our gate at seven." She glanced at her watch, abstracted. The pruning shears kept tapping. "We are part of West Berlin," she said, "but we are inside the East Zone."

"I was told Schatten was a peninsula."

"No," she said. "The highway under the bridge belongs to the East. The bridge belongs to the East. We are enclosed on all sides."

"I see," I said.

"They have the curfew right."

The shears dropped. I could have reached through and picked them up. But she bent down instantly, forestalling me, as if not even recognizing that gallantry was possible. Yet when she straightened up, she gave herself away. Her hat had slid sideward. But it wasn't my glimpse of a golden wave at her temple, or of her long gray eyes. It was the gesture with which she adjusted the brim. A gesture decorative, instinctive, precise. A beauty's gesture. The next moment her abstracted voice erased it.

"If you could come back another time."

"You see," I said, "I had hoped to discuss our hotel opening with the Prince. We would like him to participate in a historical pageant."

"Yes," she said. "We have sent your office a reply."

"Oh, you did," I said. A bell began to toll from somewhere in the manor, and at the same time a man appeared under the poplars. The pruning shears still tapped against her palm.

"I am in charge of the hotel's opening arrangements," I said. "I've only got a few weeks. The hotel will be ready in December."

"I am sorry. It's late now."

The bell tolled and the pruning shears beat, and there was nothing to do but let go of the gate.

"I'll call again," I said. "Good night."

"Good night."

I went back, across the Venetian bridge, away from the shears and the bells. KarlHeinz ushered me into the car with a grandiose volley of door slams. He didn't speak a word on the ride to the hotel. I've no idea whether he smoked. I looked out the window at Berlin.

We took another route on the way back, along dusky residential streets where plants and ferns brimmed inside picture windows, all brilliantly lit, so that we seemed to be gliding through a grotto of bright miniature forests. Here and there ruins lunged up and away, phosphorescent with sunset, jagged gestures like semaphores in a lost language. And there were small lakes, dozens of them, more than I thought Berlin could hold, lakes and canals, full of boat ripples, swallows and child cries. Sometimes we rode parallel to waterways hidden beyond the next street and I saw the tops of tall sails gliding dimly above the roofs, from one chimney to another.

I should have felt foiled by the encounter at the Schatten gate. I didn't. My lightheadedness was gone. An exhilaration had come into my blood, stirred me to my fingertips. I was thirty-seven and felt something I hadn't felt for so long: the good sweet loneliness of youth, a glorious mélange of impatience, curiosity, forsakenness and hope. I was alone in a strange new place, and the strangeness was music. I felt I was going to get Prince Schatten and that velvet blonde nun-bitch inside the gate. I rejoiced in my life, my job, in this cursed and brilliant city. When we reached the Grand Hotel at the Kurfürstendamm, the great street was already blazing and dancing with lights.

I jumped out so fast that KarlHeinz had barely time to salute.

3

Despite his public opulences Dave Dowle could be pretty mean. He hated the competition with an almost indecent blatancy. He went to the lengths of not wanting his more prominent sidekicks to find accommodations in rival hotels even while we were hatching a local Dowle. That didn't bother Andy, whose extramarital embroilments solved, incidentally, his housing problem. It did bother me, because I prefer hotel service to the complications of renting a private place. But Dave had a way of souring me on other hotels by souring them on me. That week a funny little item had appeared in the "People" section of *Time* magazine, saying that since he could not yet be properly fed and lodged in the Berlin Dowle, Leon Spey, Dowle's genius, was camping out with sleeping bag and cooking stove at the Grand Hotel.

I hadn't read the item yet. But I sensed that something unpleasant had reached the Grand. The chief concierge had no bows for me, only a demand for my passport; and the deputy chief concierge said that a person had been asking for me a great many times and had been requested, since he was evidently hungry, to wait in the coffee shop.

Even before I looked, I knew. Very few people in my acquaintance have the gift for drawing down on themselves such sulfurous inflections. Besides, my parents had written me from New York that Julius would be looking me up.

I turned around, and there he really was, not in the coffee shop, but in the outermost lobby armchair just before the coffee shop. There, ostracized, he slumped, wrapped in a big black overcoat despite the late summer heat. His black hat, too large for him like all his clothes, was of a piece with his large scuffed black shoes from which a loose lace dragged on the ground. He was eating peanuts out of a brown paper bag, and stared through his glasses at the elegance all about him, and dropped shells, and ground them embarrassedly into the rich carpet like cigarette butts. His full lips were still pulled down at the ends, sensual to no avail; his bold nose had become a little more quixotic. His face, the face of a sad hawk, had grown a little grayer and sadder. Otherwise he hadn't changed at all.

"Uncle Julius," I said.

"Leon! My little Leon!"

My cheek was kissed, my hand pressed. "Here!" he said. "Look!" and hurriedly unfolded a clipping from a Berlin evening paper. It was a photograph which showed me wavering down the gangplank from the plane. *Mr. Leon Spey, Dowle hotel sorcerer, just arrived to supervise the debut of the Berlin Dowle.* The thing couldn't have been more than a couple of hours off the presses. It lay wrinkled and smudged in his hand like a page from an old prayerbook.

"And they asked me who I am," he said. "I mean, imagine. I called the paper, you see, for your address. 'Who I am?' I said. 'I'm his uncle! He's grown up, he's become successful, I was there during his graduation—that's who I am!'"

"A nice surprise, Uncle Julius."

Let's face it, the surprise was no more "nice" than he's my uncle. Actually he's a remote cousin from the Berlin part of the family. His father, dead long before Hitler, left him the largest car-rental agency in Germany. But Julius is as incapable of being an heir as of being a remote relative. His twenties were spent on several expensive schemes to save World Jewry. Exit rich young Julius Spiegelglass; enter poor old Uncle Julius.

By the time I got to know him in my childhood, he was having trouble not only with the Nazis *and* the World Zionist Organization, but also with immigration authorities in various countries—and finally with my father. He lived with us in Vienna, dropping peanut shells and phoning long distance nine times a day. I have a memory of Julius in 1939, already aged, Uncled and bankrupt, saying good-bye to us at a Vienna railroad station, eating peanuts and crying, he off to Palestine, we to the United States. Ten years later he materialized at my college graduation in New York, on his way to "personally" see President Truman about a petition. He kissed me, strewed my collar with dandruff, and within seconds got into a row because my father wouldn't pay for Julius' newspaper ad to compel the President's attention.

After that, and for many years, pleading letters from overseas, angry letters, letters enclosing bits from Zion's earth—and now he sat before me, undiminished, undampened. His long thin cheeks still trembled with a tiny tic. He still had the habit of pressing back his spectacles, making his black bewildered eyes pop forward. He was still Uncle Mushroom, the name we'd given him as children, partly because of his large hat and partly, I guess, because he was like something wild that little boys find in a dark wood.

"Imagine, our Leon on the first page!"

"I was going to look you up, Uncle," I said. "Let's make a date for—"

"Do they pay you for printing your picture? Sit down."

"I wish I could, Uncle. But I'm fresh from the airport as you see, and late for an appointment—"

He interrupted with a cough. The same bronchitic outburst. It served as his response to slights, for he wasn't capable of neat little defenses. He thundered and gasped. It sounded like a tragic guffaw, in the middle of which he put another peanut into his tortured mouth.

"I'm all right, I'm all right. I won't pester you. The main thing is—"

"Don't eat now, Uncle Julius."

"I'm all right. I mean, who is Dowle? Aren't you a literature professor?"

"That's a long story, Uncle."

"Tell me. You don't have an American cigarette? You tell me, then I'll tell you. I have a wonderful project."

I asked the bellhop, who was still saddled with my briefcase, to bring some Lucky Strikes. I said (my usual gambit with the rare people who never heard of Dowle Inc.) that David Dowle was a money-making invention specializing in hotels, and that I had switched from professing literature to professing Dowle. But it was all wrong. You couldn't smart-talk Uncle Julius. He pressed a moist peanut into my hand as a sort of exchange for the cigarette I lit him, and blinked behind his glasses, uncomprehending. So I tried to make clear at least the immediate nature of my business, the demands it made on my time, particularly on my first evening in town.

"Business?" He looked at me. "You will be a businessman forever? I mean, I cannot teach you anything, your picture is in the paper. But, you know, Ecclesiastes, *He that loveth silver, will not be satisfied with silver.* You know? I mean, I'm not against money. Money is important. I have a project—"

"Uncle," I said. I could have asked for his phone number at this point, should have promised to call and pressed a large bill into his hand. It might have worked. But the exhilaration of the ride was still stirring inside me and I felt, curiously, that it would die if I sent this old man packing. "Uncle," I said, "let's have dinner tomorrow night. Okay?"

"*Tomorrow night?*" he said, as though that were ten years away. He began to cough.

"Tonight, then," I said. "After my dinner appointment. Meet me at Dinny's on the Kurfürstendamm. Remember—Dinny's. If you have any difficulties—if the doorman acts stupidly, you just ask for me by name."

"Dinny's," he murmured, and suddenly kissed me on the cheek.

"Forgive my hurry," I said. "Tonight, then."

"Dinny," he said and sank back into the chair. From the elevator I saw that he was smoking and chewing nuts and staring at the elegant people all about him.

Dinny's. Dinny's Club, to be exact. A luxe imitation of a lawn party. Garden furniture made of spun steel, Italian

marble and black Russian leather. Lighting by way of
Meissen torches, porcelain twigs sprouting from the
walls. A good cool jazz quartet, each musician with a
green feather, playing in a latticed cage. Three tiny
wood-carved bars tended by shepherdesses. A little ex-
cessive, but it was excess with style.

There's a reason why some jump to the head of the
pack. Dinny—alias Siegwart Dinkelberger, but he swore
he would *never* speak to me again if I addressed him by
anything so absurd—Dinny had flair. His Fräulein Livia,
who completed the threesome at our table, displayed
magnificent Eurasian nostrils, a ponytail of ebony silk
dancing down to her buttocks, a tawny deep décolletage,
a prideful carriage and a silken sarong-type evening
gown.

Dinny was no small shakes either. He was very satisfied
being himself; in fact, unlike his American brethren, he
was comfortably bored with it. Sheathed in black velvet
dinner clothes, he hung like a slim lovely drape from his
chair. He was held up solely by his head, which now and
then tensed forward at me. As if he were suspended in
some delicious languor from which only my still more
delicious presence could rouse him. His red-blond bangs
glowed at me. He stroked them now and then while
pronouncing his frequent and, marvelous to say, indolent
italics.

For an aperitif we had the special vodka martini, an
o*blig*atory Dinny ritual. Followed dinner, composed
carefully of American big-shot food, diet considerations
and Continental haute cuisine: porterhouse steak, endive
salad, old Burgundy—and Dinny's viewpoint. He would
only be too *happy* to participate in a Dowle Casino, if
only one could break away from the cliché area of the

Kurfürstendamm (meaning a noncompetitive distance away from Dinny's Club); and if we would let him play a *lit*tle with the interior decor, his special hobby (meaning profitable middle-man business with contractors, furniture people, etc.); and, of course, if one gave him a bit of an in*cen*tive to play with (i.e., a hefty profit percentage).

I said that Mr. Dowle might be a difficult man to persuade on the last point but that I saw no unreasonable difficulty on the others. A signal from our table; a waltz from the band; a smile from Dinny: he had heard rumors of my Austrian birth. If I didn't ask Fräulein Livia to dance, he would never *ev*er trust a Viennese again.

Well, I got up and waltzed with Fräulein Livia. She danced well and had an unidentifiable accent and deep-toned unidentifiable peculiarity in her voice and began to close in so nicely that I began to wonder whether she wasn't being offered as one of Dinny's courtesies of the evening.

Into the middle of that speculation jutted Uncle Julius' face. Like a sudden mirage. It hovered against the black silk padding of the entrance, pressed back its glasses, then was suddenly, violently, snapped back like a mask on a rubberband.

It was replaced the next moment by Andy. Andy against the same black silk padding, Andy very red-cheeked, in a very white dinner jacket, very upright, very drunk, with a very blonde girl on his arm. He hadn't had the guts to stay away. Instinctively I pulled behind a couple so he shouldn't see us. And the pull against Livia's hand gave her away. I made my third remarkable discovery within three seconds: Fräulein Livia's hand was shaved. I saw Dinny grinning from the table. A special hip joke, no doubt, played on special hip visitors. An experience to bring home from Berlin. I even felt—or imagined—a soft pressure against my thigh, some sly little erection under Livia's sarong.

The day's strain began to tell. The martinis rose into my brain. I wanted to get out of there—away from the shaved and perfumed hand, away from Dinny's italics, away from Andy who was doing the castrating thing after all.

But I kept up a good front. I always do. I danced my shaven beauty back to the table, let him go by curtsying to him significantly, to show that I was on to it. Dinny, shaking with laughter, stopped when I asked to be excused for not sitting down again, this was enough night life for a convalescent, for a solid Jewish citizen. The last part I added because it could still be a stopper in Germany, and then I said good night.

Andy, blind drunk, thank God, was groping his way through the right side of the room. I escaped through the left.

I'd dismissed KarlHeinz. There were taxis, but I needed some air, wanted my uncle. Blocks away a shadow moved. It retreated rapidly and looked just like Julius. I began to run after him. I was burning to find out whether he'd been roughed up by the doorman, what he was doing in Berlin, what his project was, how I could help. Something childish in me wanted to spend a few minutes with him which would wash away the Dinnys of the world.

But the shadow, when I finally caught up, was a paper vendor. I bought a copy. I dragged along the sidewalk, at the deep black end of my first day in Berlin, panting, foolish, unutterably fatigued.

It was the stretch of Kurfürstendamm we'd driven through on the way from the airport. Everything struck me as a caricature of what I had seen in daylight. Women still sat at the tables of the sidewalk cafés. But not matrons sipping coffee. These were garish, strident-legged creatures, rouged cheeks flaming in the fluorescent light. Spotlights bleached the wrecked Memorial Church and the "Pandora" structure built against it. Now it looked like a giant ghost embracing its own skeleton against the night. Other spotlights, pointed upward, made the movie posters spring at the moon with incandescent lips and blinding behinds.

I had the feeling of a single enormous room suspended in black Berlin, ectoplasmic and marooned. But, by God, it was still clean. Inside the room, along the many café tables, clean women hissed to each other or cooed at passers-by. And throughout the spectral glistening hall a breeze wafted, compounded of perfume, rubble dust and the tang of dandelion weeds.

I passed a tavern called Weisser Mohr—White Negro. The women here were too young to just sit. They were fresh, well-scrubbed, rosy-sweet, the softest youngest shambles of a war they could never have seen. They gamboled despite their heavy shoulder bags, they laughed and shrilled. A group of them tittered at a bulletin board near the tavern, or perhaps at a man who stood before it.

This man I won't forget. He carried a short ladder, pail, an array of brushes and, inside the pail, a tiny slumped child, dozing. Instantly there was a kinship. I felt, as I think he did, that the only safe place for men alone here was close by the bulletin board, reading. Side by side we stood and read the notices together.

"Unconventionally-minded young married pair seeks physically attractive likewise-minded couple. Tel. 45-76-82."

"Two well-shaped youths wish to find vacation friend interested in photography. Tel. 87-09-22."

"Adventurous red-headed lady with Shepherd dog wants contact with other dog lovers. Box 884 Berlin General Post Office."

Suddenly the man next to me began to talk. He spoke a hoarse quick Prussian I couldn't always follow. But apparently he was a house painter, a certified master house painter at some unintelligible East German place near Berlin. He'd been smuggled into the West in a truck this evening. He had been told of some refugee rehabilitation centers here, but he didn't trust them. He didn't trust centers of any kind. He just wanted a job. He'd come here because the place looked so bright, the bulletin board like a Help Wanted thing. . . . His eyes again moved past all the cards, all the correctly spelled, meticulously typed, neatly tacked-up invitations to sodomy. A young rouged creature ran up, pressed a lollipop into the child's hand in the pail, and then ran back to the shrill giggles of her friends.

The man flinched but didn't take away the candy, only hunched his shoulders as if to ease the burden of ladder, pail and child. The little girl, a beautiful blonde thing in a kind of uniform smock, furrowed a tiny brow; she began to tap the lollipop against her temple. That moment I thought of Schatten, of the nunlike lovely woman with the pruning shears.

It was an unexpected image, yet somehow rooted in the Berlin night. It budged me out of my weariness. My hand shot up at a passing cab. I fumbled a bill, ridiculously large, out of my wallet into the painter's pail. The man swiveled and grunted with astonishment. The floodlit ruins hovered; the women giggled. And just as I got into the car, the little girl began to cry.

4

PSYCHOANALYSIS SAYS that every dream ever dreamed by anybody is a masterpiece of dramatic construction. We fall asleep and become Eugene O'Neill. More's the pity that I forget so fast the virtuosities I produce in bed.

In my journal, though, I recorded the fragment of a dream I dreamed the morning after my first Berlin night: Uncle Julius balancing himself like a comic circus artist on top of a tall grillwork fence, rolling his wild lost urchin eyes, while below Prince Schatten holds a safety net and bears an embarrassing resemblance to a Eurasian nightclub dancer. Sure enough, Julius fell, but not into the net. No, he plumped onto my eyelids, crashed right through them into reality.

Uncle Mushroom had waked me. He stood in my hotel room. Bodily. The double doors to my suite were both open. In the corridor a chambermaid stared. My watch on the night table said five to eight.

"Oh, hello," I said, weary.

"I'm sorry! I'm sorry you're sleeping. I had no idea."

Of course he wouldn't have any idea. He was, as a

matter of principle, ignorant of things like inquiry by
house phone, messages or notes slipped under the door.
Amenities were an insult to his nature. He stood goggling
on the threshold, glasses a bit askew under the huge hat,
his coat unbuttoned and flowing in the draft of the open
doors. But as I fully came to, I wasn't unhappy that he
was there.

"Uncle Julius," I said, "last night at Dinny's, did I see
you pop in and out?"

Abruptly he tried lighting himself a cigarette, right in
the open doorway. "That man was a savage," he said.

"Please come in," I said. "I thought it was you yesterday. But you were gone when I looked in the street."

"I told that savage," he said, "I told him, 'You'll hear
about this. That's Mr. Spiegelglass, my nephew, in there.
He's one of the biggest persons—' "

"The doorman became really unpleasant?"

"I—I shoved him right back." He still tried to light the
cigarette, but the draft through the open door wouldn't
let him. In the corridor the chambermaid still goggled.

"For God's sake, do come in, Uncle Julius."

He stepped all the way in. His eyes moved along the
length of my room, focused on the mahogany headboard
of my bed. Suddenly he buttoned one button on his
overcoat.

"Take a chair," I said. "We could prefer charges
against the man, you know."

"Charges?" he said, transfixed.

"Please sit down." He kept looking about, so bewildered. "Can I order you coffee?"

"No—no, I already had." He unbuttoned the button
again and sat down—not on any chair, of course, but
right on the bed in which I was lying. He grubbed in a

brown paper bag without taking it out of his coat pocket and came up with a huge dingy biscuit. It cheered him up considerably. He held it before my eyes.

"No, thank you, Uncle."

"Whole wheat."

"Not right now," I said. "You see, last night you asked for Leon Spiegelglass. Nobody knows me as that any more. It's Leon Spey now."

"Leon *Spey?*"

"But, Uncle, you must have noticed, it's the name under my newspaper photograph!"

He shook his head, amazed. And for some damn reason I didn't feel annoyed. Like an idiot, I felt guilty. "My father had it changed," I said, "when we came to America, when I was still a child."

"Your father must be so proud. His son's picture on the first page!" He had grabbed my arm. He could catapult himself into tremendous warm intimacy, from which he could then catapult himself right back into puzzled, outraged alienation. "And I thought about it," he said, fondly kneading my pajama arm, "I mean about your hotel opening. It came to me in the middle of the night. I said to myself, 'Leon stopped teaching to make so much money that he can have his own school, some very special project—that's why the hotel business.' Correct?"

"Well," I said, surprised because part of the guess was quite astute. "Yes, in a way."

"Very intelligent! Very smart!" Suddenly, *sotto voce,* "Careful here. The Germans want to take your money."

"What?" I said.

"They took it away from me!"

"Wait a minute—"

"Not like Hitler. But with other tricks. They took

away the money I should have gotten for my father's business."

"But, Uncle," I said, "Germany passed a good restitution law. You should do very well."

" 'I should!' 'I should!' 'I should!' I should have gotten enough for my project. They only gave me ten old Daimler-Benzes."

"Well, don't you put up with that for one second," I said.

"That isn't the only thing. . . . You have no idea. . . ." His hand twisted the coverlet; he turned away. "There's an office building on top. . . . They took away my darling mother's grave!"

"They took away her grave?"

He didn't answer. His face averted, he cleared his throat. The same old Uncle, ashamed that he was crying so easily.

"We'll investigate," I said. "It might be a mistake."

He wheeled around, furiously recovered. "Our own flesh and blood! The Jewish Community! Selling their own cemetery! For money! *I will search Jerusalem with candles*, it says, *and punish the men settled on their lees*. God is talking about Jews here! The worst anti-Semites!"

"I think you should see a lawyer, Uncle."

"A lawyer? A *German* lawyer? A Jew should fight another *Jew* in a *German* court?"

"Look," I said. Maybe I sighed a little. "We ought to discuss this when we both have a little more leisure—"

Two knocks came from the door. At the same time the whole-wheat biscuit which I had declined, and which he had held on to all this time, broke in his hand and sprayed to the floor.

"I am sorry! I'm sorry and you're busy—"

"Stay, please."

It was the bellhop with a telegram. "One moment, Uncle," I said. "Business." And while I tipped the bellhop and opened the envelope and read a fairly maddening cable, I couldn't help watching how he tried to recover biscuit bits from the floor, ate some of them, dropped some more and started to search for the wastebasket.

"Just use an ashtray," I said.

"It was clumsy."

"Don't worry," I said. "Will you please have dinner with me tonight?"

His great nose gave an uneasy twitch. He pressed his glasses back. "I'm interfering. You are an important person, with telegrams—"

"Nonsense, Uncle."

"I get carried away—"

"Dinner at this hotel at eight? Then we can really catch up on each other."

"Here? The only thing is, you know, here . . ."

"Of course. All right, a kosher place, wherever you eat."

"There is a restaurant. It's over at—"

"Well, you just come here and tell the driver where to take us. Eight is all right?"

"At eight," he said. I thought he was on the point of kissing my cheek, but the mahogany headboard deterred him. All that happened was that my wrist got pressed by both his hands.

"At eight," he mumbled, and hurried out with biscuit crumbs sticking to the elbow of his black overcoat.

And then I could really concentrate on getting mad at the cable.

That cable was a beauty. MYRON PROPOSES NIEBELUNG OPENING STOP ME SIEGFRIED STOP LET MYRON WARM UP IDEA COUPLE OF WEEKS STOP COOL PRINCE SCHATTEN WITH OFFICIAL KAPUT ANNOUNCEMENT STOP ANY DOPE DOWLE CASINO STOP LOVE TO WHATEVER GIRL   DAVE

Of course I should have been simply amused. By then I could see through Dave so hilariously well. He was much more entertaining than Uncle Julius. The message meant that Dave Dowle had come a cropper. That day the Dear John letter from my Schatten blonde must have blown up in his face. The pain ached in each flip word of the cable. Dave was very touchy about such slights, touchier still about having his touchiness exposed. Ergo his wish to have me announce the abandonment of the Schatten scheme, quite as if the turndown proceeded from Dowle Inc. Ergo the phrase COOL PRINCE SCHATTEN—"cool" meaning here both "have him pipe down" and also "get rid of him, who cares."

As to LET MYRON WARM UP IDEA COUPLE OF WEEKS, that was a deep phrase, freighted and clustered with meanings. Myron was my right hand in New York. He and Dave knew damn well we couldn't hold off opening preparations another two weeks while Myron squeezed his sweatshop brains. Dave knew damn well that with Schatten scratched I must start on the only remaining alternative. This alternative, namely the Volksrocket, Dave hadn't even mentioned in his carelessly regal communication. But it was the real point of the message. The Niebelung gambit boiled down to the reminder that friend Dave could, if so inclined, undercut me any time with my own deputy: a maneuver designed to make me snap to and not lose a moment over the thought that Dowle Inc. might have suffered a snub.

The whole cable with its fine print of allusions and omissions really meant:

DON'T YOU DARE THINK SCHATTEN KICKINTHEPANTS MEANS A THING STOP GET GOING ON VOLKSROCKET DAVE

Dear old Dave just had to be decoded.

But perhaps I should be decoded first. It might be asked: why so mad at a cable? Or, more to the point: why so mad at Dave? Hadn't my relationship with him started on a pleasant note and continued that way from there on?

Hadn't we met, as people should, mutually impressed? He, the avant-garde tycoon who attended the college trustees' meeting in bushy mustache and lumbershirt, who communicated only by offbeat telegrams, never by letter or telephone, and who was starting those far-out hotels all over the world: hadn't he impressed me? And hadn't I impressed him as the author of *Cat Quixote*, the *pièce de résistance* of the Comparative Lit. department, the ex-continental so Creative in English that I was licensed to wear sneakers to student conferences?

And didn't Dave draw me down, that first time, to sit on the floor with him—an honor, I discovered later, he bestows only on those he considers important? Didn't he say, "So you're Spey. Hey, any kookie kids in your classes? My outfit would dig one."

And didn't I sense instantly that kookieness was compulsory for Dowle executives? And wasn't my *Cat Quixote* a kookie verse play about this gang leader in Spanish Harlem who when on junk has hallucinations saintly and romantic that make him knight errant of the 144th Street turf? Is it anybody's business that I meant

"Cat" to be parody? Didn't it become a jazz opera produced at the most obscure and therefore most prestigious drama festival in the Canaries? Hadn't the *Evergreen Review* called it "a lovely, murderously empathetic ballad"? And didn't I send Dave an inscribed copy the day after sitting on the floor with him? Didn't he receive it in the spirit in which it was sent, as employment application? As my esthetic maidenhead to be ravished by Mr. Right?

Let's pursue this further.

Didn't my executive kookieness work? Didn't I develop *The Dowle Scene*, that well-known monthly with the quarterly look, distributed to each of Dave's ten thousand hotel rooms? You know, the one with a Jackson Pollock print for a cover and, inside, my advanced mingling of James Joyce and Hedda Hopper in artful strands; an impressionistic tapestry chronicling my travels on Dave's behalf, the famous Dowle guests Leon Spey saw and saw through, with a titillating irreverence which didn't spare even the great corporation that hired my perceptiveness? Didn't I create an aura around Dowle Inc.? Wasn't I better than mobiles? Hm? Didn't I make a guest feel that by registering at a Dowle he was renting a foothold on Upper Bohemia?

And didn't Dave lead me into his parties as though I were an esoteric songbird he had personally captured from the jungle of wildest inspiration, as though I were constantly on the verge of some perilous pure cry? And wasn't it nice that for Dave's sake I kept postponing that cry in favor of fine twitter? Isn't it fair that in exchange he appointed me his genius?

All that I'll concede, though I sometimes put it in an

unnecessarily nasty way. I'll concede it and I'll concede more. The year in which Berlin happened was my last Dowle year. And if my last Dowle year turned sour, it wasn't because of any change in Dave. It was a change in me.

Slowly I began to resent something, something quite paradoxical. I resented the freedom Dave always gave me. He never held me down as he held down fellows like Andy MacLister. Take my private journal, for example. I was keeping it intermittently, throughout my Dowle period. Often I used whole portions from it verbatim for *The Dowle Scene* without cleaning up or watering down—and never a squawk from Dave. In my last year I discovered why. I had started the journal as a sarcastic antagonist *against* my Dowle column, but it ended up as an incubator of negotiable phrases *for* the column— because my sharpest needlings were safe for Dave.

That was it. Dave had always known I was safe. He was a much better critic than the *Evergreen Review*. He knew only too damn well I wasn't murderous. It had always been safe to sit on the floor with me. I and everything about me had smacked of safety from the first—safe in a way that Andy was not.

I'm not sure why that should be so rankling, or why I should envy Andy's potential harmfulness to Dowle Inc. After all, it only points to the fact that I was more hardheaded and stable than Andy. Unlike Andy, I never nurtured in my soul the hope for great art. You can sum up the problem simply. Art as a mission has always been heartbreaking, particularly in our time. Art as a profession has often been rewarding, particularly in our time. I'm not a missionary. I'm a professional. I know how far you can go—how far I care to go. I know myself. Andy's the same, but doesn't want to know. And that's what made me safe in contrast to him.

I had come to terms with that privately and made private little jokes about it—jokes like *Cat Quixote*. But I disliked Dave's having such a comfortable knowledge of my moral insides. I disliked being such an obviously safe Jewish songbird, who was now to twitter over Berlin—of all places—on Dave's behalf. I disliked being such an easy safe bet from start to finish. And I think, now that I look back on it, I think that's really why I liked Schatten at first sight.

There was something unsafe about it. I guess that's why I found myself almost eager, that morning, to get back to Schatten and fence with the blonde nemesis behind the grillwork. I wanted to try for a Dowle première which, for a change, could be truly intriguing. The trouble was that Dave had smelled the unsafeness too. And so he'd up and killed Schatten, STOP, with a wisecrack in a cable. We were still sitting on the floor together, but it was beginning to occur to me that his foot was in my face.

Well, I picked some remnants of Uncle Julius' biscuits off the floor, threw them into the Louis Seize wastebasket and registered a call to Nina. She was a therapeutic thought. If I was being had by Dave, pretty soon *he* would be had by Nina and me. I showered, shaved, rammed my way through the morning papers. During coffee the phone rang.

At the other end, Nina, at three in the morning, only an hour after her last encore at Dave's Satin Room in Manhattan. Nina, keyed up, husky-tired and sassy all at once, adorable and teasable, just what I needed. I had nothing earth-shaking to say, but I knew she was pleased by these expensive no-news calls.

"Leon? . . . Leon! Flu gone? You sound disgustingly vibrant."

"Flu gone, Ninepins," I said. "I'm fine."

"Listen, it's a relapse kind of a bug going around. Don't you come back damaged."

"Listen to her," I said. "A regular, anxious, secret little bride-to-be."

"Okay, ghoul, tell me about Berlin."

"Different city, same problems, same Dave—"

"Okay, don't tell me. You probably have reason."

"As a matter of fact, I've got one," I said. "A Javanese beauty. I met him in one of those bars." I gave her a brief description.

"Lelo," she said all of a sudden. "You sound awfully far away."

"You come through well," I said. "Say, guess what's left. One Berlin Oyster opening. One Stockholm Oyster opening, then—voom!"

" 'Voom'? Isn't there some regular English word for the dreadful idea you're expressing?"

"I got news for you—it's going to be still more dreadful for Dave. Has that real-estate whiz of yours delivered yet?"

"He thinks he may have something for us on Long Island."

"He better. Tell him I'll soon be home from the wars."

"I'll tell him. Any message for me?"

"Yeah . . . it's on the tip of my tongue . . . it escapes me now . . . but it's got something to do with why I keep calling across four thousand miles."

"Yeah, why?"

"Oh, shut up and good night."

"Good night. Write me about Berlin since you won't talk about it."

"You'll get ten pages if you don't watch out."

"You bet I don't watch out."

"You asked for it. Sleep tight now, Ninepins."

"And you, don't you start any wars over there."

"I won't. You know what, Ninepins. Good night."

"You know what, Lelo. Take care."

We always telephoned well. Only, I remember that five minutes after hanging up it struck me again: what did she mean by "You sound awfully far away"?

And I was still mad at the cable.

5

My INFAMOUS lunch with Dr. Holze. Starting in sweetness, ending in rage.

At the Radio Tower Bar she gleamed from a thin bar stool like heavy foliage from a slender tree. Leaf-green tailored suit, tiny grass-green hat, grass-green gloves and shoes. The one red fruit in the foliage, her short, heavy little mouth, bloomed into *w* position:

"*oo*Wonderful to see you!"

Below the observation window, Berlin stretched away, spic and span, no giddy tricks like last night. Dr. Holze had the city well in hand. Nice, good, free Berlin offered itself with decorum under the bright noon my hostess had arranged. Her cigarette holder pointed out the Brandenburg Gate over there, the famous watershed between East and West, 'twixt Liberty and Slavery, the perilous Checkpoint Charlie; the notorious Wall, looking, where visible, like a mud fortress running through toy buildings. And, ah, over there, "our lovely Dowle Hotel," resembling from this distance less an oyster than a very pale bedbug, so far still blood-starved for lack of guests. And there, over there, on the horizon, the first trees of the Schatten estate.

But Dr. Holze pushed this businessy sight away. It wasn't part of her arrangement yet. "First, may we lift a glass to the honor of your being in Berlin? And—and in the honor of you and I being pals? With your permission—I am Ida."

Hello, Ida. Ida she would be henceforth. Ida crossed two strapping knees without adjusting her skirt, an act celebrating our new informal relation. Her cigarette holder swept across the vista beneath.

"You look at those ruins, Leon. You ask yourself— you are a thoughtful person, Leon—you ask yourself, *oo*Why has this city suffered? *oo*What was the reason? My father always said, 'Solution of the problem! by finding the reason for the problem!' And you know, Leon, this is strange, but maybe my father was one of the reasons."

Her glass tapped against the bar, signaling a second round and providing punctuation. From her *w* phonetics to her matched colors, Ida was the Teutonic emulation of the Manhattan career sylph who in the movies so outsophisticates Cary Grant that in the end he marries Doris Day instead. I think Ida felt that this sylph, buried inside her girth, needed only the right American motion, the hip New York phrase, to become manifest. And she had a definite idea of how this sylph self of hers should conduct a business lunch. The procedure consisted of: (*a*) drinks at the bar (pally toasts, crossed legs, first names, establishment of personal intimacy); (*b*) main dish (passing the salt, business at hand); (*c*) dessert (coffee, conclusions, concrete action).

We were in the final phase of (*a*) establishment of personal intimacy. The leaf-green suit leaned toward me at a confessional angle. Ida clinked the ice in her Scotch and shook her head about her father: a fine, late man, a cultural attaché in the diplomatic service. She, Ida, had acquired from him tremendously. Foreign countries. Foreign tongues. Customs, manners, *savoir-faire*. A respectable man too. Demised 1944—political heartbreak, one might say. He had really died of this perverted Germany of those days.

A pause. A sigh, marvelously combined with a fingersnap: more ice for her Scotch.

A fine gentleman, her father. But!—what kind of a *father?* Had he taught Ida maturity? Independence? This was the other side of the story. He had swallowed Ida's life, Ida's studies, Ida's social activities—swallowed all of Ida. Did I, Leon, understand this, being a thoughtful man? The same with Ida's countrymen. No fathers, only octopuses. They were all so used to being swallowed by octopuses. How could there be resistance to the biggest octopus, called Mister Hitler? And even today— must one not look around very hard for grown-up, unswallowed people in Germany? For real men?

Another drink? No? Ida gave a second sigh-cum-fingersnap. Instantly we were elevatored down the radio tower, door-slammed into the limousine. I would not mind, would I? consuming a lunchbite with her in her most quiet office dining alcove?

She sank into the Mercedes upholstery with a third sigh, expressing both melancholy and achievement. Indeed, much had been accomplished: Germany indicted, but the Germans absolved. A little Freud, a dash of guilt, and the nasty complexities of the past were cleanly unraveled, Ida's private status explained, her spinsterhood justified by the dearth of male maturity—a noble virginity imposed by historical circumstances and her own rigorous high standards. And so the last part of lunch phase (*a*)—personal intimacy—had been consummated in an ideally modern American manner: i.e., by psychoanalytic complaints about one's parents.

Ida's office was also a deft arrangement. It began with an anteroom and three assistants introduced by Ida as "My Littel Partners." They were all beyond forty, with carmine lipstick and thin disappointed noses, and bore out an old theory of mine: that spinsters hire spinsters rather than married women. The Littel Partners were uniformed in bright New York career-girl dresses. At Ida's entrance a clockwork went off inside them that produced bright New York career-girl gestures. They hello'd and how-do-you-do'd me, and called Ida "Ida" with diligent equality and smiled smiles and fingered curls and swarmed us into Ida's office proper.

An Inner Sanctum here, gray and pink in color (executive femininity). In the dining alcove, called "My Littel Den," the walls were dotted with scrolls Ida had received and with tourist-frequency curves in which she had caused erections. A feminine little executive espresso machine took up a corner. Next to it, on the white-decked table, Ida initiated phase (*b*), passing the salt, business at hand. She was wondering how I had been faring at Schatten yesterday?

I said it had been an inconclusive visit.

" 'Inconclusive'?" said Ida. "Ah, Leon, so polite! The word is 'impossible'!"

One Littel Partner poured the wine. Another served me a Schatten letter received that very day, a carbon copy of the original which had earlier gone to Dave and caused his cable. The letter simply said that the Prince's indisposition made it inadvisable to discuss his personal participation at this time. Sincerely, Ahn, Dr. in charge.

"You see?" Ida said. "Impossible! Not worth the effort. No, Leon, I suggest the other opening. Here, you must not omit the oysters fresh flown in."

Now, it wasn't any one thing. It was, in part, the return of my lightheadedness and irritability. It was also Ida's little masticating teeth. It was her constant, smooth subterranean chomping, like a tiny ship's engine. It was the merciless smooth synchronization of cooled Moselle with ice-bedded oysters; room-temperature Burgundy with sizzling steak (big-shot food again); and the secret little teeth chewing and coping with it all so well and so greedily. They were unfailing, those little teeth, invisible, imperceptible yet powerful; after a while I felt them working everywhere, in Dave's cable and even in my talk with Nina; busy, ubiquitous, they nibbled and whittled, they digested and arranged away. They made everything so dead-safe. It was a sudden, perverse, perhaps flu-born idea. I felt the need to throw a monkey wrench into those jaws and make them stop.

"Well," I said, "that letter isn't a definite turndown."

"My dear Leon, im-possible. I know them. Schatten is technically a spa-hotel under this office's jurisdiction. I possess their statistics—"

"A hotel?" I said. "All the better!"

"Only because a hotel saves taxes in Berlin. But they have no private bathrooms, no electric, no garage—"

"How fascinating," I said.

"We used to write them letters. We even offered them renovation credit—impossible. No, you have a littel cu-

cumber salad, Leon, and we chat about the Volks-rocket."

All this without losing a single mastication beat. I had lots more monkey wrench.

"Well," I said, "maybe contact with us Dowlers will get some hotel sense into Schatten. We'll benefit mutually."

The teeth did slow a bit, but only to let Ida show emphatic, almost heroic patience. The history of Schatten, she said, was a history of subterfuge (a word whose consonants ejected a steak pellet from her mouth). Not even the National Socialists! could get their hands on Schatten for a long while because the Prince had made it a spa-favorite of all the foreign ambassadors. And even when the National Socialists jailed the Prince it only entitled him to terrific privileges later on—like making the estate Western Zone. Nobody had ever gotten anywhere with Schatten.

"Isn't that funny," I said. "Many people say that about the Dowle organization too."

The teeth finally stopped—because there was no steak left. Ida distended her mouth into a charitable smile at all my endearing misconceptions. She got up. She had a pastel-green tripping kind of goose step, a compromise between energy of motion and tightness of shoes. She walked to a file case, Littel Partners fluttering anxiously behind, and returned with a card. The card showed that Schatten was infinitely the most unsuccessful hotel operation in Berlin, using nine per cent of its official bed capacity.

A nine-per-cent parallel between Schatten and Dowle Incorporation! Ida laughed a that-settles-that laugh. She sank into her chair with a relaxed tooth-picking sovereignty, indicating that her feet were once more free of shoes. The espresso trumpeted the inauguration of lunch phase (*c*), dessert (coffee, conclusions, concrete action), and the Littel Partners brimmed with chocolate squares.

Now as to the Volksrocket, Ida intended to make an illustrated booklet of the event—

"But Mr. Dowle will be charmed by that Schatten percentage," I said. "You know, that's one of Mr. D's famous sayings: 'The hotel business would be ideal if we could only do away with the guests!' "

I'm not as good as Andy, but if necessary I can laugh up a storm. Ida's face, big with chocolate square, was coerced into a crooked smile. But her cigarette holder pointed to the Volksrocket documents which had arrived together with the coffee cups.

"Another thing," I said, "Mr. Dowle will be delighted to find a hotel colleague in a personage like the Prince. That will make a very pleasant news item."

Ida's little teeth worked again, faster and more furious than ever. She wasn't miffed at me—only at the Littel Partner who had just given her a new chocolate square and who, to make up for this misdemeanor, must be an angel and bring the Schatten real-estate registration file!!

The other Littel Partners, alarmed, sounded the espresso again, a clarion to recall me, for God's sake, to phase (*c*) and the Volksrocket. Meanwhile the real-estate file yielded two cards, both marked henceforward with vicious little smears of chocolate fudge. The first card showed that the Prince, unable to pay even his hotel-reduced taxes in 1948, had to give up three acres of his estate to the city. So much for Mr. Dowle perhaps wanting to get involved with a tax felon!

"Wait," I said. "That's another of Mr. Dowle's famous sayings: 'Show me the man who has no tax problem, and I will show you a bum!' "

Ida smiled a smile of bottomless tolerance for all the intolerable things that were happening to her. One of these was a third chocolate square that had just happened to her mouth and with which her mouth bravely coped while continuing to enlighten me.

She pointed to the second file card, which showed that last year the Prince had not even fulfilled the legal requirement of answering the questionnaire of the real-estate census. So much for his willingness to work with the authorities! The Volksrocket, on the other hand—

"Fine," I said, "then we've got something illegal on Schatten. So we'll blackmail him into a little coopera-tion!"

This threw Ida into a brute fit of laughter. Her hand battered her generous pastel-green thighs, little green hat bobbing like a buoy on a suddenly incensed sea, one gold tooth glinting way back in her small deep mouth, a gilt demon raving in a cage. Frightened, the Littel Partners dropped everything to laugh with her.

"This is the funniest idea! Leon, you promise me, when we work together on the Volksrocket—we take off a littel time for blackmailing Schatten! You promise, now!"

"Of course," I said. "But first we'll give Schatten a try once more. We'll find out just exactly what the doctor means."

That really did in the little teeth. Too much was too much. Ida cleaned her chocolate-tipped pinkie with a paper napkin. "I am terribly in favor of this," she said, hard. "Fun blackmailing, and everything else. I am mad for this idea. But it is not within possibility. They have no telephone at Schatten. Maybe they don't even open mail—"

"Oh, I'm not thinking of letters," I said. "I'd like to drive out there right now, if you have the car handy. We'll get it over with one way or another."

Ida cleaned her pinkie so thoroughly that little napkin shreds fluttered to the ground. "By all means!" she said. Her stern face showed that her feet were suffering inside shoes once more. The napkin shreds kept flying, and the Littel Partners teetered helpless around a futile heap of anti-Schatten file cards. Nothing availed, not first names or personal intimacy or the cry of the espresso. The American lunch lay in shambles. The chauffeur appeared, summoned by some secret bell.

"KarlHeinz will help you get it over with!"

Aghast door-opening by the Littel Partners.

"Good-bye, Leon! Good luck! You will need it!"

My last glance took in the fact that my hostess had just swallowed, traceless, a fourth chocolate square.

6

As a rule I'm not terribly mean to people. Which might be just another way of saying that as a rule I don't care terribly much. But on my first full day in Berlin I did vandalize Ida's lunch. For some reason, I was giving more of a damn than usual about more things than usual. The fact is that all those Berlin weeks were damn-giving weeks. I had my confounded nerve ends sticking out all over.

It was unsettling, especially at first. In addition, my post-flu weakness acted up again when I had myself driven back to the Grand. To bring the Prince around, I wanted to pick up a picture portfolio of my previous openings. Only, I couldn't get my hands on it. The cursed chambermaid had erased all signs of my presence and my belongings. I had to search for the album sitting down, I felt that rubber-legged. Finally I found the thing in a secret little wall closet into which had been swept, interestingly enough, further fragments of Uncle Julius' whole-wheat biscuit. Evidently the Grand is the kind of hotel in which chambermaids do hiding instead of cleaning.

In the driveway KarlHeinz waited with his little blond goatee, his smooth subordinate simper.

"To the Schatten estate, suhr," he stated rather than asked.

"Drive me to Schatten," I said, as if I hadn't heard.

"Yes, suhr, to the Butler's Gate."

I didn't have to do him the favor of asking what he meant. He told me anyway.

"Butler's Gate is what they call the main entrance, suhr."

"Do they."

"Yes, suhr, Butler's Gate. Because the Kaiser went there once, but the Prince didn't go to meet him, he only sent his butler. So the Kaiser went away again."

"You don't say."

"They say the Kaiser was too military for the Prince, suhr. The Prince is very particular."

I leafed through my portfolio.

"He also got in trouble with Hitler."

"You mean your poor Hitler had to go away too?"

"No, suhr." Entirely unruffled. "But the Prince, he didn't like to let in the National Socialists. They say that's because he was hiding Jews."

"Is that also a story from the illustrateds?"

"Oh, no, suhr. My uncle told me, the dead one, the one that worked there."

I smelled his secret cigarette smell. For some reason he reminded me of the little teeth which must have been into the fourteenth chocolate square by now.

"Suhr, when they liberated the Prince, they say he

walked out of the concentration camp, eighty years old, just like new."

"Unfortunately," I said, "the Prince doesn't seem so healthy now."

"Pardon, suhr, you have *seen* him?"

He asked with such fascinated naïve unbelief, it almost didn't sound impertinent. He was a virtuoso driver, smoking, taking curves, and staring at me directly in the rear-view mirror with his servile half-smile.

"I will see him," I said.

"Suhr, my dead uncle used to say, 'If he won't bother with the Kaiser, who will he bother with?' "

"You think he won't bother with me?"

"Oh, no, suhr. He knows what is good for him, suhr, your wonderful openings. He would be a fool not to bother with *you*, suhr."

"Well," I said, "let's close that draft vent up front. I want to catch a few winks."

"Yes, suhr."

But there was not a single wink to be caught, no matter how firmly I kept my eyelids shut. Furthermore, the closing of the vent made the car quite hot, and I felt self-conscious about reversing my order or contradicting it by opening my own window. Even with my eyes closed I felt the stare from the rear-view mirror. Just to show him, I tried to hurry into sleep before we arrived. I shifted and stretched and, in an uncomfortable way, managed to shake off consciousness—or would have if the car hadn't yowled to a halt.

"Here we are, suhr."

I stood before the arching Venetian bridge. Below ran the empty border highway with the East German guardhouse. Above me beat the midafternoon sun.

"I think you want your portfolio, suhr."

I'd actually forgotten it. He handed it to me, then touched me under the elbow, almost as though I needed steadying. I turned away curtly while he stayed where he was, leaning against the open car door.

All that sudden sun didn't exactly cure my light-headedness. Nor did the heavy scent of late roses coming from the estate. They ambushed me. On the near side of the bridge the scent became stronger still and confused itself with the perfumes of jasmine and marigold. The estate, when it lay before me for the first time in full daylight, was quite different from the bright little spot glimpsed from the Radio Tower Bar. Ivy and wild-rose vines foamed against the fence with an extraordinary green, a chlorophyll more vivid than anything I'd seen outside. Not only the color but somehow even the scents were blinding.

I must have dropped my hand on the crossbar of the gate. It rattled like yesterday, apparently to the slightest touch. Like yesterday, she appeared from behind a pavilion. I pulled back my hand. Then I realized, as she came nearer, that it wasn't her. It wasn't her at all. This turned out to be a much older woman, more than sixty. But her face, inclined slightly to one side, was still a shell of handsomeness. She, too, wore a long-skirted gray dress. In one hand she carried a small black book with the gilt rim of a missal.

Three yards from the gate she stopped. Her eyes fixed themselves on a point below my head.

"Good day," she said in German. "Yes?"

"Good day," I said. I explained who I was and that I had asked for the Prince yesterday."

"Yes. The Prince is indisposed."

"May I talk to him briefly? He and Dr. Ahn know what this is all about."

Nothing moved, not even the inclined head.

"It isn't possible to talk to the Prince now."

"I'd like to see Dr. Ahn, then."

"Yes. The doctor is out."

"In that case his daughter, please. She and I talked yesterday."

"Irene is out too."

Her name was Irene. The voice that had pronounced her name was overlaid with a stoic grayness, but it sounded familiar. Suddenly I realized: this is the mother. Far inside the estate, by the pond, I saw figures moving. Someone with a parasol and a shape which might have been Irene herself. A mirage no doubt, but it added to frustration a sense of deception. Underneath this woman's brittle old handsomeness was something un-yielding, something impassive. Her words came at me clenched and blind. Her eyes remained fixed just below my head. I didn't care for her at all.

"Will Dr. Ahn be back today?"

"Yes. They will return at seven."

"Not before? What would be a good time to see them tomorrow?"

"I don't know their plans."

"Seven is your lock-up time, isn't it? There wouldn't be any time to talk."

"Yes. At seven they lock the gate."

The shape in front of me was absolutely immobile. The sun hammered. The green dazzled. And I—I burned and couldn't show it.

"Is there a chance they might be back before curfew?"

"Yes. They might."

"All right," I said, "I'll try. I'll be back here at half past six."

"I shall tell them."

"Thank you. Good day."

"Good day."

When I reached KarlHeinz, he was still standing by the car door he had left open, as if taking my early return quite for granted. It was an implication he managed to stress by reaching for my useless portfolio and replacing it on the exact square of upholstery from which he had removed it a few minutes before.

"To the hotel, suhr?"

"Drive me to the hotel," I said, as deafly as possible. If he had said anything further, I might have cracked down on him directly. I felt so goddamn thwarted. But he didn't say one more word during the ride. He pulled the car smoothly around the curves, smoked and whistled. That is, he whistled the way he smoked, with an underhand flair, just below the threshold of perception. A very low hiss in three-quarter time came from between his teeth, a thing resembling the Emperor Waltz. Sometimes it barely teased my ears; sometimes it became audible enough to cut me to the bone with its grating, chill, monotonous, antimelodic nonchalance. Every time I got ready to shut him up, he forestalled me by stopping. And then he began again, so softly as to hide the noise in the motor hum.

I had one hour in my hotel room before riding back once more. That hour isn't one of my favorite memories either. I ordered a double rye and called Dinny. Of my Schatten impasse I said nothing.

Schatten was a private embarrassment, not to be mentioned until it had been properly resolved. But as I talked, an idea struck home: why not put the Dowle Casino on those three Schatten acres, the ones the city had bought? I'd crash that gate one way or another.

The receiver produced some extraordinary Dinny modulations. *Ex*quisite possibility! Really abso*lutely* clear title to the land? But the Prince such an in*sane* brute . . . never even *an*swered a request to include the Schatten crest among Club decorations . . . *beast*ly snob . . . too hu*mil*iating to tangle with . . .

In the end I had to fight him into considering the idea. The whole afternoon abounded in warfare. In forcing Schatten, I was bucking not only Dave and Ida, both hefty opponents, but also Schatten's own mysterious will. It suited my mood. I fought with room service, hollering into the phone about the drink they still hadn't brought. To Dave I sent off a fighting cable: OPERATION SCHATTEN STILL HOT STOP MIGHT EVEN WANGLE DOWLE CASINO WITH SCHATTEN TWIST STOP WILL WIRE MORE SOON   GENIUS.

I was ready to tear into KarlHeinz, for I thought I heard his whistle coming from the corridor just to vex me. The fink hadn't bothered to carry my portfolio to the Schatten gate, yet had insisted on bringing it right into my suite. I was sure he was sprawling on a chair outside now, sibilating away. But when I stomped outside, I found only a bouquet of flowers on the hall stand, full of hay-fever pollen. Room service arrived at last—with a single Scotch instead of my double rye. I sent the moron flying. And then, thank God, it was time to go down for the next assault.

At 6:30 sharp we drew up before the border highway. I crossed the Venetian bridge for the third time in twenty-four hours, each time groggier. I remember wishing, suddenly, that she wouldn't be there; that there would be no manor, no fence, nothing and nobody; that I could take a deep breath, turn on my heels, forget the whole spooky place, get to work on the Volksrocket, round off my career with Dave in a nice sane way.

But she was there.

She was waiting right by the gate, and behind her, colors muted once again by twilight, the whole dim magnificence of the estate. She was dressed in that gray linen dress, evidently the Schatten costume. Next to her stood her father, the famous Dr. Ahn.

Imagine a very tall man, with a long leathered face, deep very slowly blinking eyes, a rough cane, and white hair brushed carelessly back. Very lush long white hair; a gray smock worn unbuttoned over a tweed suit; he gave not a medical but a Bohemian impression.

His daughter swung the gate back. I saw that the fingers gripping the lever had very shapely tips, small unpainted narrow-arched nails like tiny Gothic windows, in each of which sat a half-moon. I stood on the exact threshold of the estate. The gate was open at last. There were no handshakes or flowery European introductions. She just pointed and named names. I inquired, of course, after the Prince's health.

"Bronchitis," the doctor said with a small shrug.

"Not too critical, I hope?"

"A nuisance in a man His Highness' age."

"I think you know how important it is for me to talk to the Prince."

"Mr. Dowle has a letter from us," she said. "We have no further news."

She wasn't going to get off that easy.

"You do understand," I said, "time is crucial for me. I'd very much like to explore the whole problem with you now, while I'm here."

"If you wish."

Suddenly she walked forward along the path. The old doctor extended his hand. To my surprise, we were going straight toward the manor. The breakthrough—for that's how I phrased it to myself—had come so fast.

The estate seemed a good deal less outlandish inside the gate. The scent diminished somewhat past the jasmine and roses by the fence. We walked through a well-clipped maze of yew, a kind of formal garden. Beyond it, all discipline vanished from the grounds. Flowers, grass, even huge fernlike weeds rioted freely, smothering whole stone benches. But the unearthly green glitter of the day had gone. I even thought the place looked exactly like what it was: a fine old spa park gone to seed.

The pond before the castle had once been rimmed by a gravel path; now it was a ribbon of moss. We crossed an arching thudding wooden bridge, a replica of the marble one over the highway. Underneath, huge carplike gold-fish moved through violet ripples. I had the feeling they knew my presence and disregarded it. There were swans and willows—the whole works, though all in a somewhat dowdy vein. In a pergola two big glimmering peacocks stood, with their backs to me, trembling slightly.

The clack of the doctor's cane followed our footfalls against green flagstones, the sound of birds' wings and a bell high in a tower. Apart from the pagoda embellishments, the manor reminded me, now that I saw it up close, of the playful country chateaux the good Empress Maria Theresia had built all over Austria. Once I spent a childhood summer near one of them.

I felt I'd suddenly assimilated the strangeness of the place. She, too, seemed more ordinary. In her right hand she carried a small handkerchief which at every other step she flicked softly against her thigh. Except for this abstracted rhythm, she had a manner different from yesterday's. Her tone was pointed, efficient, that of a brisk matron's or Mother Superior's. She kept walking ahead; I couldn't see her face. But her voice carried the suggestion of a flat smile.

"This part here was designed as an English garden," she said. "It was quite the vogue in the nineteenth century. The Prince's grandfather had it done in the 1850's by the man who later turned out lots of English gardens for Louis Napoleon."

"Very interesting," I said.

"It's amusing. It's supposed to convey a romantic landscape. Because we can't keep it up, it's more romantic than it should be. Our former spa springs are over there—no, it's too dark for you to see them now. We have a cunning little waterfall there, and there even used to be a nice little artificial ruin."

"How fascinating."

"Oh, it's practically regulation romantic. Shall we go in for a moment?"

We stood before the manor entrance.

"I'd like to."

Again she strode ahead, again her father extended his arm. We entered a huge but very dark hall, made a sharp turn into a bright, gas-lit alcove. It was paneled in oak and had a refectory table studded with wine bottles, and not a single chair or other furniture. The doctor went straight to the bottles.

"The manor was built in 1857," she said, "a sort of

Victorian baroque with a bit of Madame Butterfly thrown in. This little alcove is pretty representative."

Her hand flicked the handkerchief against her thigh. I had a sudden misgiving. It was all too easy and glib. It was a spiel. She less talked to me than humored me. She seemed to disguise rather than explain the estate—or herself. We were all alone, we three. I noticed no one else. I felt they all waited for the intrusion to pass.

The doctor had poured wine into three glasses. He lifted one.

"We hope you have enjoyed your visit."

It was delicate, impeccable Bordeaux. I was being given a delicate, impeccable bum's rush. The kind they no doubt had ready for any inquisitive tourist.

"Thank you," I said. "The Prince runs this as a hotel, doesn't he?"

"As a sanatorium hotel," she said in her light relentless tone. "A rest home, really. Most of our guests are old retainers of the estate. That's how they get their pension from the Prince, in room and board and care. Occasionally there are dowagers, hunting memories. Or younger visitors whose curiosity we try to satisfy."

Meaning me. And obviously her ironic tourist-guide impersonation was designed to feed my shallow sensibilities before ushering me out. The doctor had refilled our glasses. I decided to make myself quite clear.

"I wish I were just a sightseer," I said, "but I've a job to do. You see, it isn't just a hotel opening we want the Prince for. We want him to dramatize the best cultural heritage of Berlin. I can't leave before getting him to participate."

She used the handkerchief to dab a tiny wine drop on her mouth. I noted, angrily, the graceful, somehow oblivious leisuredness with which the small white-mooned nails moved against her unpainted lips.

Then came the blow.

"The difficulty is that the Prince is away," the doctor said.

I tried not to oblige them with too much surprise. It was hard.

"Away? Since when?"

"Oh, a few days," she said. "For his bronchitis. In Davos. Didn't you know?"

"It's not in the letter. I was never told!"

"Weren't you?" he said. "I'm sorry. Will you take this as a souvenir? One of the few twenty-year-olds we have left in the cellar."

He handed me a bottle with a courtly little bow.

"Thank you," I said. The gesture was just a sardonically vulgar extension of the tourist-guide bit. Free souvenir included. The bottle made me look even more foolish. And they were a damnably excellent team, father and daughter. The old man now looked at his watch with an "oh dear" expression.

"We'd better not let them lock the gate on you."

"When will the Prince return?"

"In about a week."

"Not for another week?"

"Unfortunately," he said. "With time being so crucial, you probably won't want to wait that long." He lifted his glass in a conclusive gesture.

"Good luck in your further endeavors."

Those two handsome lofty faces looked at me. Those two handsome lofty mouths were bent into the same faintly mocking curve. Father and daughter seemed quite entertained by the fatigued gentleman before them, clutching a wine bottle under his arm. It was as though they knew just how to deal with a highly competent, highly paid, highly safe lackey who bullied room service, exchanged arch obedient cables with his boss, played it smart and knew when he was being shown the door.

I put down the bottle.

"We could go ahead just the same," I said. "We're behind in our construction schedule, which gives me more room to plan the opening. Till His Highness returns, we could study preliminaries together."

"I'm afraid," he said, "I can't be optimistic about the Prince's willingness to—"

"But we can't be sure until he returns, right? Until he listens to my story?"

They both froze, but only for a fraction of a second.

"You catch us at a bad time," she said, still smoothly.

"I wouldn't ask much of you."

"It's supply-buying time. It keeps us rushing in and out the gate till seven. And after curfew one can't get in." Still bright and matronly, she was adjusting her hat, pushing the brim down still deeper.

She could push all she wanted.

"Well, now," I said, "I could cooperate there. I could stay here after closing. I could stay starting tonight."

"To*night?*" he said, and it was a pleasure to have gotten one syllable's worth of consternation out of him.

"This is a hotel," I said. "You've rooms, don't you?"

A sudden fretful cry outside the window. I can still hear it. A beating of wings.

"Our peacocks," she said. "They must have seen you in the lamplight. They can't get used to strangers." She pulled down a great scalloped window shade. Her handkerchief flicked against her thigh a bit harder. With his glass the doctor drew a small circle on the table. The bell sounded from a tower, and I was triumphant because I had finally jarred them.

"Tonight could be dreary for you," she said. "I'm afraid we're tied up."

"I'll stay just in case. In fact, we may use the city's acres in your enclave for a Dowle Casino, and it might be useful for me to move in for a few days." Now it was my turn to be mercilessly glib. "I'll be right on the spot, 'on location,' as they say."

There was no immediate answer. The doctor released his wineglass very slowly, and very slowly blinked his eyes.

"I'm sure," he said, "there must be happier lodgings for you than our clumsy place."

"I'm not a bit sure," I said. "The service at the Grand Hotel is awfully unfriendly. You've been much nicer."

It was infernal cheek. Like all infernal cheek, it worked.

"The gentleman flatters us," she said. "I'll see about his room." The handkerchief flicked, sharply. She vanished.

He walked me back to the entrance, cane clacking steadily, voice calm again with courtesies. He could certainly roll with a punch. Did I need pajamas? A toothbrush? I said I was American enough to like the idea of roughing it for a night; tomorrow I'd have my luggage fetched.

After the bright alcove, the estate grounds closed around us like a dark rich blindfold. I felt crazy and comfortable. My voice seemed to echo foolishly across the perfumed pond. I didn't care. I was headily tired, beautifully victorious. Beyond the fence, silhouetted against the last livid flush of twilight, stood two East

German soldiers with their collars turned up. One squeaked a key in the gate lock. The other one, a bit hunchbacked, observed me through the bars with a kind of merry incredulity, quite as though I were a new three-headed hippo he had just spotted in his favorite zoo cage. I still didn't care. I went right up to the gate, for my final victory was there.

"*Good night*," I shouted across the marble Venetian bridge. "*I'm staying here!*"

I saw KarlHeinz come out of the car and snap to attention. His hand went to his ear.

"*Suhr?*"

"*Dis-missed. Come tomorrow at ten.*"

For about five seconds he stood transfixed. He stared at me, at the two soldiers walking away from the locked gate. Then he slowly got into the car—but emerged again to give me a long-distance salute.

The car roared off. We turned and went back, the gravel creaking under our stride.

7

OFTEN I THINK that maturity is just a fraud; that there are no people over fourteen, only children buried in wrinkles and pomposity; that I myself am only a makeshift adult, stilts inside my long pants and manhood painted on my face—a fraud easily found out; and that suddenly, say during a Dowle board meeting, these trappings will drop away and expose the midget kid underneath with his fingers in his mouth.

And there are other times when being grown-up seems so real because you feel it has just happened—again. On my first morning in Schatten I felt as though I'd had a singular bar mitzvah, reached some thundering new majority attained so far by no one else. In fact, I kept smelling out the midget-child in others. To Dave I sent a cable that was on the borderline between the joshing and the uppity: MOVING INTO SCHATTEN STOP DON'T FALL OFF CHAIR STOP CABLE ADDRESS C/O BERLIN PROMOTION OFFICE LOVE GENIUS.

Probably he did fall off the chair, because it was a pretty poor day for most of my adversaries. KarlHeinz, for example. He drove me back to the city with a red nose and a handkerchief squashed in his fist—and not a word. I had him turn on radio music, a fine conversation-killing device I should have used the day before. I hummed the beguine. He sniffled. Sweet justice. The loyal boy had my flu.

And Dr. Ahn, a little earlier. We met as I came out of the manor.

"Good morning," I said. "I think I'll move in before lunch, if that's convenient."

He put his cane under his arm.

"With your luggage?"

"Sure, so I won't have to pay my bill in advance."

"For how long may we count on you?"

"Oh, as long as it takes to wait for His Highness and make him one of us."

He didn't appreciate my good mood so terribly much.

"I'm afraid," he said, "we have no telephone or desk service or any of the things you are used to."

"I can always work with long-distance semaphore," I said. "Could I have more of your wonderful food at one?"

A very small pause.

"We'll be ready for you," he said.

Probably he still hoped I'd change my mind. But I was enjoying myself too much. I had enjoyed myself since opening my eyes. I'd waked up ravenous—no more headache or fatigue. I loved having breakfast out of china marked with a tiny crested unicorn. Tiny unicorns were branded everywhere, into the Black Forest furniture of the room, into the sepia tile oven in the corner, even into each of the embossed ceiling beams. I found myself inside a lovely giant cuckoo clock. And the hike to the john was like a grotto ride at Coney Island—the corridor vaulted with gas lamps at every other arch; at the landing two Afghan hounds and a black Shepherd dog suspended dreamlike on the upper steps. I would have thought them procelain rather than alive, except that one scratched. The john: a parquet-floored hall, the fixture mounted on three marble steps so that you might answer the call of nature with the pedestaled dignity of a national monument.

Back in my room, the baroque pitcher on the washstand contained the most refreshing chill water. To top it off, I had no razor with me and therefore couldn't shave. For the first time in years I didn't have to start the day by punishing my jaws. It put me into a positive holiday mood.

And just my hairy chin aggravated Ida's shock in her office. Poor, unsuspecting, symphonic Ida. That day she appeared as an orchestration in yellow—pale golden suit, saffron gloves, yellow feathered hat, lemony shoes. She flooded toward me with ecstatic compassion. Oh, Leon! Trapped at Schatten after closing time! Had they given me anything to eat at all? Anything edible? And the beds—there were real beds there? Was I—pardon this phrase—bited by horrific littel animals? And had the Prince been rude?

I simply told her that, despite Highness' temporary absence, I'd decided on a Schatten opening and would live at the estate.

In the midst of rushing forward to me, Ida froze. Into a faint, ghastly smile. The Littel Partners suddenly straightened, as if all three had just been discreetly but cruelly goosed. The entire Berlin Promotion Bureau was desperately trying to come to grips with the news. Ida's eyes focused on my stubbly chin; to her it appeared to incarnate incomprehensible evil. My stubble undid all the fine Anglo-Saxon *w*'s she had ever enunciated. In fact, for the next few awful minutes she would attempt those ultra-*w*'s no more. All she could do was come to a stop beside her desk, one saffron-gloved hand finding support on the espresso machine, a smile clinging like a dead cobra around her white little teeth.

Move in there, she whispered. Bravo! She didn't want to pry what promise of theirs had made me do this, she would just say Bravo! . . . A coup! . . .

" 'They'?" I said. "Who?"

It didn't matter, she whispered. Whoever had put me up to it, whatever rival city office . . . they had made the most clever possible move to exclude her. . . .

"Wait," I said. "This wouldn't exclude you—"

Ah! . . . she whispered. Even better! They had not even informed me it would? That her office had removed Schatten from the Berlin Promotion Federation? . . . Removed Schatten for non-minimum-fulfillment of hotel conditions? . . . So that the estate was beyond her liaison-competence? Not a word about this? . . . Nothing? Marvelous!

Poor Ida stood very brave and erect against the espresso machine, the yellow feather of the yellow hat trembling slightly. Brilliant! . . . she whispered. Hats off to them! She would, of course, turn over to me all her Schatten materials and informations . . . I had all her most sincere wishes. . . .

There was now a distinct odor of St. Joan upon the pyre. The Littel Partners stood petrified, perhaps praying. All this business about liaison-competence had, up to this point, been quite brilliantly suppressed by St. Ida herself. But I was in too good a mood.

"Ida," I said, "I see no reason why we should stop working together—"

But she interrupted me with a shudder. No! The feather in her hat quivered. No, no, whoever was responsible for this, another city office would do the liaison now, no matter how unequipped for a personality like the Prince. No, they would just eat up the glamor of it all . . . but the Prince would eat *them* up, and Mr. Dowle's money too. No, she, Ida, was just a useless, well-wishing sideline watcher now.

"Wait," I said. "Why don't you go into this together with whatever other office—"

No! In her voice the flames of the auto-da-fé had already started crackling. No, shivered the yellow feather, that would be catastrophe, two offices participating. . . . That meant fratricide, death, in Germany . . . two bureaucracy offices mixing things up, fighting horrifically. . . . No, I had her best wishes. . . .

"All right, then, let's limit it specifically to your office."

Oh, no, she whispered. No, no American could comprehend this German bureaucratic cesspool. National Socialism was nothing but German bureaucracy gone mad. . . . No, it was inconceivable; even such a thing as my preference of her office over another . . . even *it* would have to be an official note to the city commissioner. . . . She almost sighed her last. . . . It would have to be done right now—

"Fine," I said. "Let's."

One of the Littel Partners had suddenly grown a dictation pad. Toward it Ida dropped a murmur which had the audio-visual quality of a saint's last will and testament. This low, holy chant affirmed that Dowle Inc., on its own initiative and regardless of the choice of its opening celebration, would prefer to use the Berlin Municipal Promotion Bureau under Dr. Ida Holze as its sole and exclusive liaison agent with city authorities, and that this decision was not the result of influence, direct or indirect. . . .

Moments later a typewriter transformed this incantation into an official truth made out in triplicate. And, as seems only good and proper in the lives of saints, miracles transpired. Tragic Ida of Arc turned into a bustling department head. The yellow hat feather, instead of shivering, jubilated. All her Anglo-Saxon *w*'s were restored. The espresso machine broke its stark silence and burst into a veritable 2 1-gun salute of steaming cups. My ugly stubble became an apostolic beard. And the move into Schatten changed from perversity to a deed of wonder and of daring.

"You see?" Ida said vividly. "*oo*What happens? An American—he makes a bold move! *Zuck*—right into Schatten! Into the lion's den! And what does a German do? He must write a littel official paper. Terrible. Terrible and typical! Swallowed by the father mentality! This is *oo*where you sign, please. . . .

"The Old World is theory," she kept saying as we sipped our *cappucinos*. "The Old World is theory, but the New World is action!"

Well, the Old World was action too. To save time, the Littel Partners phoned the Grand to pack my bags and prepare my hotel bill. They dispatched my check via sniffly KarlHeinz, who was to bring back my luggage on the return trip. But the Old World was not enough action. An hour later the Grand called back. Some mysterious snag had developed in the luggage room— could I come in person?

There was, come to think of it, hell to pay that morning for the night before. I ran into a second tempest. And the tempest in Ida's office was milder than the one that now followed in the Grand's luggage room.

The foul-up here had nothing to do with any last-ditch nastiness of the hotel's. It was Uncle Julius. He stood, pale and clenched, blocking the porter's access to my Val-Paks. At sight of me his mouth opened. Something like glorious relief passed through his glasses. But glory never lasts in my uncle.

"You're free?" he breathed.

"Hello, Uncle," I said, surprised. "How do you mean?"

"You were not abducted?" He began to cough and pushed his spectacles against his nose. I looked so incredibly and intolerably unabducted. The drought was back in his face. He turned to the porters. "Take it away! *He* doesn't care about his luggage, *I* don't!"

"But these people are only doing their duty," I said. "They had word I'm leaving the hotel."

"Everybody should leave this hotel!"

The porters cursed in Berlinese and began to throw my bags on the luggage cart.

"Everybody had word," Julius said icily to his feet. "Everybody except me."

Only then did it hit me. "My God!" I said. "Our dinner last night!"

"One shows up at the hotel last night," my uncle said to his feet. "One tells these persons that one's dinner appointment is missing. Better one should be talking to a wall. Eleven o'clock, twelve midnight, one o'clock. Useless. They won't do anything. The East Zone is half a mile away, people vanish every day. Constant abductions. But they will not notify the police. Oh, no! Not even this morning when he still hasn't come. On the contrary! They pack up his luggage and take it away!"

"Uncle Julius," I said. "Will you forgive me?"

"Even the police, after I tell them myself. They won't move a finger. They would just let the luggage be robbed."

"Uncle," I said, "I simply didn't have a chance to let you know. If you have time now, please have lunch with me."

He stood there.

"At least ride along and give me a chance to explain."

He took a deep breath. He came along, white and frozen. He stepped around the porters as though they were lepers, much too hurt to speak one more word. He sat pressed away from me against the window of the Mercedes as we rode to the estate. His hairy hand was white with clutching the armrest. I soothed and soothed. I explained and explained. I guess in explaining it all to Uncle Julius I tried to explain it to myself.

By and by he relented. Wordless, he lit a cigarette for himself and let me show him the elegantly recessed limousine ashtrays he couldn't find. He produced a brown paper bag full of lovely but not quite ripe apples. I had to take and eat one to the core.

A crisis during our disembarkation at Schatten. An ancient handyman loaded my luggage into a donkey cart, and Julius got very alarmed when the luggage took a different path leading to the servants' quarters. The luggage absolutely had to go where he could keep an eye on it. It was thus—preceded by the cart, followed by Uncle Julius (munching grimly) and observed from afar by KarlHeinz's cold watering gaze—that I moved into the estate.

More difficulties in the hall, where Ahn waited for me. Poor Julius addressed him as "Prince." My introduction corrected him. Whereupon Julius, boiling with embarrassment, ran away to my biggest bag, dragged and panted its weight up the stairs, protests notwithstanding.

It was too bad. The new mishap again delayed a rapprochement. Though the estate kitchen came up with a second lunch tray, my guest would neither eat nor talk. Instead he tried to open my bags. I gave him the keys. But the newfangled locks were too much. He could deal with them only after instructions from me—a new source of vexation. With grunts and gestures I was driven back to the table. He rushed about in an irate anarchy of unpacking, flinging shorts and shirts every which way. He still wouldn't talk to me, but after a while he at least began to talk to himself for my benefit.

"Can't just be a lock . . ." he mumbled. "Has to be a trick. . . . Can't just talk to the Prince—has to be some doctor. . . ."

"You're right, Uncle." I wanted peace at any price. "You've got a point about the locks."

". . . always vicious complications . . . *The spider taketh hold*, it says. *It dwells in the king's palaces. . . .*"

This I couldn't follow.

"People don't even know the Bible any more. Even brilliant people . . . Everything doctored and tampered with . . . One wants to reach the Prince, instead the spider takes hold. . . ."

I tried to find a foothold for a positive conversation. I knew how petition-prone he was.

"Uncle," I said, "do you want to get some message to the Prince?"

". . . nothing left but spiders and tricks . . ."

"Seriously, now," I said. "Are you interested in reaching the Prince?"

But he was not yet ready for friendly dialogue. He began to hiss at the jacket in his hand. It wasn't enough people couldn't keep dinner appointments? They didn't even know how to eat any more? People weren't capable any more of just attending to their food and minding their own business? And not exposing their ignorance? One had to be a dietitian to know the rules of good digestion?

So I just attended to my food. In accordance with the rules of good digestion, I tried not to look too closely at what he was doing. But I knew he was stuffing socks into the remotest corners of the remotest drawers in the remotest cupboard. He deformed collars and perverted trouser creases. At last, though, he thawed toward the possibility of direct communication with me.

"Wouldn't get to the Prince in a hundred years," he opined to a vest.

"Uncle," I said, "I guarantee you. I'll meet the Prince himself soon. Anything you give me will get to him directly."

"This—this spider won't get hold of it?"

"Of course not."

He stood there, face averted, crumpling a paper bag in his overcoat pocket. Everything had been unpacked, including my ties, which he had wound wildly around and around a hanger, but he still wasn't ready for a direct dialogue.

"Look, come to think of it," I said, "the Prince's name might really help you in your restitution. Why don't we try him? And why don't we talk about this whole problem now?"

He pressed his glasses against his nose. He lowered himself into a Dante chair far away from me, and even that only distrustfully, as though the seat might give way under him. He was that impossible thing, an avuncular waif, and my heart went out to him. At the same time I enjoyed disconcerting this troublemaker with friendship.

"Another thing," I said. "In that pageant we use for our opening—we might want to rent those marvelous old cars they gave back to you already. We ought to discuss that too."

He gave a small bewildered nod. Now he had really let himself in for a chat with me and, what was worse, for a cordial and positive chat. It seemed to confuse him. He took the roll that lay beside his plate of now cold meat, bit into it, then changed his mind and put it into his pocket.

"I'll tell you what," I said. "We'll draft a statement of your restitution complaint and ask the Prince for moral support."

But Julius simply couldn't participate in such warmth so soon.

"Maybe tomorrow," he said gruffly.

"Okay."

"Documents take time. The day after tomorrow."

"Fine," I said. "The Prince isn't back yet anyway. But let's really have lunch. Let's meet at the Grand, since you're familiar with—"

"No!" he said. "Not that hotel! I'll come here—"
"I don't want you to come all the way out—"
"It's all right. Never mind."
We agreed on the day after tomorrow, lunch, at the estate. He got up.
"The chauffeur will drive you back—"
But he pressed my wrist, pressed back his glasses—gone.

The funny thing came afterwards. I followed his progress from my window as he rushed down the path, crossed the bridge over the pond, disappeared into the high yew, materialized by the gate and vanished altogether. It was my first discovery of the window.

I began to re-unpack his unpacking, recovered my socks, untangled my ties, rehung my suits. I pushed around the two big oak dressers until they were cozily juxtaposed with the Chinese screen and the fireplace. Then I tackled the escritoire. I spilled my briefcase onto it, arranged portable, dictaphone, papers, portfolio into working order. I pushed the most comfortable of the four chairs before the desk. And then, having completed a ritual that gives the most arid hotel room a kind of lived-in litter, a homey feeling—I felt completely strange. I didn't know what I was doing here. It was as though the chain of cause and effect had broken the moment I hit Berlin. I stared at the patina'd miniature gargoyle sitting on the inkwell lid. I tried the paw-shaped knob of a bureau drawer. It resisted opening. I forced the drawer. It rumbled open, showed nothing but dusty emptiness inside. Suddenly I began to write a letter—something fairly rare for me—a long rambling letter to Nina.

JOURNAL

September 12th

The window's got me. Maybe the journal is really just self-defense.

I mean my Schatten window. Not the one at Ida's office. At Ida's all goes well. The Littel Partners have rigged up a nice little desk for me, with a travel calendar and an ivory extension phone. Andy slapped me on the back nine times before flying off to Stockholm to complete the Swedish Dowle and recomplete his marriage. At Ida's I know that Schatten is no mistake. Let's get that straight. This could be a fine and, for a change, even authentic opening stunt. It was right to pursue both the opening and the Casino right on the spot, to move right in. And much can be accomplished before His Bronchitic Highness' return. The library alone is worth weeks of research. And still the window's got me.

After the office morning, after the drive back to the estate, I stare at all the objects in my room. I watch them in the heavy afternoon light as they turn their backs to me. The weighty cupboard with its labyrinthine inlaid design and cupolas surmounting its upper corners. The big white four-poster which lies in state in the middle of the room. The Chinese screen full of preoccupied fishermen and devious rivers. The broad windowsill with sharp bladelike iron flowers along its outside rim, and the chestnut branches rocking abstracted just beyond. Sometimes they seem to sway right into the room. But they are beyond arm's reach. I know. I've tried it.

Everything's like that at good old Schatten. It has a
funny childhood smell. All the objects around breathe
with a secret soul, and each hides its secret soul from me.
For the first time in thirty years objects have been snub-
bing me again. They keep driving me back to the window.

At the window you must be patient. If you wait long
enough, you'll see Schatten residents walk singly or in
pairs along the pond, the men's hands anchored on large
lapels, the women's feet moving slow under long black
skirts. Crones and he-crones in dreamy conference.
Never more than two at a time, so that they appear
forlorn and otherworldly against the heroic park. Such
ancient lunar dolls. Superlunar Dr. Ahn only seldom
consents to materialize, and only very seldom Miss Moon
herself, his daughter, the Nun . . . the pin-up Nun.

One Schatten creature actually comes into my room
with the meal tray. An old retainer with a long mustache
much too well kept for his green apron, and a bald
noncommittal head. His greeting, a dim bow, always
takes place on the threshold, entering and leaving. Technically, he approaches within three yards of me. Yet he
never seems nearer than the figures I glimpse from the
window. In fact, he has something of the astral distance,
the remote fairyland pathos of the fishermen on the
Chinese screen.

Even the pages of the Nina letter which I started
yesterday read like some dusty *billet-doux* found here in
a forgotten drawer. That letter seems as remote as the
Chinese screen. So I didn't go on with it. As substitute, I
suppose, I'm at the journal again, hereby resumed as a
serious, daily, going concern. It's a more constructive
form of loitering than ogling at the window.

Though, mind you, window ogling got me to the library. After lunch today I noticed her standing almost directly below my room, on the gravel path outside the manor. She was talking to her mother. I saw the breeze tug at the one blond wisp not imprisoned by her coif-hat. I was that close, and the window open. Yet her voice remained inaudible. Through its very whisperedness the damn conversation seemed to announce its importance, while at the same time mocking eavesdroppers like me.

I wanted to look at the grounds anyway. I was out of my room, down the stairs, into the lobby. But I never made it outside, to her.

Ahn came swooping out of some alcove. Gray smock open, his long arm extended in an "after you" sweep that gathered me up and along. Into the wrong direction.

"Do you find the meals adequate?"

"Yes, I was just about to walk off lunch—"

"Good. May I show you something?"

Instead of going to the door and the Nun, I was being escorted deeper into the hall. But I had no chance to protest. He threw open two tall oak-paneled doors.

That was it. I was hooked. The library. My salt mines for the next few weeks. It's an astounding place, even for Schatten. Huge, with stained-glass windows and heavy-chained bronze chandeliers. An ecclesiastic symmetry and yet a pagan air. On one side a gigantic fresco of Goethe pensive in a chair, topping a wall studded with German classics. On the opposite wall, Clio, the muse of history, a little near-sighted, bent over some parchment: she presides over the history shelves. The third wall holds drama, dramatized by the masks of comedy and tragedy in bronze bas-relief. All well done, considering the almost intentionally naïve conception of the room. Like an apse filled with fine primitive old saints.

"How nice," I said.

"I think this is what you want."

He pointed to the fourth wall, filled with books, albums, portfolios.

"This is all about us."

"About Schatten?"

"It's amusing." And he hoped I wouldn't mind the rule that no material was to leave the room?—and left the room himself, with a bow.

The rest of the afternoon was strictly between myself and the fourth wall. On its top panel are the Schatten arms, simple, dainty, and unmartial for major nobility: a snow-white unicorn garlanded with flowers, rampant against a mauve shield—the same motif as the stained-glass windows. On the wall beside the bookshelves, framed in gilded wood, is a hand-lettered parchment which I've translated for Dowle use. Hear this:

Schatten estate was founded in 1774 by August Eduard von Schatten, building contractor to the Prussian government. Frederick the Great raised him to the peerage for exceptionally distinguished repartee at a table conversation with Voltaire.

The first Schatten manor stood on this site, hospitable to the intellect and fashion of its time. It did not, however, take kindly to fire. In 1854 it burned down in a great blaze, though without loss of a single soul, for which God be praised.

Prince August Eduard II raised the new manor in 1857. But Schatten still found it difficult to agree with the ruder elements of the age. August Eduard II did not serve in Bismarck's army, as he considered the killing of foreign men much more barbaric than the killing of domestic foxes. For this he suffered tax reprisals and complete loss of government patronage.

Providence rewarded the Prince with the discovery of medicinal springs on the estate. His son, August Eduard III, converted Schatten into a spa that entertained and watered and billed the beau monde. Prince August Eduard IV, continuing this policy, had to fend off the deadly new vulgarities of Wilhelm Hohenzollern and Adolf Hitler. In 1945 the Prince was released from the cellars of the Secret Police. By fidelity to tradition and by excluding the recent excesses of history, the Prince has restored Schatten to itself. God be praised.

Get the dry, ironic flavor. It goes well with the four portraits of the four Princes August Eduard which are gathered around the coat of arms. Clean-shaven peculiar old men, all of them. The gilt plaques under the portraits show that the first two Princes Schatten attained the ages of 92 and 85, respectively; the third died at 79; the current Highness has no death date, of course. He must have posed in his eighties.

A sturdy tribe, those Schattens. The clothes of their generations progress from ruff collar to shirt frills to cravat and tie. But they all have in common a fine long nose, craggy chin, short thick eyebrows—and more than that. I mean a sidelong, black-eyed, lush-lidded and really derisive glance, quite odd when you find it darting out beneath such venerable white hair; a gleam suggesting will power and a sensuous wryness. All Their Highnesses glimpsed the same piquant, slightly ridiculous mystery.

Whatever it is, this traditional object of ironic Schatten contemplation, it won't be contemplated much longer. A small curlicued family tree indicates that whereas the older generations always came up with a single male as well as several female offspring, the present Prince had only one daughter, deceased in 1913. *Schluss.* That funny glance is dying out.

Still, in its time this place magnetized the stylish pilgrims. The shelves of the fourth wall are loaded with mementoes of Schatten observed. A number of English and French landscape painters—even a surprising Manet —put Schatten on canvas; and here they are, the prints bound in gold-tasseled folios, showing younger poplars and blue-liveried servants against the same lake and the same pagoda'd manor in which I live today. And who had a romance here? Who squeezed a remarkably banal sonnet out of squeezing a lady's bosom? Lord Byron, lui-même. "How once in Schatten's petalled mist we dreamed. . . ." Oich.

Later on it seems that half of Britain's lordlings went literary over sojourns at Schatten and sent the Prince genteel, privately printed effusions with a silk flower for a bookmark. Then, Currier-and-Ives-like photograph albums catching the old century as it turned, superbly, to the sweep of embroidered skirts at ladies' lawn tennis, to the gallop of His Imperial Highness, the Austrian Crown Prince, along the lakefront. And what's fin-de-siècle hip without Victoria's Prince of Wales? Here he is, smiling at little countesses in a dozen different get-ups. The Edwardian éclat of the place is, of course, just the thing to appeal to DD's esthetic nostalgia. Why, Schatten even beats Dave's office bathroom with its Limoges toilet bowl and medicine chest disguised as a hand-cranked wall telephone. Dave'll just lap it up.

But apart from that—and in all seriousness: tremendous raw material for a fin-de-siècle opening. It'll take tremendous sifting and processing, to judge from a quick survey. It may also take my eyesight and my ego.

My eyesight because the stained-glass light in the library is precarious even in midafternoon, and the windows have northern exposure. No electricity or even gas lamps, of course, which meant that eye strain drove me out even before the onset of twilight. Whereupon it was my ego's turn.

In the hall I found the whole manor population—some ten of them—spread out across a few tables in the alcove. Each table had its own little hooded gas light, reflected by lace doilies, swan-spouted silver pots and snowy porcelain cups. I'm not kidding. In a recess, a small upright, before which my tray bringer bent his head nearsightedly (just like the library's Clio) toward the music stand. An old Lanner waltz, obliquely out of kilter, merged with the smell of hot chocolate freshly poured and with the tinkle of silver spoons. It added up to a Five O'Clock Tea of fifty years ago, preserved in dusky amber, yet more lofty than ever.

For these people, these damn pensioned-off valets or worn-out chambermaids or whatever—they didn't deign to see me. They had absorbed me, taken my measure, thrust me aside, even before I'd come through the library door. From Spider Ahn and his wife I got one impervious polite nod each. The pin-up Nun sat between them, her youth flashing out among all these crones. Her fingers tapped the table. She gave—or rather dismissed me with —the same concise head motion as her father's.

I went on, up the stairs, straight to my room. I had plenty of Dowle research to organize, cables and letters to dictaphone. But something stopped me on the way from my door to my desk. Guess what.

The window, the window.

September 13th

Apparently there's a conspiracy on to keep me lonely, irritated, off balance. A pretty good trick because

ordinarily I am—Nina claims—a rather smug character.
But something happens to me every time I return from
Ida's office. It's fairly maddening.

Uncle Julius says "people" whenever he refers to me in
anger. I could adopt the same parlance. People are so
stupid. The understanding is that all Schatten interviews
and discussion—with the exception of library work, of
course—must start with the Prince and therefore await
his return next week. All right. But meanwhile people
experience a perhaps natural personal and professional
desire to talk to other people at the estate. But whenever
they approach a point of possible contact, such as the tea
gathering in the hall yesterday—why, then people get
pridefully, heart-poundingly, stiff-neckedly self-conscious and walk straight on. And afterwards people accuse
themselves of having missed a chance, of not having
raised a finger to break down the all-round stand-offish-
ness. People start stewing over lost opportunities. The
whole matter becomes ridiculously and painfully inflated
beyond its proper importance.

In brief: people kept brooding over the thing at Ida's
office. People were still brooding over it at lunch, since
people's uncle wasn't present to offer distractions. And in
the library, where people tried to start a systematic study
of the material at hand, why, there they brooded still
more. They knew the Five O'Clock Tea was waiting in
the hall—i.e., waiting to ignore somebody.

And it did. I walked out of the library into the hall
with its chocolate incense and ghost-sonata *Gemütlich-
keit.* I got the touch-me-not nod from Ahn and daughter.
Her finger tapped the table in three-quarter time. I had
sworn not to be put off. I went straight for their table.

"Good afternoon."

Ahn rose at once, eyebrows ever so slightly raised with the question of why in the good Lord's name I was barging in.

"There's no light left in the library," I said.

"Yes, I'm afraid we're quite dark and backward."

"A gas lamp would help."

"We are rather inflammable too." He smiled. "Especially in the library."

"I see," people said. People's hand fell, not by accident and with too much eagerness, on the unoccupied chair at the Ahn table.

"There's plenty of daylight left outside," Ahn said. "I've been wanting to show you the rest of the grounds."

Up he scooped me on his outstretched arm, up and along with barely a chance for people to bow to the ladies.

It was a clever way of not asking me to sit down. Clever and viciously graceful. He didn't just pack me off without further ado. This deflecting maneuver, like the one that shunted me off to the library yesterday, had its rewards. He's such a goddamn gentleman.

He ushered me away from the white tapping finger, out of the manor, onto the path along the shore. Willows and fern, jasmine and wild-rose bushes. Under the shrubs it was already evening, but much sunlight still hung high in the leaves.

"We call it our feeding walk." His courteous cane herded me along. "When the Prince is here we usually take it together. You don't mind being a substitute?"

"Not a bit."

"Tuk, tuk, tuk . . ." he said. Things shivered below

the lake surface, stirred in the trees. "Tuk, tuk, tuk
. . . Nobody hungry? Everybody shy today? . . .
This gentleman bother you? . . . Tuk, tuk, tuk . . .
he's just curious . . . he can't hurt you . . . he came all
the way from America just to look at you . . . all he
does is look . . ."

He spoke to them much as he spoke to me, from his
fine, divinely amiable Buddha height which he increased
still more somehow with his long, open gray smock
trailing behind him, the long bamboo cane and the long
artist's hair. And they listened to him, his creatures. He
reached into his pocket and sprinkled nuts and crumbs
into the twilight. They burst into visibility. Goldfish
freckled the water. Rabbits stood up under sunflowers.
Small birds made twigs tremble.

"What's the matter? . . . Think he'll hurt you?
. . . Don't you worry . . . come on . . . tuk, tuk,
tuk . . ."

They came on. A flicker of squirrel tails, bird beaks,
fins flirting and swans' necks uncoiling. They do have a
mess of swans at Schatten. Then the courteous cane
steered me away from the pond, through a birch copse,
into a meadow filled with jonquils and grass-choked old
marble benches and some very peculiar things.

"Tuk, tuk, tuk . . . Nobody home here? . . . Nobody at all? . . . If you go up there, you'll get a view of
our amusement park."

This last to me, pointing to a tremendous dead oak tree.
A ladder led up to a platform among the branches. I
climbed up the few rungs because his smile seemed to
have something of a contemptuous dare in it. The moment I stepped onto the platform it sank, to my shock,
right into the tree trunk, which turned out to be fake and

hollow. The "tree" is really a little trysting house; it still has a huge voluptuous chaise longue with crimson upholstery in half-rotted disarray. Something made me look underneath and I found—I don't know why I was so startled by it—I found a small pile of very recent movie magazines. There is a doorknob inside the trunk, and when I pressed it and came out I saw him sowing his morsels and smiling the same smile.

"Anybody in there?"

"Just some magazines," I said.

Within a second he was inside the trunk, within another second out, the magazines flaming from the match he had set to them. They dropped, consumed, to the ground and he stamped out the ashes, smock flying, like a tall fierce male witch.

"Now, how do you suppose they got in there?" he said, apparently still bland. It's a question *I* wanted to ask; I couldn't see anybody at Schatten reading that kind of thing.

"My chauffeur likes illustrated magazines," I said. "Maybe he sneaks in here."

He laughed briefly, scattered the ashes by kicking them into the thick dark grass. "Shall we go on?" he said.

Next came a miniature Arch of Triumph, rearing up in the most ridiculously truculent Prussian manner, mobbed with eagles and lions in marble bas-relief. "Highness' father built it as a wine cooler," Ahn said. He pushed a button, and suddenly one whole side of the arch swung away, to reveal bowels filled with moldering bottle racks and jarred indignant red spiders. "Amusing?" Ahn asked. "Tuk, tuk, tuk . . ."

We passed the waterfall the Nun mentioned; it falls *upward* onto a hillock, being really a broadside of fountains. And, bang, we almost ran into an East German border guard. Just like that, among all those nineteenth-century follies. We'd been jaunting right along the edge of the estate. I hadn't realized it because the fence is matted with jasmine bushes and beech trees to the point of concealment. Of a sudden all the green is cut clean away. From the other side the clapboard of a small guardhouse jumps at you. The grillwork splendor of the fence is printed on it like a fancy Tudor façade.

"Tuk, tuk, tuk . . ." An Ahn bow to the chubby young soldier, who grinned and scratched his shoulder with his tommy gun and was erased the next moment by more jasmine and beech leaves.

After this, remnants of the stables— "We tore them up for firewood—had to keep warm during the war, you know."

And then the old spa pump room, now an outsize dovecote. White wings snowed down on us, pursued us along the empty arcades, and then fled before the two big hysterics of the place—two big wild peacocks looking like fairy vultures, with tremendous rainbow-colored combs hanging down their beaks. Their breasts puffed up, their tails touching, they strutted toward us with tiny high-heeled steps, two feathered transvestite Idas—till they shrieked out a joint jagged peal of laughter, stabbed at Ahn's crumbs, minced off together toward some Sodom and Gomorrah of a coop.

And then, finally, guess what? *I* was fed. We had come almost full circle. The last phase of the walk took us past the small but high-spired chapel—quite new-looking, by the way—in back of the manor. Nailed against a tree there is a castle. A complete little medieval robber baron's castle.

"We used to have children here, you know," my host said. The fact is that I remembered the castle from my very early childhood thirty years ago, when old specimens of the thing were still surviving: a genuine, antediluvian, pre-World War I chocolate automat.

"Would you like one?" he asked. "Tuk, tuk, tuk . . ." He dropped a coin into the castle keep. The drawbridge croaked down and slid a small purple-wrapped chocolate bar into my ready hand.

"There you are, Mr. Spey."

"Why, thank you, father," I said smiling, and he gave a short deep chuckle that didn't change his mouth a bit. The poplars under which we walked were like my host. They sounded without moving; their leaves hissed high up in the breeze with no apparent motion.

The lanterns had been lit. A lazy gust carried the scent of roses from the front gardens and echoes from the peacocks still shrieking madly. I smelled a boundless animation in that wild midway of an estate. I don't think I've even touched its surface. Maybe I came closest to touching something when I found that weird cache of new magazines inside the tree trunk. Something very alive smolders and pulses beneath these antique grounds. Even the dead garden conceits have the breathing, unkempt look of live things. The grass grows here especially green, with an insidious vitality. Which, by the way, was partly explained as we returned to the manor.

"You can't complain about a lack of plant life here," I said.

"Thank the Cold War for that." He sowed his last morsels and explained that West Berlin, being without sewage outlets, used the nearby fields for drainage.

"No fertilizer problem now." He smiled. "We never

could grow cyclamens before '45."

"Really," I said.

"If you don't use history, you know, it'll use you. Nice of you to come along."

When I walked up to my room I saw her waiting for him in an alcove, her white smooth finger tapping against the wall.

It wasn't the last I saw of her last night. I was quite hungry—perhaps only natural after all that *tuk, tuk, tuk.* I sopped up the very last drop of beef stew (Schatten seems to favor plain gastronomy). The chestnut leaves swung outside my window, and the haughty furniture averted its sundry souls. My footfalls and me started our trek to the john later than the night before. I noticed that of the three dogs guarding the upper stairs (the Prince & Ahn floor) two—that is, both Afghans—were gone. When I returned and was about to climb into bed, a faint yelp fetched me to the window. In time for a momentary glimpse: her, in slacks, the wide slacks of the 'thirties, her hair a loose swinging rope, romping with the Afghans in the moonlight. She flashed up and away like a lantern slide. Woosh, vanished in the thicket by the lake.

The bitch. She refused to reappear. Even a ten-minute vigil wouldn't bring her back. I returned to bed. I still had the little chocolate gift from Ahn. As a child I used to reserve this sort of treat for a pillow feast, in the very teeth of the toothbrush law. That's what I did now. I peeled away the faded paper wrapping, undid the foil. The gray chocolate emerged underneath. An ancient little sweet from the ancient robber-baron automat. I touched it. It crumbled into nothingness and a sweet nostalgic scent.

Just as I brushed the gray powder off my sheets, I heard another yelp. She was coming back. But I didn't go back to the window.

I had enough.

September 14th

Today Ida rushed up with a confidential air, in a pink-and-mauve ensemble, and took me on a conference-walk around the espresso machine. A littel bird, she whispers, has told her a littel secret from the City License Department—she has a littel friend there. The Prince's hotel license is due to expire on November 30th and *must* be renewed in person by then. Nice? Why not set the hotel opening for that week? No? If His *oo*wonderful Highness is healthy enough for a license, he should be healthy enough for a pageant. True? Good idea? Good idea! *oo*Wonderful! And she rushes away laughing, to exhibit Checkpoint Charlie to one hundred and eleven Daughters of the American Revolution.

She confirms the attitude Andy and I like to take: that Dowlification is just a glamor prank, just fun toil. As for Dave himself, I think he's impressed. He squawked only once, about the lack of communications with the estate: WHY NO CABLE OR PHONE AT SCHATTEN STOP NEED LIVE WIRE IN BERLIN. Whereupon I got back to him with NO ELECTRICITY AT ESTATE STOP JUST CLASS ALAS.

That did it, that and my preliminary budget estimate falling well below our Tangier or Madrid costs. But most of all it's JUST CLASS ALAS, plus the circumstance that Schatten's intractability has only increased its desirability in Dave's eyes. His Genius sailed right into the den of the lion who dared defy dread Dave himself.

My Schatten invasion also set Dinny back on his ear. Oh, my, yes. At first—we talk mostly by phone—I got nothing but dire italics from him. He was *terri*fied on my behalf. They would *cut* me to pieces there. A *blue*-blooded quagmire. But after I could report all that useful library material, the melody changed. *Dear* Mr. Spey, whatever *do* you beguile them with? And yesterday Dinny went so far as to produce a Schatten slogan of his own, not a bad one either. The idea is to actually brag about the main difficulty, namely that any evening customer of the Schatten Casino won't be able to leave before the 4 a.m. unlocking of the gate by the East Zone police. Dinny's inspiration would make an outlandish virtue of necessity: "Don't you see? The Berlin Dowle *Dawn* Casino—Europe's *on*ly make-a-night-of-it Sunrise Gaming Place!" I agreed that this was the germ of something brilliant, and today Dinny sent us roses. Ida a dozen ivory ones, and me three big black-red masculine beauties.

Maybe the flowers celebrate the fact that I've become friends with the fine old city of Berlin. It looks so nice and tidy and daylit after the blurred vistas and green silences of Schatten. When KarlHeinz chauffeurs me away from the estate and through the city streets each morning, everything brightens and shrinks, crystallizes into such pretty toylike definition. Even the rush-hour traffic, even the Cold War yawps, even Ida's office. And of course Ida herself.

Ida, thou hast altered. First of all, she's become less frequent. I see her much less often, which improves her no end. Mornings she usually takes American senators or Mideastern princes on Iron Curtain tours. Afternoons I'm back at Schatten. But when I do meet her, she's no longer such a relentless chic chunk. She's taken to dressing in two colors instead of one. If she has something to say, it's brief and to the point, as about the Prince's hotel-license bit. She's been relaxing ever since Schatten was included within her liaison-competence. Now Prince Schatten is no longer a noisome, boorish villain. Now she finds him just a naughty old boy whose tricks are really *oo*wonderful fun because *oo*we—she and I—will out-naughty him. No?

The Littel Partners, taking their cue from her, are spoiling me studiously. To Dinny's flowers they add carnations renewed daily at my desk and arrange things into a pleasing bouquet. My desk equipment now includes, besides floral cheer and extension telephone, a Pan-American calendar, a gigantic green blotter and a specially printed memo pad headed, in English, *Of the Desk of Mr. Leon Spey* (sic).

Re Littel Partners: At first I had a hard time telling them apart. After all, they finger the same dyed curls, titter the same politely dyed titter, flurry the same religiously chipper print dresses. But now I discern that Fräulein Edeltraud has a virginal little lisp; Fräulein Ursula, a tiny triangular wart placed in the precise middle of her cheek; and Fräulein Lieselotte, rather daring harlequin glasses. These audacious spectacles, together with Lieselotte's distinctively L.L.-initialed chair cushion, indicate that she is *prima inter pares* and Ida's vicar in her absence.

They are useful, too, the Littel Partners. I have asked Fräulein Ursula (with her wart's promise of exactitude) to conduct a telephone census of Berlin's costume shops and seamstresses; she is compiling a report on how long it would take, how much it would cost, to either rent or manufacture a hundred first-rate nineteenth-century costumes for the opening pageant, most of them to be patterned on authentic material from the library. Our authoritative Fräulein Lieselotte canvasses consuls and cultural attachés of the resident diplomatic corps: I want the procession of Daimlers and *fin-de-siècle* coaches to roll from Dave's disembarkation point at Le Havre, through France, Italy, Switzerland and West Germany, with changes of horse, official pomp and mounting press coverage all the way.

Fräulein Edeltraud of the lisp has a littel comptometer and does my cost statistics as well as my letters and my long-distance set-ups. The lisp, coupled with Fräulein Edeltraud's slight asthma, makes her effective on the telephone; it imparts a breathlessness, an urgency to the announcement of my person and my mission. It came in quite handy today, with Nina.

"Nina," I said across four thousand miles. "Wake you?"

"*You!* . . . My operator's been after you for forty-eight hours!"

"Mine's been panting after you!" I said quickly.

"You've vanished, you know. Nothing at the hotel. No forwarding address, no new phone number. Simply not a trace."

"That bitchy hotel!" I said.

"And li'l deserted Nina ain't gonna go whining for your address at Mr. Dowle's!"

"That damn hotel knew damn well where I went. I had to move overnight, Ninepins. I'm sorry."

"Anyway, you don't exist, so you can't possibly be interested in good news."

"Don't tell me."

"Yes. We've got the place."

Our real-estate man really found an excellent proposition on Long Island. Two well-kept spacious Hampton cottages, the bigger one to be done over into our own supper club, the smaller one for our private house. Good site, feasible mortgage. She sounded excited. I was glad, not only because of the find, but because the excitement of the find might make her forget that I'd forgotten. Somehow, God knows how, it never occurred to me to cable her my change of address when I moved to Schatten. "Listen," I said. "Option instantly."

But you can't get by Nina that easily.

"Yeah," she said across the Atlantic, mock-pouting in her quite adorable mock-Brooklynese. "Yeah, yeah, yeah."

"Have my lawyer look at it," I said. "If everything's all right, grab it altogether. And if you ever stop yeahing, you beast."

"Yeah, yeah."

"And case the contractors for estimates on renovation. And audition me a Justice of the Peace. A real nice, corny, moom-pitcha Connecticut type."

"I thought it was going to be just sensible City Hall! Is this assignment making you romantic?"

"Ninepins," I said. "This could be one Dowle insanity that's fun. Almost as much fun as ditching Dave right after Sweden."

"Yeah, yeah."

"Don't you want me to leave Dave in a blaze of glory?"

"Just leave a phone number when you move, thank you."

"Listen, Ninepins, I *had* to move into Schatten at a minute's notice. It was the only way—"

"You *live* at Schatten? I thought you had to be a princess—"

"Technically it's a spa hotel. But no phone, and no way to cable. You should see it. Belfries and bats—"

"And princesses?"

"Sure, with long white hair and little mustaches. Even a crazy uncle of mine. I'll write you—"

"Yeah. That ten-page letter."

"Five pages are finished."

"Oh, shut up. Just come back soon."

"Listen, you can always reach me care of Berlin City Promotion Office, where I'm calling you now."

"Shut up. I'm going to sleep and dream about Long Island. Just City Promotion Office?"

"Right. Call you in a couple of days. To get cussed out a little more."

"Promises, promises . . ." she said softly, sweetly.

"You know what, Ninepins."

"You know what. Good night."

"Good night."

And then the Littel Partners and I had a terrific fight about who was going to pay for this long-distance call. I declared I would, of course, since it had been strictly nonprofessional, private to the point of being semi-intimate. This reddened the six spinsterly office cheeks; it doubled over three print dresses with uneasy merriment; but it didn't stop the argument.

"You money iss not good here," said Fräulein Lieselotte with tremulous pride in this American expense-account gambit, while Fräulein Edeltraud made such wild exorcising motions at my hundred-mark bill that, just to calm her, I put it back into my pocket again.

All terribly cozy in Berlin.

September 1 5th

Uncle Julius is back. Should I laugh or cry? He stepped out of the shadow of the estate fence as I returned for lunch.

"I came on foot," he said. "You know, Rosh Hashonoh."

It turned out to be the tail end of the Jewish New Year, which is why he didn't ride. That I didn't appear at the synagogue he found headshakingly incomprehensible, in view of Rosh Hashonoh; but, in view of Rosh Hashonoh, he forgave me. Julius' mind works that way. I got a good wrist squeeze, implying our relations were okay again.

At first we didn't get much beyond that. Just inside the gate, and directly in our path, Ahn's daughter. She straightened up from some strenuous yew-pruning. My first good look at her in the full light and heat of noon.

A single small bead of perspiration glinted on her forehead. Her full dark-blond eyebrows are untweezed; they curl slightly, in the form of a horizontal question-mark, the left brow more curled than the right. Her high cheeks were slighly sucked in. She stepped to the right to let us pass, but my uncle had also edged to the right, and the result was a brief impasse during which the little bead ran down from her forehead onto her nose. It's the clearest, most satisfying close-up I've yet gotten. Then she moved to the side, nodded, my uncle tugged at his hat, and we were past.

We walked to the manor. On the stairs he suddenly said, "And that? That woman?"

"I'm sorry, I should have introduced you. She's the daughter of the doctor in charge."

"She was laughing at me."

I realized that, by God, he might be right. Maybe those sucked-in cheeks had suppressed a smile.

"Come on, Uncle," I said. "You're imagining things."

"Oh yes, she was laughing at me. She can't laugh at *you*, you're their famous guest, your picture is in the paper. But me, she's a beautiful woman—what is this, in the Bible about this, about this very thing . . ."

"Believe me, Uncle—"

"Ah: *Beware the serpent when the serpent is of gold.* You see? Beware. At me she can laugh. She's the doctor's daughter? The Spider's?"

"Yes," I said. "But it's quite unimportant whether she laughed or not."

Thank God, the sight of my room swept the problem from his mind. "Your luggage! The suitcases? What happened to them?"

"Nothing's been stolen, Uncle. They've been put under the bed."

"Ah."

He checked to make sure, then made directly for the double lunch tray I'd ordered. By the time my hands were washed he had already nibbled away the salad. His frame, black overcoat and all, was pressed into the small Dante chair by the window. He was bent over a small notebook, an unused 1949 diary printed in Syrian.

"Now the petition?" he said.

"How's that?"

"You know, the petition." He pressed his glasses back and read from the notebook the title he had already written down. *"Petition to Prince Schatten Concerning the Illegal Removal of Julius Spiegelglass' Mother's Grave and the Good Use to Which Financial Compensation for Such Injustice Will Be Put by Julius Spiegelglass Aforementioned."*

He looked at me, pleased by the formal splendor of the phrase. "Go ahead, lunch," he said. "I do the writing. You just supervise for style. Go on."

"Oh, yes," I said. "We were going to draft a statement."

"All right. Fine." He pressed himself back into the Dante chair, took an old-fashioned ink pencil out of his overcoat pocket, moistened it with his tongue, pressed his glasses back against his nose, sighed, bent his face deep into the notebook. Suddenly his hand moved like a small possessed animal in writing spasms across the paper. His voice couldn't keep up with it, except in breathless catch phrases.

"Honorable Prince . . . undersigned Julius Spiegelglass . . . not *Dr.* Spiegelglass, though passed most medical examinations by the time Hitler . . . world going up in flames, more important things than medicine . . . 1938 founded Jewish Peace Farm Foundation . . . settling persecuted Jews in famous battlefields . . . Waterloo, Gettysburg, Thermopylae . . . swords into ploughshares . . . blood into bread . . ."

I cut into my steak, wondering how to stem or organize this flow. "Uncle Julius," I said. "We don't need quite so much background."

"Of course . . . not so much . . ." he murmured, but hunched himself still closer to the notebook, unquenchable, unreachable inside his litany. "Honorable Prince . . . to sum up . . . undersigned Spiegelglass walked a thousand miles for Blood Into Bread . . . rich man to rich man . . . horrible secretaries . . . vicious underlings . . . the spider in the palace . . . war killed project altogether . . ."

He stopped and looked at me. "The horrible war," he said.

He unbuttoned his overcoat; coughed; remoistened his ink pencil.

"Uncle—" I said.

"Right," he said. "Not so much background. . . . To sum up. . . . . Only to show my experience in this field. Like after the war . . . undersigned Spiegelglass started New Solomonic Temple Incorporated . . . grand artistic and religious undertaking . . . also employment of stranded Jewish artisans . . . attract worshippers from all over the world . . . re-creation of a great shrine . . . British obstruction . . . unfair bankruptcy laws . . . Letters, Honorable Prince . . . dozens of letters from saved Jewish handicraftsmen . . . letters undersigned Spiegelglass wishes . . . he wishes his late mother should have seen . . . unforgettable lines . . ."

He reached into his overcoat pocket as if to prove these letters really existed there. He failed to find them, and their absence seemed to be the last straw. "Honorable Prince . . ." he tried to go on, but couldn't. His writing hand went limp. He straightened up, reached for some of my lettuce leaves. As he slowly ate them, his eyes wavered into mine, each one sheathed in a big tear.

"They killed my poor mother," he said.

"Look, Uncle," I said. "We needn't get upset. A petition should be factual."

"Yes . . . all right. Factual." He tried to smile gratefully, and actually galvanized himself again into his writing stance. "Honorable Prince . . . to continue . . ." He continued long after I'd finished the fruit on my tray, and still, I could see, he was far from having exhausted the heart of the matter. It was after two.

"Uncle Julius," I said. "You must excuse me. I wish I didn't have so much work."

"Oh?" he said, shaken out of his incantation. "Yes. Naturally! Apology. Apologies! I'll make up for it. I'll help you."

"No," I said, "no, really, don't bother—"

"I mean it! Apologies!"

We left the room together. He's such a poor heartbreaking pain in the neck. He's inconsolable, intractable and unpredictable. At the landing he grabbed me by the hand.

"Killer dogs!" he whispered.

His chin twitched at the two Afghans and the German Shepherd sitting on the upper stairs.

"Trained to kill humans!" he whispered. "You can tell by the red eyes."

"What?" I said. "Where'd you pick that up?"

"I'll show you," he whispered. "Watch . . ."

He stepped forward, toward the upper stairs. That moment all three animals sat up as one, ears vertical, teeth showing. All three let out the same sound, a very low, deep, trigger-ready growl.

"You see?" whispered Julius.

Another reason why he's such a pain in the neck is that he pours his emotions over you with a ladle. No matter how corny they are, no matter how you squirm, you can't escape them. He trembled so enthusiastically, I think I almost trembled too. For a moment I was really scared of those dogs.

"Naturally, they are watchdogs," I said. "Those are the Prince's private quarters upstairs."

"And the Spider's too?"

"Yes," I said. "The Ahn family's too."

"You see?" he said, grabbing my hand even harder in triumph. "The Spider!"

"Come on," I said, and pulled him away. He followed me down into the library, his shoes creaking, his lips blue from the ink pencil, the old gentlefolk staring. I've no doubt that from some alcove corner the pin-up Nun sucked in another of her wretched smiles.

In the library itself, though, Julius took the chill off the place. He wasn't astonished by it. Not a bit. Out came the Syrian notebook and ink pencil. He burrowed into the photograph albums, making a chronological list of pictures and captions for me. Again his voice began to sound in intent snatches.

"Emperor Franz Josef . . . Schatten cure, 1890 . . . nice man but goyish beard . . . Baroness Julia von Rothschild . . . visit, 1893 . . . you try to reach a Rothschild about a project . . . 1895, the singer Melba. Fat! . . ."

He was almost fun, even while being a nuisance. And later, when we walked out of the library into their confounded impenetrable Five O'Clock Tea, he came in handy. I hardly knew their Tea existed. I was involved in a very deep conversation with my uncle. The Ahns were worth just a slight absent bow to me, even less than I was worth to them. I was much too absorbed in the discussion of why Julius had even more trouble reaching the Rothschilds on behalf of New Solomonic Temple Incorporated than Theodore Herzl had on behalf of Zionism.

I accompanied him through the gardens. We agreed he'd return for lunch tomorrow to continue petition and library work. After I'd said good-bye at the gate, a funny thing. I turned around and found those two effeminate peacocks with their overblown combs and limp tails. They stood a bare two yards away, tremulous, staring at me. They must have followed us down the road. Suddenly they shrieked out their laugh together and ran away.

The cowards. Waiting till I was all alone again at Schatten.

September 16th

Tremendous jollification at Ida's. Yesterday Dave wired her an offer to send a CARE package containing one life-size phone booth so that her office could set up a wire connection with me at Schatten. This strikes the whole crew here as the living end in wit. To sneak into the estate at night and put up this foamboof! Everything so practical in America—even the jokes!

They were absolutely in stitches. Note that Dave cabled Ida instead of me. Is Mount Olympus clouding? The fact is that I'm not delivering as fast as I should. Now I'm told the Prince won't be back for perhaps another ten days. There's still no firm commitment on his personal participation. I've sent a cable to the Villa Husli, the

Prince's address at Davos, given to me by Ahn with a shrug. As prophesied by that shrug—no answer. Steady silence. What's more important, I still haven't been able to present Dave with a specific boffo plot for the opening, and usually I'm way past that at this stage of the game.

Somehow too many other momentous problems come in between. Paris has been phoning me daily for hours. The manager of the French Oyster needs just me to straighten out a number of kinks too ridiculous to detail —my reward for being the organization genius. But Paris is nothing compared to Julius and his collected works. The library notes he's doing for me are crammed to the margin with his blue ink-pencil scrawl; full of thick underlinings, CAPITALIZED phrases and arrows pointing to especially important asides of his own. Sigh.

I asked Fräulein Ursula (of the precise wart) to type a transcript of the mess. But Uncle Julius' script put a bad strain on the sobriety of the Littel Partners, who were still giggly over Dave's foamboof. For an hour, typewriter clatter, silence, desperately choked-back titter, more clatter. Fräulein Ursula returns with Julius' editorial eruptions neatly hemmed in between parentheses, like

In the motor car (sitting down very arrogant) CROWN PRINCE RUDOLPH (who later committed suicide, a sin to God!)

Fräulein Ursula puts down the sheets, desperately striving for gravity, retreats toward the anteroom already whinnying, and goes to pieces behind the door.

Then Julius' Petition To The Prince. I decided not to expose it to such Gentile merriment. I asked for a typewriter to do the job myself. I was given the office best, a futuristic electric monster with more bells and signals than a fire engine, the dear Littel Partners full of curl-fingering and still tittery instructions. Now, Julius' petition is worse than his library notes. A regular decoding job. You have to learn to fill in his omissions. Often he forgets to write down that part of the sentence which isn't grieving or accusing—mere grammatical completion doesn't interest him. You have to cut away rambling commentaries and irrelevancies, watch out for *t*'s looking like *b*'s. Of course I realize that I'm expurgating a work which could be known henceforth in Judaica as the Schatten Talmud. But I'm also beginning to realize that there won't be an end to it.

For an end to it there won't be. Serves me right. I had to go and ask our Dowle lawyer to recommend a Jewish restitution specialist. To this man I sent Julius' first cleaned-up petition installment. Alack, the case looks good to him. He wants more background stuff. I can't even tell Julius to shut up. I'm not going to do the poor devil out of a hundred thousand marks; certainly I'm not going to save our German friends such a sum.

But while I'm happy for Uncle, I'm sorry for me. I envy my father, who could tell Julius to scram without the slightest remorse. There was a second petitional chaos at Schatten yesterday, occasioning my second struggle with the typewriting fire engine today. And still the Littel Partners go *hee-hee* behind the door.

And you know something funny? The eyes of those animals on the upper stairs really are rather killer-dog red.

September 17th

Such ups and downs in a single day. And moving on such cat feet, particularly the downs. In my morning innocence I walked to the car. Ahn appeared and casually remarked that the workmen would be arriving soon.

"Workmen?" I said.

"We're having the front part of the manor renovated," he said. "But there's time for you to make hotel arrangements. They won't get here till the day after tomorrow."

"You mean," I said, "you want me to move out?" The morning seemed much too nice and sunny to do such a thing to me.

"Unfortunately," he said, "our first floor, our guest floor, won't be habitable for a while."

"All of a sudden?" I said.

"You know how masons are these days," he said. "Very difficult and capricious. I was just notified myself."

"Just when I'm settled in," I said.

"You see, we want the worst part of the work to be finished by the time the Prince arrives," he said.

"All right," I said. I wasn't going to start crying in front of him.

"Of course," he said, walking along with me, and with a vicious air of consolation quite as if I *were* crying, "of course you'll be welcome to visit us any time during the day."

"All right," I said. "Thank you."

The first thing I did on getting to the office was to call the Prince in Switzerland. I had Fräulein Edeltraud find the number through his address, Villa Husli, Davos. I felt it was time to force the thing, right through all the prevarication and delay. Fräulein Edeltraud got through fast, and the receiver was picked up almost instantly. It was the most frustrating experience.

"*Ja, bitte?*" said a pleasant voice.

"Good morning," I said, also in German. "Prince Schatten?"

"*Ja,*" the voice said at the other end. "*Bitte?*"

I think I was so amazed I may have spluttered a little. "I'm Leon Spey," I said. "You have a cable message from me. It's on behalf of Dowle Hotels—"

"How very nice of you," the voice said. A mellow, somewhat orotund tenor.

"We've been hoping for a commitment from you on helping to open our hotel here in Berlin—"

"*Open* hotels?" the voice said with lilting amusement. "I'm rather better at closing things. Do you need any help in closing something, by any chance?" It was really an almost decadently accomplished voice, speaking the King's German with no local inflection, just a glossy stagy aristocratic one. But at the same time it was faintly off key, off balance, as though the speaker were drunk.

"Is this Prince Schatten?" I asked.

"Yes, yes," the voice said. "Are you there?"

"My name is Leon Spey," I repeated, "I sent you a cable—"

"How very nice of you," the voice said, and went on with its slightly foppish and rabid frivolity, "Of course, I could open your hotel and close it the same day again. Wouldn't that be chic?"

"All right," I said. "Someone is playing a nice little joke."

"Not a bit," the voice said. "You wouldn't want your hotel open for longer than a day, would you? Nothing worthwhile lasts longer than that—" And then the phone went clink-clink. The dial tone hummed in my ear. We'd been cut off.

I had Fräulein Edeltraud try the number again immediately. Actually she tried it three more times. Each time a deep voice came on, saying yes, Prince Schatten was here at Villa Husli; no, the Prince hadn't talked at the phone before; he couldn't talk now; he never took calls while taking the cure; no, no one had called the Villa Husli earlier in the morning.

I didn't believe it—long distance seldom makes mistakes. Just to be doubly sure, I then saw the call through myself. Same result, the deep voice getting quite impatient.

Okay, so some drunk Swiss prankster had a little fun with a wrong number. Rather interesting to be evicted *and* misconnected so thoroughly on the same day. I really didn't want to brood about it. I drove off to inspect progress at the hotel site.

Of course the whole damn hotel is sort of a vile prank. But at least I'm in on this particular joke. At the plaza in front of the building they were hoisting into place an enormous, enormously modern sculpture which looks like two giant bronze jellyfish with skin trouble copulating unsuccessfully. It's called "Space Age," and Dave is mad about it.

I walked through a good deal of the hotel, past all those rooms consisting mostly of huge windows and low ceilings, rooms still mobile-less and Matisse-less and indirect-lighting-less and therefore naked and rather sordid. I went to the Royal Suite—if I had to be evicted, at least I'd be evicted into a Royal Suite. The construction manager said it could accommodate me, with improvised furniture, in ten days if necessary.

For some reason the barrel had already arrived, though, weeks ahead of schedule. It's a petite barrel, made of artifically aged wood, gorgeous brass hoops and baroque brass trimmings, which should blend well with the artificial antiques yet to come. It will be filled with excellent Rhine wine; each tenant of the suite will get a rack of ten bottles bearing his name and a legend saying, in Gothic letters, "Personally casked at the Royal Suite of the Berlin Dowle." My idea this, and really in the *Cat Quixote* genre, and like *Cat Quixote* taken very seriously. Dave Dowle took it so seriously he raised the daily price for the suite from $120 to $160.

I walked around the barrel. The insane Davos phone conversation kept buzzing in my head. Also a certain question, a question people past thirty-five should never ask themselves. The question is: "Did I take the trouble to be born, to grow up and struggle, for *this?*" Unfortunately I asked myself the question as I walked around the barrel.

What really bothered me, of course, was that I haven't even been doing *this* very well any more. Since Schatten it's been all commotion and no inspiration. I haven't even evolved a specific pageant idea to present to the Prince when I see His Mysteriousness. I seem to be much too

busy typing up Julius and getting booted out of Schatten.
I don't know why, but the barrel made it all especially
painful.

Ida arrived during this low and began to admire the
hotel, the suite and the barrel, with deafening *w*'s.

"Ida," I said, "Dr. Ahn just told me that they're going
to renovate the manor at Schatten."

"Ah?" Ida said. "Is this so? This is such a *oo*wonderful
suite. I think we will make an illustrated booklet of the
most beautiful suites in Berlin."

"Ida," I said. "The trouble is that Ahn said they'll be so
busy renovating, the Prince will probably not be able to
pay attention to the opening."

I don't know what made me distort Ahn's renovation
news like that. Perhaps the idea of being kicked out by
Ahn, and of feeling so rotten about it, was too humiliating
to be passed on to Ida in unvarnished form. Perhaps it was
just a lucky instinct that I put it the way I did. Suddenly
the world turned brighter. They couldn't kick me out.

"Ah?" said Ida. "This is nothing. They need a building-
police permit for the renovation. I have some littel friends
at the building police. You tell Dr. Ahn there will not be
a permit until after the opening."

"Ida," I said. "Are you sure?"

"Of course," she said. "You see one mason at work,
Leon, you report this to us. The next moment they will
have fifty building policemen down there. The building
police want to get in there anyway, because the Prince
has not removed some war bomb. I think a Most Beautiful
Suite booklet will be extremely stunning."

And that's how the radical up occurred after the
radical down. I loved Ida and told her I loved the idea of
the booklet, and I went right back to the estate, eager to

throw my counterpunch.

It was thrown almost immediately. I found Ahn by the entrance. We remarked on the fine day.

"Incidentally," I said. "I talked to Dr. Holze of the Tourist Promotion Office. She's very excited about your renovation plans. Only she was afraid you might have the building police on your hands."

He smoothed his Bohemian white hair. "I hadn't thought of the building police," he said. "I should have realized other people would."

"Dr. Holze suggested you wait a few months," I said. "She could exert a little pressure on your behalf if you give her a little time."

"The Prince doesn't want to wait too long," he said.

"Oh, but he wouldn't want the place full of building police," I said.

"No," Ahn said. "You're right. We're very good at patience here. And the additional advantage is that you'll be with us here much longer then." Frosty smile. "Won't you?"

"Yes," I said. "Thank you, Dr. Ahn."

He didn't faze me one bit. And a moment later something still better happened. I found my pin-up Nun in a tree. Repeat: in a tree. On a low branch, with an ornamental basket slung around her waist, and the leaves dappling her dress, and her coifed face like an extravagant blossom half-hidden in shade. She looked like a figure in one of the old Schatten prints in the library, like an eighteenth-century court lady caught in a pastoral pose. And she had, as I looked up, a good curve at the back of her knee, an excellent line where most women are rotten, a most delightful promise of thigh.

"Hello!" I said.

"Hello!"

A "Hello!" from her, even as mimicry, is way above par, way beyond her usual formal acknowledgment of my salutations. I saw that she was dropping small apples into the basket as she picked them.

"How nice," I said.

That instant she came down. Her hand touched my shoulder for support, a careless, lightning-fast, impudent touch, a knowing hoyden's touch that was perfectly at home with men's shoulders.

"We're making apple jelly," she said, standing next to me. I'd never seen her quite so close or so open before me.

"Good," I said. "I'll be able to taste your apple jelly." I took an apple and bit into it. "Your father just postponed the renovation."

She looked at me. She swung herself onto the low branch of the next tree, without resort to my shoulder, not showing so much as an upper calf.

"These apples are too sour for eating," she said.

And then I understood that the "Hello!" and the shoulder touch had been things premised on my imminent eviction; things that could be done safely with a deportee who was really no longer there. But now she knew that I was here again to stay, and she instantly switched on her old remoteness once more. It was a wrong connection all of a sudden, like my Swiss long-distance earlier. It was the second down after the midday up. And it lasted, for some reason, through the rest of the day, which I spent in a rotten mood.

Maybe I'll move that baroque barrel into the manor and get drunk here.

September 18th

Thank you, KarlHeinz.

This morning I had to cheat on Julius. I phoned him on the way from Schatten to the office. Since he wasn't in, I left a carefully worded message. It said I wouldn't expect him for lunch the next two days because I was suffering from an infectious cold—that kind of sickness being, let us pray, a valid excuse even in Uncle Julius' book. I called from a public booth because I didn't want the Littel Partners to listen in on a lie (however white and necessary) foisted on Julius. But I'd forgotten KarlHeinz.

My fine chauffeur, you see, has recovered from *his* very real cold. His whistle is back and so is his secret cigarette smoke. Lately he's taken to asking, "How *are* you, suhr?" as if wondering how I could bear the strain of Schatten. Sometimes he tries to reinforce this idea by a helping touch under my elbow as I get into the car. In addition to such virtues, he's just marvelous at eavesdropping.

"You are all right, suhr?" This after he had helped me back into the car seat.

"KarlHeinz," I said, "you should have become a nurse."

"Well, suhr," he said in his inimitable simpering smoke-smuggling way. "Many people cannot stand the estate climate, suhr."

"Have you taken a survey?"

"I mean, suhr, my uncle always said so, the dead one that worked there." And then he went on to tell me about the drainage fields near Schatten and their influence on the flora and barometric pressure of the place.

"I know all that," I said, taking out my morning paper.

"My uncle always complained, suhr. It made him tired."

I wasn't tired. I was very lively and mad.

"KarlHeinz," I said, "that's very strange, because I find Schatten terribly stimulating. It makes me extremely energetic. In fact I think I'll stay there all day, for the rest of the week. You won't have to drive me in. I'll get much more work done that way."

"Yes, suhr."

Which is how it happened, on the spur and provocation of the moment. For I hadn't intended to do anything beyond keeping away Julius for a while. But now I found myself in an altogether new momentum. Man, I was swinging. At the office I got Uncle Mushroom's outpourings taken care of, got rid of my entire backlog of cables, correspondence and phoning, then asked the astonished Littel Partners to give my love to Ida (currently touring the Wall with the treasurer of the South Korean Rotary): I'd be working at Schatten all day during the week, important stuff to be forwarded to me there by messenger, thank you, good-bye.

KarlHeinz was very quiet on the drive back. I was very grateful to him. That's the thing about my good chauffeur. He may enrage you, but it's a cold, constructive rage that knocks away the cobwebs in your thinking. It made clear to me at last why nothing's been getting done in Berlin. I haven't had a schedule here, only a kind of helter-skelter rush. All my noons and afternoons are taken up by listening to Uncle Mushroom's orations; my

mornings frittered away by typing up same, and ridiculous Paris on long distance, and calls to the the bloody
long-winded restitution lawyer. I simply haven't had a
chance to come to grips with Schatten, which happens to
be my reason for being here. I haven't had a chance to
touch the people or the soul of this crazy place, to bear
down on its potentialities, to find something genuine and
creative if you'll forgive the expression, something better
than our safe standard opening stunts. I live at the estate
technically, but not actually. I've been treading air. But,
man, I'm coming down to earth now, or at least to the
Prince's highly fertilized portion of it. The rest of this
week I'm going to really *stay* at the estate, stay put and
zero in. Kick me out of Schatten? I'll kick myself still
further in. Just watch me.

For which decision thank you, KarlHeinz, thank you
and your smoke-smuggling smirking villainy, thank you
very much.

September 22nd

You might define the day as a progression of silences. After breakfast I sit in the angled morning light, a
green glow churned by the chestnut leaves beyond the
window. I listen to the small sputter of my portable. Pingping ping pingping ping. Ping. The sputter sounds
smaller, the framing silence is so large here. And nothing overcrusts the silence, neither traffic screams nor Ida
espresso. The portable sputters; the portable stops. I begin to shave.

This shave is quite different from the water-faucet
drone I've been used to all my life. It's an unfamiliar job,

centered around a hot-water pitcher; clinks, splashes, sudden soundlessness. . . . Then I go down to test the mettle of the silence, to come nearer to its core.

The grounds are empty. The pin-up Nun has left a few minutes before. I know because I've watched her from the window. I also know her present whereabouts. Am I in a particular hurry to get there? I am not. On the contrary, I amble into the spa park. An interesting stroll, because my presence acts like a vacuum cleaner sucking away all animal life around me. Gone all squirrels, birds and feathered hysterics, all fading from my sight and hearing. This manifold absence accompanies me with a certain blatancy, almost like a motorcycle escort. It produces a stringent noiselessness which I elect to interpret as flattering, a very special silence moving with me through the over-all silence of the estate.

Arch of Triumph, pump room, upward waterfall, fake oak tree. This time, no mysterious magazines in the trunk. Without Ahn, and thus without animal life, all these garden conceits look dormant, as though they had just been put into summer storage, as though someone had thrown a dust cover over them so they wouldn't be soiled by trespassers like myself. The garden smells, however, are kind enough not to boycott me. I walk through clouds of hyacinth, roses, lavender. Sniff, sniff. Much obliged, garden smells. I walk across the pond bridge, above immobile swans, along the main path toward the gate. And beyond the gate, across the Venetian bridge, into the first street of West Berlin itself.

That's where she is most of the morning, shopping from motorized vendors who drive up. Vegetable trucks and grocers' trucks and a baker's station wagon and one of those horse-drawn fruit stands. The old servant hovers by her side, pulling the cart that once transported my luggage. It's very hot here on the asphalt street, away from the luxuriant shade of the park. The old man sweats. Not she. Oh, no. No, she will not gift me with the sight of one more bead forming above the dark-blond S-shaped eyebrow.

As I come nearer, her shopping choices grow more and more engrossing, more complex. She must turn over each apple carefully before surrendering it to the tradesman's scale. How she does search for worms and blemishes. No time for any kind of conversation, except a strictly proto-col *Guten Morgen* to me, and some utilitarian instruc-tions to the old servant with the cart. Not a teeny pearl of perspiration. Very stingy. Only as I stand next to her, waiting and myself perspiring, only then does she suck in her cheeks slightly, her foot begins to tap, all by way of some indistinct, veiled impatience and annoyance.

But I have my own impatience and annoyance. That's because the taxi with the messenger usually arrives a few minutes late. I use the tardiness. I can ruffle again through my papers. I look at my watch, walk up and down.

When the taxi arrives (yes, taxi, not limousine; it's one of the luxuries of this Schatten stay that I can do without KarlHeinz altogether)—when the taxi comes, I can exchange important documents and whispered words with the office messenger inside, items involving cables and registered letters forwarded by the Littel Partners, items possibly more important than the rottenness of apples or the freshness of eggs which so concerns the lady nearby.

When the taxi leaves, I walk away with a polite greet-ing, but never a turn of the head. Back at the manor, I lunch off my tray, with all my Schatten notes so far propped up in front of me for reading. This is to stimulate me to get down to work right after the meal. Supposedly.

But other thoughts come crowding in, not so much thoughts as admonitions and suspicions, with Jewish question marks at the end of each. For example, could it be that I'm really ashamed of Uncle Julius' presence here? That perhaps I uninvited him so as not to be seen with him before Ahn and the Nun? And that only out of sheer guilt am I so damn active on behalf of his restitution? And that Julius could well be right, that she's indeed laughing inside those sucked-in cheeks, laughing at me beside the Venetian bridge? And that the dogs are really killers and the whole place a weird conspiracy? And why haven't I finished, let alone sent off, my letter to Nina? Why am I wasting all this time thinking undisciplined destructive ideas, and being so terribly sleepy?

The tray is borne away. I can hear the others come upstairs from their exclusive little lunch. The hour of the nap is upon Schatten. It has its own powerful new brand of silence. Even the chestnut leaves outside my window stop their infinitesimal soughing. In Julius' presence I could fend off the nap. Alone, I sense a sudden heaviness in my head.

I try to conceive brilliant Dowle-opening conceptions. My body receives angry, brutal instructions to walk over to my work desk. It obeys. It walks over. Invariably I wake up three quarters of an hour later, and lift my truant head from the typewriter which makes such a damnably good pillow for a nap.

Later I do work, but never for long. You see, it's not only I that's waked up, but the whole estate with me. Its silence is now defined by low bird calls, gravel crunching

under shoes, a small laugh. Who laughed the small laugh?
Who can help going down to find out? Actually it's not a
distraction from my work but part of making more contact with the place, or so I inform myself.

At this time the Old Tribe—that's what I call the
inmates—are out on the grounds. They're usually by the
lake shore, playing cards. Though the afternoon sun is
still powerful, they never enjoy the shelter of the lakeside
pergola; that, I've been told, is reserved for the Prince
even in his absence. They sit on stone benches at mossy
stone tables, men and women separately, playing cards.
The ladies whispering and tittering under a cluster of
parasols, some still holding the cards as if they were girls'
fans; the men with high-crowned hats, sucking their
pipes.

All this, from afar. From afar it looks like a cozy
bridge game. But as I approach—I, with my escort of
silence—they change. They grow dead quiet. The parasols stiffen; the faces are switched off like lamps. Even the
cards change. The things they hold in their veined fingers
now are not bridge cards but weird things painted with
passion-play symbols, tarot cards perhaps, grinning with
death and villains. I can't make head or tail of them.

I stop for a minute, just the same, to drop a random
remark about, say, the weather. Yes, comes one reply, yes
it is indeed still so very summery. Yes, allows an old
gent—to his pipe, not me—yes, remarkably rainless. A
thin liver-spotted lady quavers that the swallows are flying high. Others chime in: yes, high swallows mean high
heat. Yes, more summer weather tomorrow . . .

They've all turned into marionettes; on their mechanical faces nothing registers except the hope that perhaps
enough conversation has been accomplished to make the

gentleman go? All right, the gentleman goes.

But it isn't pleasant to be high-hatted by marionettes. I feel a crazy itch to shake them up. On another day I come at them, really burst in on them, and say blithely, "Good afternoon. Haven't you heard? The Prince has just come."

Man, it shakes them up. The robot game they play for my benefit, it just falls apart. The cards drop to the table. One parasol crumples. It's dandy. They seem positively frightened by the return of their beloved Prince. But someone—I think my tray bringer—makes a gesture that recomposes them. After that they know it isn't so.

"The gentleman jokes," he says, and the parasol reunfolds.

"The Prince should stay in the mountains till it gets cool," someone else says.

"The swallows are still out."

"Yes," my tray bringer says, "high swallows mean high heat."

And the non-cards begin to move again through their non-game; these non-faces have accomplished their non-conversation with me. And so I leave as I always do, nonplussed. And the further I walk away from them, the more it always strikes me that their witchy old voices are snickering up their sleeves behind my back; that they're running me through a gauntlet of madness and mockery.

But if I turn half around, to catch from the corner of my eye some confirmation of all this—why, then they have all gone, God knows where, into the oak tree, or jumped into the lake or turned themselves into swans. They've vanished from my sight like all the other Schatten fauna.

Shall I hound them down? No. I'll rest content to have

learned the valuable lesson that high swallows mean high heat and to return to my room. Furthermore, I've promised no interviewing until after the first meeting with the Prince. Furthermore, there's Ahn's daughter.

Of course she's draped around herself her own kind of exquisite unapproachability. In midafternoon—and in my rendition of the Book of Hours we have reached three p.m.—in midafternoon she is usually clipping the topiary yew by the gate. I see her whenever I take a little time off from the dictaphone and go over to the window. She stands or kneels, and her hands move in a steady, abstract rhythm, a rhythm that rejects a priori any outside approach or interruption.

Later, after four, though, she stops; begins to make a systematic circuit through the estate. The rhythm is still there, self-contained, self-absorbed. Her legs swing in her long linen dress like slim tongues in a dainty bell.

One could bump into her, quite easily and quite accidentally, after one's library stint. One could ignite a little chat, not out of desire or loneliness, but simply to spite her. But it isn't easy. There's no getting near the woman without a special, obtrusive effort. Wherever she walks, along the pond, by the chapel behind the manor, she throws up a rainbow barrier between herself and her pursuer. Every few feet she bends down (a linen buttock blooming dimly among the buttercups) and turns a spigot hidden in the underbrush. And suddenly another garden spout weaves a veil of water 'twixt my walking belle and me. I keep hoping fervently that she'll get drenched. The whole park sparkles and drips, jasmine scent floats on pearly meshes, the matted green glistens, and the socks of Dave's genius become gently soaked.

I know she must get back to her quarters to get ready

for the Five O'Clock Tea. She arrives at the manor, powder-dry. I watch her walk upstairs, up beyond my landing, right through the sentinel dogs. Their tails flick; their snouts nuzzle for a moment against her hand. Then they lapse into immobility and stare at me, not so much with their eyes as with their teeth. It's as though she'd passed through a bead curtain that rustles briefly while she parts the strings, then hardens into bars of steel.

The Five O'Clock Tea. Correction: the library, for the Tea tolerates me only as a passer-through with transit visa to the library. There I get some work done, mainly by studying old prints and moping over what members of Dave Dowle's celebrity entourage would best impersonate what nineteenth-century VIP's in which costume?

All along I eavesdrop on the piano and spoon tinkle. I listen hard from the stained-glass stillness among the books. As soon as my watch lets me, I walk back. The Ahns nod from their table with much courtesy but not an iota of invitation.

Of course one jaunts up to them all the same. One asks the daily question: when will the Prince return? And Ahn's friendly outstretched hand rises up as if to welcome the query, but then merely touches my arm with a hail-and-farewell tap. His eyes are only painted on in washed-out water-color blue. His real pupils function on the brainward side of his eyeballs, where they watch very superior and fascinating things. His lids blink very slowly. Dr. Ahn moves like a superb artist constantly gazing at mental spectacles the rest of us slobs can't even imagine. What's worse, he is a very polite superb artist, who gives irrelevant creatures like me a tolerant look, an impeccable nod.

"When will the Prince return? By next week, Mr.

Spey, depending on the weather. He never sends precise word, you know. Aren't our petunias handsome this week?"

I nod. I smile. I go. Of course the petunias are handsome. And high swallows mean high heat. What makes the brush-off worse is being all alone, Juliusless; and that I'm not even sure whether or not she sucked in her cheeks. Worst of all, the cockamamie Five O'Clock Tea stops the moment I've reached my room. It lasts just long enough to enrich my sense of isolation.

And in my room? In my room I stand by the window and watch Ahn go down the path, open smock flying, on his feeding walk. He returns. Two servants stride through the grounds with flame-tipped lances and touch them against garden lanterns, turning them into silent, saffron-luminous blossoms. Beyond the fence I spot the two East Zone soldiers who've just locked the gate, one hunchbacked, the other smoking. They walk at the same pace as the lantern lighters. All four seem to be in step, and for a moment the whole Schatten day embodies itself in syncopations and silences, glissandos, harmonies and chords which ought to coalesce into a single pattern. They ought to, but refuse. They fade away instead and yield to the footsteps of the servant with the dinner tray.

Dinner must be eaten and one more fine little frustration accomplished. After dinner the Old Tribe shuffles upstairs for bedtime on my floor. Just at that juncture I always contrive to journey toward the toilet. I manage to meet my fellow inmates at the landing. But she's never among them, though I've established beyond doubt that she dines with the whole gang. What would such an encounter bring? Very little. But the spoiling of even this trivial satisfaction is the final brush stroke on the day's long and intricate masterpiece.

Now, I may not exactly enjoy the masterpiece. But I do admire the skill, the downright virtuosity, of a series of maneuvers which can make a man with a quite estimable record in matters social and romantic, a man whose fiancée happens to be one of the more glamorous women on the New York scene—which can make such a man feel like a wallflower. There's almost as much craftsmanship in that sort of thing as in a Beethoven symphony. I mull over the subtleties involved while the green apron removes the tray with a good-night bow, while the lanterns go out in the garden. I mull it over while I stand by the window, waiting.

I know she's basically no more than an oddly gotten-up handsome female ghosting around a dowdy estate. And if it's any of the journal's business, I am not in love with her. But just like brushing my teeth and placing my handkerchief under the pillow, so waiting for her has become part of my lay-me-down-to-sleep ritual. So I wait. I wait at the window, in the romantic raiment of pajamas. At last she appears down there, flashing up in the moonlight together with the dogs for five whole seconds before the black trees swallow her.

Thank you, Madame. I can walk slowly to my bed.

September 23rd

Sometime early in December Teddy Roosevelt will land in Cannes, and in a stately progress of great-wheeled steam locomotives and silvered landaus pick up a Habsburg on the Riviera, a d'Annunzio in the Dolomites.

He and his friends will change to Daimler-Benzes in Germany, drive up to West Berlin via the Hanover access route, stop at Schatten, and in exchange for so many chivalrous hospitalities enjoyed there, invite Highness to an evening in a great new hostelry. D'Annunzio may show a piquant resemblance to Noel Coward. Under the Habsburg decoration you will, if we're lucky, find Sir Laurence Olivier, and old Teddy of San Juan Hill will certainly be Mr. Dowle of the many oysters.

Now, Dave is both stout and mustached and the Teddy R. proposition just about sure-fire. We'll have gold ducats struck (gilt veneer, brass inside) with Teddy's profile on one side, Dave's on the other, and Teddy-Dave will sow them into the populace during his triumphal ride from country to country. This will get us not only spectators and photographers but perhaps also money, because the coins will be accepted as come-on chips for any Dowle Casino. I might even get some of the countries on the route to issue special stamps with the Prince's face in honor of the event, and transport mail so stamped in our inaugural postchaises. We'll have the whole inaugural tour photographed with nineteenth-century cameras borrowed from the Smithsonian, and print the pictures as lithographs. Period albums of the event will be presented free to all those staying in Berlin Dowle suites costing over $50 a day. You ain't heard nothing yet.

The scheme really can't miss. And yet it had such a laborious birth during my four think days at Schatten. Even after it was born, and some of the preliminary logistics worked out and shaped into a presentation and phrased into a cable—I never believed it had a chance with Dave.

Toward the end of my four days' imprisonment I just

didn't believe anything any more. I wasn't in an exactly positive mood when I took up my station at the estate entrance yesterday morning. She was buying her famous supplies as usual. But I didn't stand next to her. Let's be frank. I sort of took cover behind the Venetian bridge. I didn't feel up to the let's-ignore-each-other game. She was much too good at it. The sun was too hot, and the probability too great that the taxi would bring a great big jeering NO cable from Dave.

But it wasn't a taxi which finally drove up to the Venetian bridge. It was something different, yet old-familiar. For four days I'd wandered through perfumed and iridescent hieroglyphics, and here a solid letter of the alphabet appeared in front of a dust cloud. I could read it so well. I could tell just from the way KarlHeinz brought the office limousine to a most gentle stop that someone important sat inside it—at least someone the old rascal didn't want to irritate.

Behold Ida, emerging with a flash of knee and a pink-wrapped pink-bowed package she dangled by a string. My melon-hefting Nun paid no attention to the visitor. Whatsoever. With a talent peculiar to all Ahns, she managed to ignore Ida even while returning her good morning.

Then, something rather nefarious. The only way to get to the bridge was through a gap between the butcher's and greengrocer's wagons. The gap was narrow and Ida—how else put it?—too fat. She stood there, dangling the pink package. The Nun chatted with the tradesmen; wouldn't dream of helping. Back and forth she walked through the gap, easily, teasingly, slimly, several times. Poor old Ida stood there; the color contrast deepened between fawn hat and stymied cheek. Ida reddened; Ida nearly purpled. It was the sort of incidental humiliation one woman can suffer only at the hands of another.

I came forward, through the gap. By a triumph of will she produced at least eleven teeth of smile.

*oo*Well, hello! Long time not see, Leon! Would I accept this littel token baked by the Littel Partners on my anniversary—the second *oo*week of my stay in Berlin! She just had to give it to me in person, and there was this cable from New York, and many phone calls, and everybody missed me so, but—convulsive turn-away from the apple-hefting Nun—it was difficult to talk here. Could she not abduct me to the office?

She certainly could.

Well, it was a joy-fest coming back. The moment we were beyond sight of the estate, even before opening Dave's cable, I knew it was all right. I was sure he'd love my Teddy Roosevelt. And he really did, with bells on. Ida waxed incandescent when I told her the idea (though she confused Teddy with Franklin D.) and the Littel Partners gave me a momentous curl-fingering welcome, Fräulein Ursula being in such a hurry to renew the flowers on my desk that she almost fell into my lap. I cabled Dave, fleshing out the Teddy R. While the going was good, I also sneaked in a hint to give Andy a crack at the Casino design. And then I worked the phone with great relish, really reveling in the sharp clicks, the janglings, the crisp operators. I never liked noise so much as after that huge dose of silence at Schatten. I checked out our preparation for the Casino-site bid at Schatten, called Dinny on Teddy Roosevelt costumes, and left a message at Julius' hotel asking him to please come for lunch tomorrow as usual, I was recovered.

I did *not* go to Schatten for lunch today. This at the office's unanimous insistence, even KarlHeinz', who seems downright lovable. I would never ever be forgiven if I wasn't Ida's guest in her dining alcove. So I had *oo*wonderful beefsteak with her, and afterwards the anniversary cake, pink like the wrapping and producing a tiny pink mustache on Ida's lip, and nobody with enough courage to tell her about it.

After lunch came Dave's interestingly fast reply, okaying most of my Teddy amplifications as well as Andy for the Casino. I called Andy right away at Stockholm, saying nothing of my intervention, only telling him the good news, and found him sober, full of beans, planning to come here next week to stake out the Casino site—only would I please not breathe a word about his return, as he had phfft with his German dish, he was really, repeat REALLY making it with his wife?

A golden day all around. Worked the phones some more, and the six hundred bells on my electric typewriter, but I did skip a heartbeat when I found my watch saying ten past six. We yelled for KarlHeinz and, bless him, he got me back home in time, before they closed the Schatten gate.

September 24th

Now we have it—a certificate of their ordinariness, of their very common fallibility and vulgarity. My lofty friends, the Ahns!

Easy. Deep breath. Let's have a nice orderly sequence. The charade begins with my uncle. He showed up for lunch today, the same old Julius, only a bit more so. In principle he did accept my "cold" as valid excuse for having kept him away, which is white of him. But he suspected my inadequate symptoms. He sat there, pressing his glasses back, listening to my careful coughs like a disgruntled music critic.

"Why don't you go on with your petition, Uncle?"

He ruffled through the typed-up petition installments I gave him. No, he said, he couldn't go on. Too much time had passed, he had lost the thread now, the mood was wrong—it was almost the eve of the Day of Atonement. It just wasn't any good trying to reacquaint himself now.

All this by way of oblique accusation. Then he followed me downstairs to the library, murmuring, blackly, his gratitude for the typing up. That was the fine thing about the Day of Atonement, it wiped the slate clean of debts and resentments among true Jews, it left only generosity and thankfulness; as far as he was concerned, he felt he owed people thanks whether these people deserved it or not.

Thus radiant with mercy, he resumed cataloguing pictures for me without any of the usual vocal comments, just toiling and moiling along. And then it happened. A grunt. A sharp intake of breath.

He stood by the window, clutching a heavy morocco-bound album.

"Come here!"

I ran, sure I'd outraged him again somehow. He's a great boy for arousing guilt feelings.

"You see?"

Trembling with effort, he held the album higher and higher in dark triumph, as though it were the severed head of an enemy general.

"There?"

The photo was very recent for the library. Probably the end of the 'thirties, taken not at Schatten but at some huge church. I saw a young man and woman kneeling, obviously at their wedding. Their faces were tilted upward and slightly blurred. But after a moment I could distinguish Ahn, standing behind the bride. An Ahn with much darker hair, oddly turned away from the nuptial pair and looking toward the margin of the picture. His carriage was unmistakable, though. Even the tails of his formal frock coat hung off his back the same way as his open smock now.

"You see?" Julius demanded. "You recognize that?"

"It's the doctor," I said.

"Yes, yes, the Spider. *And?*"

And my Nun! She was the bride. The same long blond hair I glimpse now and then as she romps the dogs—here it fell down her lace gown in long fair folds. And the mouth that likes to close itself into such tight impassivity now, sucking in the cheeks—here it was open in a vibrant young smile, a dimple in the left cheek and the suspicion of a tiny gap between the front teeth. I stared voraciously. The damn picture was like a keyhole which would undress the stoic queen into a live and eager virgin.

"Let's see," I said. "That's the doctor's daughter getting married."

Uncle Julius virtually stamped his foot. "Yes, *and?* To whom? . . . There! . . . To whom?"

The bridegroom was handsome, with gorgeous eyes, elegant sideburns that looked theatrical on such a young face, a strong well-formed chin. He, too, seemed vaguely familiar.

"Don't you see?" my uncle said. "You still don't see!"

The ink pencil circled what I'd taken for a button on the groom's collar. A tiny swastika. It was so unexpected because everyone else was in civilian clothes, because the groom's cap was off and his kneeling hid most of what I now recognized as boots—and finally because this involved supposedly holy Schatten people. My good Nun had married a man in SS uniform.

"I'll be damned," I said.

"I had an idea about her," my uncle said. "I could smell it. The Spider! And I tell you, maybe the Prince doesn't even know. He wouldn't have let her! We'll give him a hint in the petition! What do you think?"

"I'll be damned," I said.

"You see now? We discuss it on the way. Yom Kippur starts in an hour."

He shut the album before I could put my finger on the page. And then I realized he actually expected me to come to his Day of Atonement, to the synagogue.

"Uncle," I said, "I can't go to the city at this time of day. I'd never get back before they lock the gate."

"You won't come?"

"Don't misunderstand me—"

"I understand!" The album dropped on the table with a small thunderclap. Our rapprochement had cracked again. "You make your own decisions. You're a grown man, with your name in the paper. You're too big for Yom Kippur!" He stared at me, pressed his glasses back. He was even beyond coughing. He put three nuts in his mouth and made for the door.

"I'll pray for you!"

And I, who had to deal with his cursed temper, with the ridiculous no-material-must-leave-this-library edict and with my own insane desire to look my fill of the photograph—I stripped off my jacket, wrapped the album inside it and ran after him.

It reached that degree of ridiculousness. The idea was to catch Julius and ask him up to my room for a reconciliation drink—to use that as camouflage for getting the album into safe home territory. But Julius, fleet-in-anger Julius, had vanished past the manor door. At the same time I heard Ahn stir out of an alcove. The damn jacket hung in a bloated and unnatural curve from my arm. What happened next? What did Leon Spey do, a thirty-seven-year-old $50,000-a-year vice president of Dowle Inc.? He took his good tweed jacket with the album inside it, and he shoved it under a chest.

"Good day," said Ahn, with an ironic glint at my shirtsleeves. "How clever of you not to bother with a coat in this heat."

"Yes," I said stupidly.

"Let me show you a cool place."

Arm extended, he scooped me along in his inimitable, infernal fashion.

It's partly the toll taken by my solitary Schatten days. They've kept treating me like a clumsy juvenile intruder until I actually started to behave like one. And it's partly that as a cold fish with slow reactions, I'm seldom at my best in moment-to-moment emergencies. If you look close, you might find in my wake a whole series of good tweed jackets moronically stuffed under chests.

And yet I have a saving grace. A faculty for recompo-
sure, for calming down angrily and icily. This happened
today while the doctor ushered me through the gardens. I
began to see that photo as proof of the Ahns' ordinariness;
of the fact that Schatten—untouched, exotically pure
Schatten—sports some very ordinary garden-variety ex-
Nazi pimples. My great Nun-Queen has the same fallible
thighs, the same moral acne as the next German woman.

I began to regard my knowledge of the fact as a useful
thing to keep in reserve. By the time Ahn led me into the
pine copse behind the chapel, I was fine. I was all
blandness. A narrow path ran through the copse to a
clearing scattered with crosses. Had I ever been to the
cemetery before?

"No," I said. "I had no idea. It's all very cunning
here."

"Oh? Did you notice that? At any rate, this is the
coolest place in the summer."

It was cool all right, and quiet, quiet even for Schatten.
The plots are islands of moss on a ground full of pine
needles. I decided that perhaps he wasn't playing with
me. Perhaps I was playing with him; the photograph was
like money in the bank, to be taken out at the optimum
moment and used for all it's worth.

Meanwhile he was talking about the cemetery, explaining that the graves were of guests and servants. "Quite a
few here were both," he said. "When a guest dies, the
Prince replaces him with a servant. It's a sort of pension
for our staff."

"Really?" I said. "I'm learning a lot today."

"Good!" he said. "You see, the world is running out of
our kind of guest. Now we groom our guests in our

porters and waiters—what's left of them. Once upon a time you had to be a page to become a knight."

"You make everything sound so reasonable," I said.

"*Reasonable?*" He laughed. And then, of all times, he picked this one for a sermon. With one of his urbane, imperious motions he sat down on a cast-iron bench and drew me down beside him. "Nothing *reasonable* here at Schatten," he said. "All the reasonableness takes place outside." His cane pointed. "There: East Zone, West Zone, they're both reasonably organized, wouldn't you agree? The radar screens and the exhaust pipes, the barbiturates and the bomb shelters, each one of your enlightenments—they're all reason or the creation of reason. They're not for us. We keep them out."

I was thinking of the perfect reasonableness of participating in a swastika wedding during the Hitler era. Aloud I said that I felt we might give reason a little more credit than he did.

"Oh, yes," he said, "reason is now being put to social purpose. The social application of reason must now catch up with the scientific. Isn't that the slogan? I read it in all the newspapers that come straying in here. Reason will make society into something electronically perfect, perhaps like one of those anti-water-pollution systems in your excellent American cities? Or like a well-run parking lot? Or any of the other idylls of our time. Or should I say, *your* time?" He chuckled.

"You put things very vividly," I said. The blighter is an intellectual snob as well as the regular kind.

"And you shouldn't encourage me," he said, smiling. "But you must understand, to the Prince a reasonable society is just as hopeless as a reasonable religion. A reasonable God, a God like a good football referee, isn't worth believing in, is he? Nor is a parking lot. No, reason is all right for making motors or pumping water, all the lowlier conveniences. But it should be kept out of important affairs. There it's poison. It poisons our stars at night. The Prince will not compromise with reason. Once you start, you die like the others out there. Of gas fumes and emptiness. I think we'll find a much better thing to die of."

His mouth turned grim. The cane had been driven deep into the moss. But on the instant he became urbane once more. "A bit chilly?"

It *was* getting clammy in my shirtsleeves amid the pine shadows. "I feel a little cold," I said, "but very much instructed."

He honored me with a long amused glance. "This is just echoing the Prince's thoughts," he said as we were walking back. "He believes that a decent society is like a decent mystery play. It's a romance, a performance. All the durable institutions are—the Holy See, the English Crown, the Knights of Malta. Society is a vehicle of fancy, which may puzzle you young people because you've grown too sophisticated to enjoy your imagination. The Prince thinks that society should be a work of art. Perhaps you've noticed that at Schatten."

"Perhaps I have," I said. Again I thought of the photograph and what a sly unctuous fake he is. I asked him, pointedly, whether his Prince left any room for truth in that work of art.

" 'Truth'?" he said, putting sardonic quotation marks around the word. "That's very much like 'reason.' 'Truth' is a word invented so that people may lie to each other about it. Don't you think? The Prince feels that the moment society takes itself seriously as a big reasonable 'truth' it becomes vicious. It wants to truthify the rest of the world. The Prince feels that truth has nothing to do with man. The small truths—I mean the little mechanical platitudes about oxidation and construction and so on— they belong to the motor and to the screwdriver. The great truths belong to God. In between, here we are, a little shadow, a little fantasy. That's enough to get along on. At least in Schatten it is."

"This," I said, "is the age of the screwdriver."

"Oh, we may outlive it," he smiled. "We outlived the other truths. The Prussian empire. The republic and the dictatorship. We got past the war and the bombs. And the Prince was restored to us whole. We just may survive the screwdrivers too."

"Well," I said, "we'll try to make the hotel opening untruthful and unreasonable enough to satisfy His Highness. He'll return next week?"

The good doctor smiled and held the manor door open for me. "As far as we know. His last letter said so."

"The earlier the better," I said. "Good night."

It was Five O'Clock Tea in the hall. Tinkly piano, doilies and silver pots. They were all there, the Ahns at their table (he excused himself to join them) and all the others. Her little white fingers tapped to the music. The whole blasted Five O'Clock Tea was like a barricade thrown around the chest and the tweed-wrapped photo album underneath. There's just the chance that I was conned away from the chest, knowingly, by the smoothest, most treacherous exercise of reason.

I wished my doctor friend a nice long screwdriver up his altitudinous behind and walked, since there was nothing else to do, upstairs, to my room, to the window.

September 25th

Spent most of the day in Paris.

The French nuisance, which has been building up all along, came to a head. A morning call from Paris did it. Nothing but shrillness and confusion. I realized that if the mess was going to be resolved at all, it would have to be resolved brutally, in my presence. Drove straight to the airport while the Littel Partners phoned ahead for reservations. Made the morning flight by the skin of my teeth. Landed Orly at noon. In the limousine that took us to town, a brief victorious scuffle with our French promotion *maréchals*, each one a Bourbon in dignity, a Mitty in effectiveness. During a hundred-minute lunch at the Crillon finalized (a less poetic word would not do justice to the matter) our switch to another advertising agency. Back at the airport, a bottle of champagne sent me by the head of the newly chosen *publicité*. Berlin at 6:10. Couldn't get to the office before closing. KarlHeinz considered this a shame because Ida "has something most special to report, suhr." Didn't gratify his expectation by asking what. He deposited me at Schatten's gate a comfortable twenty minutes before lock-up time.

Whew.

Funny. Paris, which I love, and which I saw for all of an hour in the silkiest fall weather—Paris made no dent on me. Nor did the whole jet-age fantasia of the day. I performed as if in a dream, though I performed very well. The fact that I refused to stay in France for longer than lunch, my brief mysterious high-powered swoop—all that gave me an edge on the French boys which I exploited competently. The whole foray was brought off by a kind of automatic pilot; a decision-making attachment screwed onto your brains which sees you safely through difficult weather without recourse to your living core. The core remained in Schatten all along. Within a thirty-yard circumference of a photograph wrapped in a tweed jacket, waiting under a chest.

Once you get back here you realize that you've never been away. Here each shadow carries, as it grows, the whole weight of the day. I looked out of my window and watched the shadows of the poplars smother the gregarious glitter of Paris. The chestnut leaves hissed, the lanterns in the garden flowered one by one. I felt I'd never been the terror of the Crillon. The Pan-Am tag on my briefcase is a mirage. Her eyes in the wedding picture, her bright sixteen-year-old virgin's eyes burned through the album cover, through tweed and chest and hall ceiling into my room.

My dinner tray arrived, but I wasn't much for eating. I was for going down to snatch the picture—if it was still there. The crew below began to make their good-night pilgrimage up the stairs to my floor. Her footfalls were not among them. I turned to the letter I've been trying to write Nina for days. After two paragraphs I bogged down. I dictaphoned my cable on the French shift, but killed no more than a few hundred seconds. Of some help was the bill which had arrived together with the dinner on the tray. Someone—her?—always writes out the figures with an inkwell pen in thin-and-bold-stroke calligraphy. But the bill only took a few minutes to check. So I totaled up my expenses for the Paris trip. It didn't keep me from feeling forsaken.

It was Saturday night. Just Saturday night it had to be.

I knew that at the Ku-damm, just two miles away, braided doormen were saluting ladies in satin whose legs flash as they swivel out of cars. I thought how sensible it would be to dip my last bachelor days among those legs, to surround myself with a different pair each night. I thought of Paris, of this season's discotheque, where perhaps one of those pert copywriting redheads was dancing right now, one of those girls who had witnessed my classic four-hour raid today and who imagined Monsieur Spey in God knows what momentous and high-speed revelry.

And Monsieur Spey, the high-speed reveler, stared at his cooling beef stew and sat alone, quietly mooning in a quietly decaying house.

The hell with it. That's when I decided to fetch the thing, the photo, to my room. I could bring it close to the lamp. I'd bare her face to the light; she'd have to smile at me helplessly with her young naked bridal face in which everything could still be seen all at once, and I'd stare my fill of her, all night long if I wanted to, at my leisure.

Only the first-floor corridor was lit. The downstairs loomed with pitch-dark quiet. Above the landing, on the steps, the German Shepherd dog sat in stone repose, alone, ears upright, eyes gleaming. I groped my way down the black well of the stairs.

The hall was like an unknown forest. My flashlight carved out of the void chairbacks and pillars I couldn't recall from daytime. Like mushrooms they had sprouted within a single nocturnal hour. I thought I was halfway to the chest when the entrance door rattled.

I wanted to switch off my flashlight, but in the abruptness of it all couldn't find the button. The two huge Afghan hounds tumbled through the door. Both held leather straps in their mouths from which lanterns swung and swooped. The whole hall turned into a riot of glows and shadows. I just stood there. It took me seconds to make sure that it was actually her all right, holding the leashes. But she wasn't my daytime Nun. She had on those wide old-fashioned slacks I'd glimpsed before from my nocturnal window, the single blond rope of her hair flinging back and forth. Her face glimmered up flushed and vibrant, much more akin now to the one in the photograph. Against her surfed the dogs.

They all froze at the sight of me.

A defense formula rattled off my tongue. I said I was just about to go out, to walk off a headache.

"Don't," she said. "It'll make my boys wild when they hear someone outside."

She patted the Afghans. Her voice wasn't the voice I knew but a high-breathing whisper still warm from her romp. She was out of breath with a magnificent breathlessness that heaved along her black sweater, her whole slim electric shadow-confused figure. Then she said something quite ridiculous. "They're smelling a bitch in the East Zone," she said. "They're bad enough tonight."

She pulled at them. They pulled back at her. The whole procession of gleams and blacknesses, of suddenly lit paws, hair rope, fangs and sweater bosom swarmed upstairs.

It was intolerable just to let her recede like that. I scrambled after her up the steps. I told her I'd go back to my room in that case and try to ventilate my headache by opening the windows.

"Thank you," she said, climbing away.

In Paris, where I didn't care, I was a lion. Here, where I do, I'm butterfingers. Nothing occurred to me except to ask, stupidly, why she didn't provide her dogs with female company.

"Their bitch died a year ago," she said. "I can't get quality Afghans to breed them with in Berlin."

We had reached the first floor. Her whisper had changed to her daytime tone. At some secret signal the dogs subsided. She took the lanterns from their mouths and blew them out. The wild spookishness between us died. The Lion of Paris, me, stumbled over the top step.

"Good night," she said, ascending.

"Good night," I said. The Afghans sat alert, immobile, below the landing, just as the German Shepherd did above it.

With the stairs sealed off both ways, I had to go back. Back along the corridor, back to where I had started, back to my room with its familiar, revolting leaf-hissing solitude. And to defy it and everything else defiable in that damnable house, I slammed the door right in the night's face.

September 26th

A remarkable Sunday command performance at Ida's. The whole morning turns out to be rather military, an overture quite in key with the main event. Rain squalls, short and swift, like cavalry attacks. The showers kept them all in the manor hall, blockading the album chest. I'm harking back to my unreal, all too briefly visited Paris with its unreal silky weather, away from this very real Prussian madness.

Can't get over that amazing performance at Ida's. Setting: Fräulein Lieselotte, the Littel-Partner-in-chief, is drawn up dagger straight in the inner office, a sheet of paper in her hand. The very espresso machine breathes solemn significance. KarlHeinz hasn't removed himself as usual. In a stance of semi-attention, thumbs hooked into his pockets, he leans ever so faintly against the wall, half lout, half sergeant-at-arms. The other Littel Partners finger their curls in exact synchronization, with the same relentlessly nervous rhythm. Ida, clad in field gray, trip-struts toward me.

"My dear Leon." Deep breath. "I have been *oo*wanting to trouble you with a littel info. But you came back from Paris too late yesterday for this." Deep, grave, official breath. "You will understand, there are some German people who have not been able to entirely avoid the National Socialist era—" to my surprise, she points at KarlHeinz, who grins faintly and leans faintly—"but who are now doing constructive labor. There are other German people, female persons often, delicate snob ladies, exactly the types that upraised Mister Hitler. They start by marrying a National Socialist Schatten grandson—"

This, of course, brings me up short.

"Yes!" Ida pounces, snatches Lieselotte's paper, flourishes it high like a captured regimental flag. "That's *oo*what she did, this slim delicate lady—married a National Socialist!"

"Schatten grandson?" I say skeptically. "The Prince's daughter died—"

"Right!" Ida jams the paper back into Lieselotte's hand. "The daughter demised right after her marriage to a Baron Lausche. *But!* Lieselotte!"

"Anno 1913," Lieselotte rattles off, "demise in child-bed Baroness Lausche, infant boy Helmut surviving.

Anno 1933 young Baron Helmut's first motion picture, *Achtung, Liebe*. Small featured parts till war. Anno 1938, Baron Helmut appointed Assistant Secretary National Socialist Actors' Front. Anno 1940, married Irene Ahn."

"Ah," says Ida, watching me. "Exactly my reaction, when I investigated this yesterday. Now you understand why she gives herself airs, our slim snob lady at Schatten? She married the Prince's grandson. Not really a Schatten, just a grandson female line, even a disowned grandson because of the National Socialist connection. But airs! The *oo*wedding was not even permitted at Schatten. Our snob lady was not permitted either. Not even after the separation."

"Separation?"

"Se-pa-ra-tion." She points to the sheet in dainty disgust, as though it were the slim snob lady's uterine X-ray. "In 1940 National Socialism was a very excellent bet. Thus marriage. After 1942 an incorrect bet. Thus separation. This is a very clever record. Lieselotte!"

Lieselotte, gravely: "Anno 1942, separation granted Berlin City Court. Baron Helmut killed, Kharkov, Russian front. 1945 . . ." Lieselotte pauses. Ida raises her hand to compel attention and to turn up Lieselotte's sound. "1945," Lieselotte rings out, "December 27, 1945, marriage of widowed Baroness Helmut to Colonel Roger du Sard, French occupation force."

I give a soft whistle.

"Now! You see?" Ida is very pleased by this American response. "What a special person! An occupation officer, the most excellent bet of all!"

"Anno 1946," reads Lieselotte, "incorporation of Schatten estate, originally East German, into French

Berlin zone, due to influence of Colonel du Sard. Anno 1948, divorce from Colonel du Sard in Cannes."

Ida, obviously languishing for another American whistle, gets one. "You see? Exactly! Already through with him. Millions of women manless in Germany, *she* divorces her husband on the Riviera. Lieselotte!"

Lieselotte snaps to. "Anno 1949, return, Irene Ahn, to Schatten—"

"The Prince took her back?"

"Precisely the question!" says Ida. "The Prince! So holy during the National Socialist era, so un-Hitler they even had to put him into prison. And when it is all over and he returns—he takes back this very mixed-background person. The question is *oo*why?"

*oo*Why is Lieselotte's cue, but for some reason poor Lieselotte misses it. "*oo*WHY?" Ida reiterates, stamping her foot the tiniest bit.

"Anno1947," Lieselotte reels off in a panic, "salethree acresSchattenestatebythePrince—"

"There, you appreciate?" says Ida, perhaps bucking for a third whistle. "A poor, a poor sick old man, down to selling off estate pieces! But with *her* he has a rich divorcée, an *Allied* divorcée, on his side. That's *oo*why! No hunger, no black market. Nothing of what *oo*we all had to suffer." She sighs, to excite comprehension in me. At an eager but respectful distance of two seconds follows Lieselotte's sigh.

"With her he was above the bad days. Just like he is above the good days now. He is above electricity, this Prince Schatten, above the telephone. He won't even permit the bomb-removal squadron—"

"Above the Dowle pageant?" I asked.

"Bravo!" Ida says. "Bravo, Leon! Touché!" Sotto

voce: "And, a secret: *she* wants no Dowle pageant either. No outside influence. Only that way she will inherit the estate!"

"Is that what she is after?"

"I told you. Everything is very clever!"

Ida smiles implacably and steps aside for Fräuleins Ursula and Edeltraud wheeling in a table set for two.

No use saying that I had planned on my usual lunch at the estate.

"No, no, Leon. No. I am—*oo*what is the delightful American phrase—I am queering this. She will not have you today. And she will not have the estate the way she thinks, the snob lady. *oo*We *oo*will queer this too. All the privileges, the tax exemptions and the hotel license, they go with the Prince. We have made our littel inquiries. What kind of hot sandwich, Leon? Lamb? Chicken? Steak? We have the restaurant standing by. Pork? You say the *oo*word."

It's one of Ida's very, very strong days.

"Steak? Two steaks, Ursula." She begins to take off her field-gray gloves with slow, severe triumph. Vanished, Lieselotte, Edeltraud, Ursula, KarlHeinz. The court-martial is over.

"I hope I'll be as incisive as you are," I say.

"Ah, you are *oo*wonderful, Leon." She beams. She sits down. Her face relaxes into a shoes-off expression. "Edeltraud!" she releases a mighty crescendo. "*Ketchup!*"

September 26th

That was the first half of the day. I came back to

Schatten for the second. The Prussian weather let up. The sun came out. But I was not *oo*wonderful. Not at all.

It's always like this. I feel cocky, happy, witty about Schatten as long as I'm away from it. Then I walk through the gate—and everything wobbles.

It was siesta time when I returned today. Not a soul about. My first chance alone with the chest. Finally I could lie down on the hall floor, and peer and reach under and squirm and dirty my shirt cuffs at my leisure, and find nothing. Nothing. No album, no jacket. I ran into the library, plowed the shelves. All the old albums were there except the twentieth-century one with her bridal smile. I ran upstairs. The first thing I saw was my tweed jacket hanging newly pressed in my closet. The handkerchief gleamed newly laundered from the breast pocket.

Around me the estate dozed with consummate blandness. In the whole manor only the dogs were alive, forbidding the upper stairs with their grinning ice-cold teeth. I didn't feel like taking it. Not with Ida's powerhouse momentum still inside me. The court-martial still struck me as funny. The Nun's copious past still as rather a riot, and no skin off my back. Why should it be? Only the idea of queering them wasn't such a joke. It began to seem like a most satisfying idea. I burned to revenge that mockingly pressed jacket, to find someone to say something absolutely point blank to.

Downstairs the hall lay deserted. I combed the gardens, chased peacocks out of pergolas, frightened lizards out of the follies. And inside the new chapel, where I've never been before, I found Ahn.

I almost missed him. The door stood open, but the interior was so uninviting. Empty, glacially neo-Gothic,

with no saints or decorations to soften the stern arches
and the sharp angles of the pews. In a stained-glass
window, a Jesus with jagged arms and a sun bursting
curiously beneath him. Behind the altar, a flight of stairs
down to a crypt. From those steps Dr. Ahn's head
emerged just as I was about to leave again. He didn't look
any less startled than I.

"A surprise visitor," he said.

He slammed the stair gate shut behind him, the first fast
movement I've ever seen him make. There was no point
wasting time on amenities.

"Hello," I said. "I'm looking for a vanished photograph
album from the library."

"Why, we must have thieves here," he said. "Then it
was careless of me to leave the chapel door open."

"Yes," I said. "They're a cunning bunch. They'll steal
a thing no matter how cleverly you hide it, even under a
chest."

"Nice of you to warn me," he said. "We've got
Schatten jewels and mementos in the family crypt. You
just keep alerting me, Mr. Spey, whenever you find me
negligent."

That cold ironic bastard. Nothing throws him. He
scooped me up once more, on that unbendingly cordial
arm. "Mustn't let you see the chapel before it's finished."
Smile. "The Prince is bringing some beautiful things for
it. Next time you surprise us, we'll surprise you."

If he'd tried to chuck me out just a shade less amiably,
I'd have had a foothold for a fight. But this time he even
put his arm round my shoulder as he steered me to the
door. "Let me show you the really finished part, the
tower. I think you'll like the view."

With his relentless chattiness, his damn politesse that

left no room for objections or interjections, he ushered me across the vestibule and up a whitewashed spiral staircase.

"The thing cost a frightful lot of money," he chatted sweet as you please, "particularly the family crypt. The Prince started building in '49, a somewhat bankrupt year, and he's finishing only now. The point is, during the war a big bomb fell on this spot which didn't go off. In fact, we defused it ourselves. The Prince thinks there are too many memorials to exploded bombs, don't you? To battles, victories and whatnot. He wants this to be a memorial to a dud. He thinks there are just two things that can save us today, love and inefficiency. In this chapel we pray for both. Here you are."

We stood at the top of the staircase, he a couple of steps below me, his face flushed, hand pressed to his side. The old sonofabitch had climbed some forty steps, speaking constantly. He pointed, bowed me onto the look-out.

"Do enjoy the view." He bowed, vanished. I wanted to throw after him something like, "Thank you, I'd have enjoyed your Nazi wedding too!" Something that would splash against that lofty face like a custard pie.

I never got around to it. The moment I stepped on the outer ledge, dizziness came down on me. A terrific attack. The chapel roof below, sheet tin, gathered up the sun and poured it as a single savage reflection into my eyes. All I could do was clutch the parapet. Only my hands preserved me against incandescent vertigo. I didn't dare let go for minutes. Then the vista reassembled itself below: the pond with the two swans nailed motionless in the middle, the poplar peaks next to the pagoda roofs just underneath, the lush stolid lawns, the whole noncommittal splendor of the estate.

All the anger had gone out of me. I leaned away from the parapet, limp and sort of futile. The bridal photo, and all the fuss, and my desirous conjectures and the Nun's damn sundry marryings and Ida's infos and courts-martial—all nothing but futility, a long laborious tunnel with a mirage at the exit.

I still haven't recovered from that moment. It gave me a sudden middle-aged ache, a feeling that it's a little late for the truth, the pure noble young truth, and that this quagmire of deviousness is an absurd place in which to search it out.

I grew very tired up on the tower top. I envied, and still envy, Uncle Julius, who had his Yom Kippur yesterday. All day yesterday Julius struggled with something as grandiose as God, while I couldn't grasp something so obvious as Paris. I really envied him. I envy him still because I'm at least one generation more tired than he, so much less simple, so much more naked to death. I was tired of the highway I saw from up there, curving away from the gate, one side lined with pseudo-Mediterranean villas (good West), the other with scraggly barns (evil East). I was and I am tired of West vs. East, of me vs. Schatten, me vs. Dave Dowle, me vs. a smiling bride. Tired of all sources of solemn human excitement. Tired of feeling a rotten let-down over my multimarried Nun.

I saw two East German guards strolling under the Venetian bridge, one hunchbacked, the other dangling a cigarette. Tokens of the world's most terrifying confrontation, yet so small and piteous and mortal at this distance. Up there the whole Iron Curtain seemed like a frantic trap invented by man so that he can riot busily, importantly around it and turn his face away from the truly big brink. Perhaps it's much the cozier abyss to divert yourself with.

It didn't divert me at all this afternoon. I felt the weight of a gargoyled, excruciatingly apathetic universe against my skin, and, inside that skin, nothing but urgent and forsaken mysteries.

And then I thought what a lousy *Dowle Scene* feature *that* would make, and slowly climbed down the staircase.

September 27th

Rain, rain, rain. It's touched off a conversation with KarlHeinz that I've long wanted to have. One of those sudden cold showers came down as we drove to the estate. Hear this.

"Suhr." Spoken with the patient superiority of a baby sitter. "If you are afraid of catching cold, I can get a blanket from the trunk."

"Never mind."

"Yes, suhr. You must live here many years to get used to the weather."

"Apropos of living here," I said. "Dr. Holze mentioned something about your life here during the Hitler period."

"Yes, suhr. I was drafted into the SS, suhr." He was smoking and whistling in his virtuoso below-the-board fashion. The steady simper on the rear-view mirror did not admit for a moment that he had just been counterattacked.

"I must be badly informed," I said. "I thought the SS

was a volunteer organization."

"Yes, suhr. Their typical propaganda, suhr. I was drafted as a driver-orderly."

"Looks like they were anxious to have you."

"The Prince's grandson forced me in, suhr."

"Uh-huh," I said.

"Because I once helped out at Schatten, suhr. So he could say he had Schatten personnel. Even in the SS he was Schatten-crazy. He always talked about this connection."

I decided to venture it. "You must have gotten to know his wife."

"Oh, no, suhr. The marriage was short, suhr. I was strictly in the official car."

"How interesting," I said.

"Yes, suhr. Interesting hard work. He was a maniac about his work, suhr. Organizing soldier shows right up to the front, right till he was killed."

"Too bad," I said. "Such an active life."

"Right, suhr. Precisely what I testified at my denazification. A capable but misguided man, suhr."

And then we were there.

A sweet man.

A swell fellow.

September 29th

Yes, Virginia, there *is* a David Dowle. Yesterday he materialized unexpectedly at Frankfurt. The telegram summoning me to the presence only said: WANT TO HELP ME PICK A SPINET STOP YOU MUSIC LOVING VIENNESE STOP LOVE DAVE.

For additional details I got hold of our Frankfurt manager by phone: DD was on a one-day stopover on his way back to New York after a week end in Greece. Dave is thinking—God help the Gods—Dave is actually thinking of an Olympus Dowle.

So I hopped over to Frankfurt yesterday morning and "helped" Dave get a spinet. A real flying week for me. At the showroom of the biggest Frankfurt piano outfit I found my employer among dozens of lovely antique spinets specially corraled for the occasion. In attendance were the proprietor, the manager, plus a salesman, all in tight white collars, tiptoeing gravely behind Mister Dowle, who strode around in his lumbershirt, mustache rhythmic with chewing gum. I hate to admit it, but he sounded the spinet keys with melodic deftness.

"Hey! How's the old genius?" he said. "You look a little pale. Take care of yourself. You're the most indispensable madman I've got. Now dig—those cats want something special."

"Those cats," it developed, are a far-out jazz combo using antique instruments. Next week they're to blow at Dave's pad, and he promised them a real groovy eighteenth-century spinet, air freight.

Okay, I played the Indispensable Madman game; let Dave have it for not flying me to New York for a ball like that, then stabbed at spinet keys myself and talked to the salesman in a combination of German and beatnikese which just flipped Dave. It just broke him up, for a little while. But then he squinted at the mahogany finish of an instrument and, quite incidentally, came to the point. "What's new?" he asked. "You beat old Schatten out of the bushes yet?"

I had my report ready. I said that the Prince's coming

(which is acquiring the expectancy and mystery of Christ's) has now been definitely fixed by Ahn for Tuesday, October 5th, less than a week from now. Also that things are zipping along apace at the Berlin Oyster, including the Teddy Roosevelt suite (guns); the Richard Wagner suite (Valkyrie wallpaper); the Rudolph Archduke of Habsburg suite (much plush); and the Lola Montez suite (much bed). Each great impersonated member of our opening pageant will be immortalized by impersonated interior decor, down to the individualized matchboxes in each suite. At this very moment, I said, Dinny was designing gangs of Götterdämmerung for the Wagner suite.

Dave laughed at that and said they were playing Leonard Bernstein's biblical thing at the Frankfurt Konzerthalle tonight, strange groove for a German outfit, how about him and me digging it together? I said great, and both of us continued to poke spinets. It dawned on me that he considered my progress report poor or that something was wrong.

"Your pal the Prince thinks he's better than Winston Churchill," Dave said all of a sudden.

"Churchill?" I said.

"Well, I cabled an offer to fly this Schatten character here chartered for a lunch—"

"But wait a minute," I said thunderstruck. "He isn't even in Berlin yet."

"I know. I cabled to Davos, that address we got, just to smooth the way for you a little. Last cat turned down a plane of mine was Churchill. Except this fella goes him one better. Old Churchill wrote me back a whole long letter saying why. This fella just sends back the cable unopened. That's one up on Winston."

"I'll be damned," I said. "I'll ask him about that when I see him next week."

"You have a definite appointment?" Dave asked, and the chewing gum stopped in his cheeks.

"Not yet," I said. "He's hard to pin down in advance."

"How the hell does he get away with it?" Dave said, low.

He'd swiveled slowly around on his piano stool, his back coming to rest heavily against the spinet top. For an instant his face was silent, stymied, stationary, cheeks sagging down from the up-brushed mustache. That instant Prince Schatten scared me terribly, because the very idea of the man seemed to defeat even Dave. It also made me see for the first time how very tired Dave was, how very far into his sixties. Greece, Germany and New York in a single week, twenty-five hotels, millions of dollars, and a hip spinet brawl coming up—it was a lot for a small-town boy from Nebraska. But it wasn't enough. Even with all that, he wasn't getting away with it, compared to the Prince. And maybe Dave's summoning me to Frankfurt was to find out why, how come he wasn't, and to make sure somehow that I wasn't either.

Anyway I felt, to my amazement, sorry for him; he looked gray and old in that rich virile young lumbershirt and tried so hard and so well, and poked the spinets so feelingly. And after making a lot of money out of him, I'd desert him so soon.

But you can't feel sorry for Dave for longer than a second. He's too swift and insidious. The chewing gum resumed in his cheeks, moving slowly, cunningly.

"Tell you what." He grinned the old Dave grin. "Needn't let on the cable was from me personally. I'll tell

Mr. Prince myself at the procession and watch his face. Crazy?"

"Crazy," I said.

"Apropos the procession. Know what'd be a gas? Fly a white horse to Berlin. You know, like the biggest. And photograph it in advance with the horn attached?"

"Uh-huh, with some feudal jazz in the background," I said, "to show it's the Schatten unicorn."

"Now you're swinging," Dave said. "And, say, know what else'd be the end? If I'm going to open as Teddy Roosevelt, some sort of cute malarkey about Teddy hunting a unicorn."

"Hm," I said.

"Right," Dave said. "And here's another thing you'd have a ball with." Actually there were a number of things. Each time Dave sat down before another key-board and let his fingers roam into a fragment of Stravin-sky, each time another ball for me occurred to him. Like my taking photographs of sexy German Valkyries astride the unicorn—for release to the Sunday supplements. That would be a ball. And a few bright new Teddy R. quips for me to plant in the Ivy League student papers. Crazy? Also for strictly serious and class purposes, a booklet called "Invitation to Yesteryear," an atmospheric glance back to all the great Schatten guests of bygone days; each one to be featured in the booklet in the form of a full-page period etching or lithograph, and on the reverse side a photo of the celebrity who will impersonate him or her in our procession. And for the cover of the booklet, a photo or drawing of the Prince. Balls, every one of them.

All this between migrations from piano stool to piano stool, and deft chords, and Dave taking in with a sidelong glance that my notepad and pencil were duly in action now. When he finished, the phone rang and the stiff-collared manager handed him the receiver, and after Dave hung up it turned out that this had been Mrs. Dowle who'd just sacrificed our proposed *Konzert* evening to some social bit with some goddamn Krupp. Dave sighed and said what a drag and asked if the alarm clock had arrived yet—he'd sent it to help me wake up Schatten—and if *that* didn't work, he'd send me Big Ben. And, with a comradely pat, pushed me back to the airport to Berlin.

Now I don't mind this kind of dismissal. It was sort of a relief; I could catch the same five p.m. plane I'd gotten on the way back from Paris. I don't even mind the whole Bohemian comedy for whose sake I had to fly four hundred miles in one day. I do resent the real purpose behind it, which is to make the Schatten operation (and particularly the Prince) Dave's personal baby. You see, Dave doesn't mind enthusing when his genius conceives a kookie idea. But as the idea unfolds into a practical exciting plan, old Dave grows jealous of the man who dreamed it up. He muscles in. In his offhand, spinet-poking way he insists that he, and only he, is really with it, only he can really swing with the Prince. Which makes me, in the end, rather glad the cable came back from the Prince so nicely unopened.

The only thing I'm not at all glad about is that this time I made muscling in so inviting to Dave. I'm way behind with my own idea work. By now I should've gotten much more mileage out of the library. I guess the thing is that I hang back; I don't want to let Dave make another standard kookie opening out of Schatten. I want something more because I smell that there's so much more to the place. I'd hate to give Schatten and its stuck-up denizens, particularly the bloody-lovely Nun, the satisfaction of cheating me of their core. Of staying so bloody untouched.

This morning Dave's alarm clock really arrived at the office. It's the size of a lantern and, when it goes off, plays "Onward Christian Soldiers." The Littel Partners are so titillated they can hardly be set to work. But I did get Fräulein Edeltraud to phone all the German animal brokers till we were promised delivery of a huge white horse from Hamburg within twenty-four hours. Just about the only positive outcome of the day. The feature on Teddy hunting a unicorn should have been a cinch. But somehow my fingers don't connect with the typewriter keys.

In fact, I don't seem to be touching anything. The sun slams limpid, heartbreaking late summer against the panes. Before I can open the window, Ida tides in on high decibels of curiosity and helpfulness. Did I have a successful conference with Mr. Dowle yesterday? If this is permissible to inquire, is Mr. Dowle wedded? Ah! . . . And the Mrs. Dowle, she is always traveling with him? Ah, ah! . . . This is an example German husbands should be taking! Speaking of traveling, Ida has established a Good Relation with some littel customs people at the airport. Her Littel Partners *oo*will get *oo*word of the Prince's return before the Prince can even pass the barriers. She *oo*will ensure! his cooperation. *Before* his delicate ex-granddaughter-in-law can lay another finger on him. Shall we drink a littel cup to that?

She and her espresso machine are in excellent voice. So

is Dave's alarm clock. Onward Christian Soldiers. God help the Jewish ones.

September 30th

At least somebody has touched somebody. I'm trying to look at the day's mess the positive way.

Andy flew in today from Stockholm to do a preliminary design survey of the Casino site. At first, like a fool, I was glad to see him; after all, I maneuvered Dave into giving him the job. There were some storm signals, it's true. He turned up at the office before noon, complete with attaché case and Polaroid camera, fresh from the airport, very red-cheeked, with a slight soddenness of tongue, a great burst of greeting all around and an appalling series of jokes.

Had King Dave ordered a Stockholm canal to flow through the Stockholm Dowle lobby? Yes, Dave had, and he'd get it too, with a secret lever that would turn the thing to sewage! Why the hell couldn't something be rotten in Sweden as well as in Denmark? Right? And hadn't King Dave decreed the biggest sauna in Scandinavia? Indeed he had, and Andy was adding one of those Scandinavian conversion chambers so that after King Dave inaugurated it, he'd be Queen Dave and pregnant too! How about that?

The Littel Partners flushed, clutched their curls and fled into the secretarial room, where they stopped up their ears with typewriter clatter. Ida, on the other hand, seemed to think at first that Andy's was some chic new ultrademocratic way of talking about one's boss. She tried to keep up her end with a jest about the mayor of

Berlin. But suddenly she smelled Scotch and remembered a luncheon appointment.

Andy roared on. I steered him out and down into the car. On the way to Schatten he became quieter but also a bit surlier. He said he realized I'd always been a cold fish, a tight-lipped bastard. But did he have to drag it out of me? What had it been like, being in bed with Dave a couple of days ago?

His ruddy forehead had a glaze of moisture across the furrows. Poor Andy. He was ashamed that I'd wangled him the Casino—a job he had been unable to get on his own. In addition, he must have heard all sorts of rumors about my Frankfurt meeting with Dave. And, worst, Dave hadn't bothered to see *him* while in Europe. So Andy had to show me all over again that he didn't care, his being on the outside and me being in; that he could blaspheme Dave as much as he pleased. It was terribly important to him to prove that he didn't give a hoot.

While KarlHeinz watched in the rear-view mirror, I administered therapy. I related how Dave in his insidious buddy-buddy manner had really put me down. I gave a few graphic details. Andy relaxed. He punched me in the shoulder, a magic and liberating motion for Andy. Through that shoulder slap flowed the fondness we reserve for those of whom we know that they suffer no less than we.

"For bleeding Christ's sake," he said, "oh, for bleeding Christ's sake." That was nothing, that put-down. I didn't know the joy *he* had been through. And he told me an old familiar story of Dave's torments, as well as a new story about his wife, his almost-reconciled Barb, supposedly an intelligent attractive girl but to her love was a form of aggression. She'd found one old ick-liebe-dick letter and threatened to fly off to New York to attach his salary as separation income! How about that? When he had broken off entirely with the ick-liebe-dick proposition! And when, for Barb's sake, he hadn't even banged a number he'd run into in Stockholm, an out-of-this-world broad, Icelandic-born, hair down to here, knew the Vedas by heart, yet not one of those castrating intellectual bitches, a piece of tail with a real soul for a change—I must meet her sometime—so he was really between three chairs and nothing sure but a half-built Swedish Oyster, and no time to think because of a last-chance, last-ditch reconciliation try set up by his lawyer at Stockholm tomorrow, which is why he had to fly back from Berlin tonight. Paradise, huh?

He fumbled out his pipe. At moments like this he always thought he was the M.I.T. halfback again; and that the tragic clichés of life were just a practical joke played by the fellahs, a thing which can be licked by playing some big practical joke in return. So he slapped me on the back again. He said he'd chuck the whole business, Dave, Barb, Icelandic hair and all, get away, and found a chain of art hotels with me, art hotels like there were art theaters, in the hip off-beat off-Broadway fashion but applied to hotels—in fact, he'd call the chain "off-Dowle." Off-Dowle! Off-Dowle-International! How about that? He roared. We had to drink to that from a flask cunningly embedded in his attaché case. We had to drink to it again, and the only reason we didn't drink to it a third time was that we had arrived.

The estate had a funny effect. It subdued him. He became surprisingly tame; tiptoed on the gravel of the garden path. He took the Polaroid out of its case and held on to it and to his attaché case tightly. The sun had broken out again after a shower, and from poplar and pergola the water dripped with Schatten's special gleams.

"Lenny! . . . Wow! . . ." he kept saying softly. "You got it made. . . ." He said it as though the estate were my own creation, my personal and somehow secret achievement.

In the hall we passed the Nun. Removing a hat is always a major operation for an American. Andy's problem was aggravated by the fact that his hands still held the attaché case and the camera. The gesture didn't succeed until she passed from sight. We negotiated the staircase in silence.

"Who was that?" he asked in the safety of my room.

I explained. My words didn't seem to register. He made no comment on my room, though it widened his eyes. He sat down by the food tray—decked for two as always when they saw me with a guest—and began to eat and talk.

"Wow . . ." he said several times again. "You dog, you . . ." All of a sudden he was deeply, bitterly among his erotic adventures, eleven of them since he had married Barb, even including the ick-liebe-dick.

"Exactly eleven," he said. "Think that adds up to something? It adds up to nothing." He went on about how he couldn't really remember one of them; he hadn't gotten a single memory out of a single one of them, which is what Barb refused to understand. Could *I* understand that? He wanted to come back to Barb, but with a memory of someone, with some fresh romantic ventilation. An intelligent, well-preserved girl, Barb, but a castrator; he had to come back to her refreshed. Otherwise he wouldn't be any good to her, he wouldn't be able to stand up against her. He wanted just one good memory, like maybe the Icelandic hair. A man had to have something to keep on taking life.

I suppose I should have taken him straight back to the limousine. But the food did seem to disperse the alcohol, and his tongue worked well again. He didn't have one drop during lunch, nor tried to. I thought that his talk—I never heard him go on quite that way before—was really a form of emerging sobriety. I also put it down to the impression the estate made on him. Strangely enough, the idea flattered me. It turns out that I've become possessive about Schatten. I took him down to the library —it became "my" library in the presence of this big silk-suited man who tiptoed and gaped like a child at the strangeness before him.

He was particularly fascinated by the portrait of the current Prince. "Tricky stuff . . ." he kept muttering. "Very good. Another league from the older boys' pictures . . . Not like the older boys at all." I disputed this, probably because it was "my" library and I hadn't noticed a difference before. But he insisted that only the bad light kept me from seeing his point. Finally he flashed his Polaroid bulb at each of the oils.

He was right, by God. The photographs proved it a minute later. The current Prince wears the same face as his forefathers and even a similar expression; yet a nervous impressionist glimmer plays across his features, and his eyes aren't perfectly aligned, jarred apart by something, by some sudden but veiled disturbance. It amounts to no more than a nuance—perhaps added by the portraitist for the sake of "character." Andy had seen it in the half-light at a glance. It made me decide, excusably enough, that he was in condition to work on his own.

I led him to the proposed Casino site, the city-owned acres near the gate, and left him there to take photographs and notes. Then I returned to the library, with the idea of finding some drawing of one of the older Princes that would do as a reproducible likeness of the present one. But I went through all the albums without hitting anything satisfactory. In a pinch, of course, I could always use the Polaroid photo.

My watch said four when I stopped. I went back out to the Casino site. On the grass I found Andy's attaché case. An open pad lay on top with a sketch of the projected Casino, pagoda-roofed, blending dexterously into the background of the manor. He had done it that fast.

But I couldn't see him. I was just about to call when a peacock came hopping along from behind a pavilion. It cried in tail-spread fury and was followed a moment later by the Nun. She flashed up, flashed past; it seemed to me there had been a redness in her cheeks. The next moment Andy slumped around the corner, in wobbly pursuit.

I am, as Andy likes to say, a cold fish. I was boiling within a second.

"You goddamn fool," I said. "What did you try with her?"

I was so angry that I had to keep my hands in my pockets for fear of punching him. He leaned past me, grabbed for his things on the grass. Suddenly he ran out of steam. He just stood there, weighed down by camera and attaché case, huddled in a mist of Scotch.

"She's a witch," he said. "Whole place's a witchery. Better get out of here, Lenny. Better get out."

"*That's enough.*"

I pushed him toward the gate, the whole heavy man

with his expensive clothes, his expensive gadgets and expensive plights, the words dribbling helplessly out of his mouth. "Can't touch her," he kept saying, "she's a witch." KarlHeinz loomed up poker-faced and helped me stumble him across the Venetian bridge. Together we dumped him in the back seat.

"Better get out of here," he said, and mercifully the car took him away.

Maybe I'd feel better now if I *had* punched him.

Tonight she was nowhere, absolutely invisible.

October 1st

Either be good or be unforgivable. Don't ever stoop to something so half-assed as the forgivable. Should I be blessed with a son, I'll pass that wisdom on to him. Poor Andy is forgivable. In fact, I'm no longer mad at him, and that's just his tragedy. But the unforgivable ones are the people who matter. They inherit the earth, like the Nun. No wonder she always married superbly. No wonder she's magnetic. I think that the moment I first laid eyes on her, I already didn't forgive her. I don't think I forgive her now even when I sleep.

I came on her at last this morning, as I was rushing from breakfast to the limousine. She kneeled in the yew maze, combing one of the Afghans and humming softly.

"Hello," I said. The damned thing is that I never know by what name to address her. "I just want to apologize."

"Pardon?" Blandly, brushing.

"I just want to say that I want to apologize for my associate's behavior yesterday."

"That?" Her hand untangled one of the dog's knotted tresses. "It's not worth fussing over."

"If he took a liberty, I'm responsible."

"Let's not get upset about it."

"I mean, his condition was no excuse."

"Was your friend taken care of?" She patted the dog because the untangling seemed to have hurt a little.

"We got him into the car," I said. "It won't happen again."

"Well, everything's all right then," she said and, humming, began to brush the dog once more.

Not a sign of concern or even interest. She'll never give me any such satisfaction. The only motion to which she condescended was that of her small hand with the green ring, caressing the dog in smooth rhythm.

I resisted the impulse—though I was tempted—to whip out a certain page of vital statistics, to throw at her a brief contemptuous question about a wedding picture. I'm glad I didn't, because I wouldn't have been rewarded with any embarrassment or anger. No, she'd have pulled a Daddy Ahn, she'd have maintained the same stubborn pigheaded pleasantness, she'd remain safe within her well-mannered armor, and the small white hand with the green ring would have gone right on, up the Afghan fur and down again. No, I cherish my trumps against her much too much not to reserve them for the most deadly possible time and place. A way will be found to jolt this tranquil kneeling goddess, to tear the coif off her blond hair, to stop the white hand with the green ring. Everything in its own good time. Meanwhile casualness will be met with casualness.

"Did you say you couldn't breed these dogs here?" I gave an absent tap on the Afghan's head.

"Oh? Do you know that?" she said, having apparently forgotten our nocturnal meeting, a most unimportant encounter.

"Somewhere I remember your saying you couldn't find the right thoroughbreds in Berlin."

"I did?" she said. "Yes."

"We're setting up a pet shop in the hotel now," I said. "I'll ask them for a good shipment of Afghans."

"Really, you needn't bother," she said.

"No bother at all," I said. "Do remind me, though, if I forget." I bowed and left, quite in the manner of her father, after another absent tap.

I hope it sank in.

October 3rd

All right, the roof has fallen in. Hooray. And not even over the Princely bombshell. Over a much smaller, a most banal, murky, itchy and tawdry little spectacle.

But I must take this slowly, sensibly, one by one.

The whole day started in a muggy, oppressive temper. Neither sun nor rain at first, none of the outspoken weather of the last few days, the sky barricaded. When I walked downstairs, I found no one but old Frau Dr. Ahn, kneeling on a *prie-dieu* in the hall, her hands covering her face. I assumed the others were at the chapel; it's the Sunday custom here.

In the gardens the birds seemed especially irritable. All around me an irate gorgeous vibration of wings, volleys of furious titter. I was fretful myself, worried about my uncle who hasn't been around for days. Suddenly—guess who? My good friend KarlHeinz. KarlHeinz of all people, minus cap, in a well-cut gabardine jacket, a regular Sunday suit, smiling as though his presence were the most natural thing in the world.

"Good morning, suhr. Lovely day."

"Did Dr. Holze send you?" I said. "What's up?"

"Oh, no, suhr. Everything is quite fine, suhr."

"Are you looking for me?"

"I have been visiting my uncle's grave, suhr."

"I see," I said. "All right, KarlHeinz. Good morning."

It was entirely in order. Sunday *is* the day to visit graves. And in a sultry sort of fashion it did become a lovely day. When I met the Nun a couple of minutes later, she already had a parasol out against the heavy, misty sun. She held it above a little-old-lady inmate with whom she must have been cutting flowers; her other arm brimmed with red roses. I got a correct, short good morning. She too was entirely in order (and a bit in a hurry), and she too was a cheat. She cheats with her courtesies the way a magician cheats his audience with small talk while doing his trick. Some essential part of her is always caught up in some trick. Some part is tightly wound around it even while she holds up a parasol and nods good morning. I didn't feel like letting her get away.

"One moment," I said. "A favor, please."

She stopped, but only just. To show that she needn't expect any Andy-like overtures, I maintained a good seven-foot distance.

"We very badly need a picture of the Prince," I said.

"Will it keep till tomorrow?"

"I wouldn't trouble you on Sunday if it weren't urgent."

"The Prince may have something," she said. "My father will take it up with him."

"I'd cable the Prince about it," I said, "but he doesn't seem to—"

"The Prince is here," she said.

"*What?*" I said. I was dizzy. "Two days early!"

I may have shouted. Probably I did. Ahn appeared on the double with a handful of carnations.

"The Prince arrived early this morning," he said and took the roses from her. "We are picking him a welcome." The implication was that Herr Doktor's presence relieved his daughter not only of her flowers but also of other burdens, such as conversation with me.

"Nobody bothered to tell me," I said, furious.

The familiar, accomplished, negative smile.

"You need your morning sleep, Mr. Spey. And the Prince needs a good deal of our attention."

"You will let him know that I look forward to an interview at his very earliest convenience?"

"Of course. After he's had time to get back his breath."

"You mean I can't see him now?"

"We must let him rest for six or seven days after his cure, Mr. Spey—"

"Six or seven days!"

"—particularly if we expect exertions from him later. He's had a long journey."

"I've had a long wait."

"We keep your problems in mind. Meanwhile try to enjoy the week end, Mr. Spey. I believe it's an American invention."

"How is his health?" I said.

"Not too poor for a nonagenarian," he said with a pre-departure bow. "He's chosen a fine day on which to return, hasn't he?"

"Yes," I said. "Let's all praise the weather."

I didn't even bother to go up to my room for a hat or coat. It was such a goddamn fine day. I walked through the gate, across the Venetian bridge and into the streets until I found a taxi.

The sense of frustration, of helplessness, was intolerable. Three hard-working, hard-trying weeks at Schatten—and still the same baffled outsider, the patsy of some miasmic sardonic comedy played way over my head. I knew that if I let them keep it up I'd never get to the Prince.

I wanted some friends, some allies, just somebody to gang up with. Above all, I wanted not to be alone. Ida had begged me to disturb her any time in case of an important development. Deep down, I guess, hid a naïve hope that if I blurted out my news at her, my grievance, she and the Littel Partners would come down on Schatten like the Jacobins on the Bastille.

But there was no Ida at her private address. Nobody answered the chimes on that lovely apartment door. I kicked it. If you don't like Mama, the worst thing is not finding her when you're down enough to need her. I gave the next cabbie the address of Julius' hotel.

I'm not quite sure why. Perhaps it was one of those occasions when guilt joins convenience. He hadn't come near me in over a week—not since I wouldn't go to the synagogue with him on Yom Kippur. By now he should be over his sulks. Anyway, I needed somebody. Since Mama wasn't there, Papa would do.

Papa Julius would, of course, live in an old pseudo-Baroque scabrous transient hotel full of lacerated potted palms and mildewed wallpaper along the corridors and brass doorknobs turned green. His own door was ajar. Julius stood before a hotplate (i.e., the kitchen of *suite with kitchen*) warming an enormous pot of milk. He actually did incarnate, *commedia dell'arte* fashion, the essence of Papa Jew, the clownish patriarch. His long gray stubble looked black because the skin underneath was so white. He wore his overcoat over his pajamas, and floppy slippers that seemed to slap flies with each step. On the most unmade bed imaginable sat two older Jewish men, both with black coats folded across their knees, bent close to each other and at the same time huddled toward Julius. The three of them composed some immemorial, intimate campfire-like theme, as though cold winter started immediately beyond the door, as though all of Berlin were a Labrador of *goyim*, with this the sole warm human room.

"Leon!" Julius said. "My nephew!" He hugged me to his stubble.

"Where've you been?" I said. "Are you sick?"

"*Ach!* Ridiculous."

Naturally he'd been sick. Thirty years ago in Vienna he had the same ulcer attacks, called them *ach*, ridiculous, and cured himself with just such gallons of hot milk.

"You will stay for evening prayer?" he said. "More friends are coming—"

"Uncle Julius," I said, "I'm on a business errand. I just wanted to see how you are."

With a cough, a kind of bewildered pride, he turned to the men on the bed. "You wouldn't believe the appointments he has. He's Leon Spiegelglass, *Generaldirektor* of American hotels. Business trips on Sunday . . ."

"It's just that I've got a taxi waiting downstairs," I said.

"Shall I send you a doctor?"

"Ridiculous!"

"The Prince has come back to the estate," I said. For I guess I had come to tell him that.

"Ah!" said my uncle. "Good! We finish the petition!"

In view of what happened right afterwards, the visit was not a mistake. Julius' milk—I'd never have gotten away without drinking some—helped. Its heat heartened my insides. A few sips from the Papa-tit and I was ready to try Ida again on the way back to Schatten.

And so the sight came down on me like some soundless express. In retrospect it seems inevitable. The whole day was built to receive it. Everything else, even the Prince's arrival, was merely overture or aftermath.

Ida's windows still looked dark. But I noticed, around the corner, a car I hadn't remembered being there before. I asked my driver to park on the curb opposite. The car was the limousine. It was unlit and dark inside—yet not dark enough.

Behind the wheel leaned KarlHeinz, our pious visitor of graves. With the half of his face that wasn't carved off by a black shadow, with one eye and half a mouth, he smiled a hideous amputated smile, grinned downward along his arm which was rooted in his neighbor's lap. From his right hand glowed, frank and naked this time, the red tip of his cigarette. And against his shoulder heaved Dr. Ida Holze in stricken and shadowy sumptuousness of bosom and jowls, her eyes pressed shut under rigid eyelids as though surrendering at stiff attention, her teeth gleaming faintly inside the open mouth, her hat, her little black hat flattened against her temple, squashed, distorted, derided by passion.

Such moments slash right through. They cut to the vitals, to the basic rapacity of life, down to testicle, womb and jugular vein; to all the demons beneath the skin, the final nakedness we dress up endlessly in vain. Such moments say that every ingenuity of mind, every fine tepidity, every sophisticated compromise is a lie, a sickness and a joke. Such moments liberate.

I wanted much more than the Prince. I wanted my Nun. And just like that.

"Let's go," I said to the driver. "To Schatten. *Los!*"

Watch out when a cold fish stops being cold.

NOCTURNE

1

_____

It's POSSIBLE that the three days following were the most exciting of my life so far. Certainly they were the most packed. No time for the journal. No time for anything but this single fierce thrust forward from the side of the darkened limousine. The image of those two, frozen together in the grotesque solemnity of lust, became a lodestar. In that sign thou shalt conquer. Nakedness is contagious. If it's intense enough, it will spread like fire among the beholders. I became conscious as never before of its powers and its uses. Puritans like me can get nuder than pagans; virginity clings to them through all violations like an aphrodisiac.

I felt a fine wicked speed inside me; a programmatic speed. I never thought of stopping for a moment to ask myself whether the scheme was fair, or sane, or feasible. I just knew that I wanted her badly and brutally, had wanted her for many days; that now I could conquer Schatten and the Prince only by first conquering her; and that love is war. I'd get her à la KarlHeinz with Karl-Heinz's help.

It all happened with such crowded speed that I must

take pains to sort out events in order.

Monday, the day following, I had the Littel Partners put in another call to the Hamburg animal broker to order (in addition to the yet hornless unicorn) a shipment of first-class Afghan puppies. Then I informed the manager of the Berlin Dowle shopping arcade that part of the pet-shop stock would arrive about six weeks early, and that he'd best billet the dogs at the Gellstrasse kennels near the Schatten estate; I undertook to exercise the dogs personally. He was quite astonished. Oh, I raised a fine crop of astonishments that day.

Ida, with a fuchsia but unsquashed hat, was terribly astonished at the Prince's lightning return and at the failure of her airport intelligence system to signal the august arrival. (Twenty-four hours *afterwards* they had informed her of the Prince's name on the arrival list; she would, she said, toothlets gleaming, give them a littel piece of her mind.) She was equally astonished at my begging off from an espresso-charged war council on the situation.

Uncle Julius was astonished at my absolute insistence that he observe the two days' bed rest prescribed by the doctor I had sent him. I did want him to get well. I also wanted him and his interference out of the way for the next forty-eight hours.

The Grand Hotel was astonished. After all my contretemps with them, I up and reserved a double room for the following night.

My favorite astonishment among them all I produced in KarlHeinz, soon after a short visit at my uncle's.

In the Gellstrasse, a five-minute drive away from Schatten, a store sign consisting of a wooden dog swung into view. I ordered my good chauffeur to stop, went into the store, verified the arrangements made earlier by phone, and returned to the car with a huge red rubber bone.

"Do you like it, KarlHeinz?" I asked as we rode on.

"The bone, suhr?" Perhaps he was already a bit puzzled because *I* had started the conversation.

"This rubber bone," I said.

"Yes, suhr. Very nice."

"The Schatten dogs ought to enjoy it," I said. I wondered if he recognized his own technique.

"They will like it very much, suhr," he said carefully.

"I think so," I said. "I like to see enjoyment, Karl-Heinz. I saw you enjoying yourself yesterday."

"Yesterday, suhr?" His voice hadn't changed pitch at all. Only his shoulders hunched together a little.

"Yesterday, in this car, in the evening."

The car slowed down. It, too, seemed to brace itself. He must have gotten rid of his cigarette, because both his hands gripped the wheel squarely.

"Yes, suhr," he said softly, but with remarkable evenness of tone.

"Of course," I said, "enjoyment isn't enjoyable if it produces complications. Nobody wants complications, do they?"

For a moment nothing but the purr of the motor. This was fun. "No, suhr," he said. "Nobody wants them."

He kept his head slightly bowed so that only the black visor and not his eyes hovered in the mirror. I had struck home. I had touched the lever that reached right through the black cap.

"I don't want complications in my enjoyments either," I said. "I might want some cooperation from you tomorrow."

He didn't even ask a question.

"Yes, suhr," he said.

We were there. The car had halted before the Venetian bridge. But he kept sitting, head somewhat bowed, shoulders hunched, waiting for what was to come next.

"That's all," I said. "Just don't forget the address of that pet shop. You'll do me some favors there tomorrow."

"Favors, suhr?"

"You'll hear about it in time."

"Yes, suhr." He got up and walked around the car and ushered me out, his visor far down over his eyes.

"Thank you, KarlHeinz," I said, all sweetness.

There was no such thing as stopping or reflecting. I yielded to the lunge inside me. Every cell of my body was pointed at her. At her, mind you, not at the Prince, not at my assignment, nor at all the comings and goings up and down the stairs since Highness' arrival, all the flower vases and food trays carried aloft—at none of that. They had their secret hubbub and I had mine. They had their madness and I my own. I'd gotten nowhere as long as I had tried to make sense of, or to, my Schatten friends. I didn't press for an appointment with the Prince. I wanted to get *her* first; after that, he'd drop into my lap like a nice ripe plum.

I watched her walking on the lake shore, standing in the hall, pruning the gardens. I didn't consider myself in love with her. I didn't even make that much concession to romantic good sense. I just wanted to have her absolutely, the way KarlHeinz had our lady friend under the squashed hat. Nothing less.

Of course, with my left hand as it were, I acted out the charade of an old familiar self. With my left hand I wrote Ninepins her ten-page letter, a very successful example of the genre. And I finally devised a pleasantry called "Teddy Seduces a Unicorn," taking up half my column, full of elegant witticisms for the carriage trade. I sent Andy's Polaroid shot of the Prince's portrait to New York, together with some clever suggestions for the artist who would make Highness a cover boy.

But I ignored these things, though I did them well, just as you ignore the breathing you do so well because it's done only as necessary background to what matters. And I ignored my breathing; ignored Dr. Ahn; ignored the dogs guarding the Prince's floor, the silver tureens borne aloft for princely consumption. They were all mere background to her.

Her I watched with a hard, sober heat all through the rest of that Monday. I followed the movements of her gray frock from the hall into the twilight green back into the manor again. I could pick out her light long footfalls better than ever. I could feel how near or how far she was; and every inch of grass or wood or mortar between us tingled.

I was not lonely when I went to bed. I was not lonely entering the limousine next morning, the morning of the crucial day. KarlHeinz had a small shaving knick on his cheek and yesterday's hunched braced shoulders. He listened, immobile, to my instructions. He said "Yes, suhr" seven times. I didn't smell any cigarette smoke; the rear-view mirror revealed only a pushed-down visor.

We drove to the airport to inspect my animal shipment just in. The white horse was airsick and noble, good raw material for processing into a unicorn. I had it stabled with the municipal mounted police (the Littel Partners, you see, had phoned the fear of God into the commissioner's office). As for what really mattered, namely the fourteen Afghan pups, they were absolutely gorgeous, a frisky silky diabolic lot of Nun bait. They took a long time being cajoled into the animal van. KarlHeinz and I followed them to the Gellstrasse and saw them safely fed and housed.

And then I was back in Schatten again, at just about my usual time. I lunched. I watched for her. I began to stalk her. The time, as they say, was nigh. It had begun to drizzle a bit, kept drizzling into the middle of the afternoon. The gardens were empty. I found her nowhere in the grounds. No matter. Inside my clothes I had turned into a fine infallible arrow. Nothing could stop me.

On my second foray into the hall I met her and the Afghans as well. They were having a brushing session in an alcove. She had such damn grace to her, even when she was squatting. Against the dog's fur, her slender ribbed-stockinged knee glinted like a seashell. I was quite calm and stroked an Afghan ear. To the animal that wasn't being brushed I gave the big red rubber bone.

"Thank you," she said.

"Believe it or not," I said, "I can match you Afghan for Afghan now."

"Pardon me?"

There appeared to be this rigid convention attending all our conversations: (*a*) she was full of bland and untouchable affability; (*b*) she forgot every shred of our previous conversations. There was never any building or development in our relationship. We must always start from scratch. It didn't faze me one iota now. I might give her something fairly unforgettable fairly soon.

I smiled and explained that her Afghan beauties were no longer the only ones around; the Dowle pet shop had just flown in over a dozen like them.

"Really," she said brushing. "It will be a good shop."

"You said you couldn't find mates for your males. Better take that back now."

"Did I mention that?" she said.

"Your dogs will never forgive you if you don't take a look at our selection."

"They've learned to get along." Polite, untouchable smile.

"Wait till they smell the bitches," I said. "We kenneled them here only a mile away, because the hotel shop isn't ready yet."

She stopped brushing. Her hand covered the seashell knee with skirt. "Here?"

"For the time being they'll be right in the Gellstrasse Kennels."

"Silk Afghans?"

"Pups, but perfect mates," I said. "The limousine's being repaired, otherwise I'd have you look at them this very minute."

"Thank you, but—"

"Wait a minute," I said reflectively. "I have that taxi coming in at six with some cables. It's riding back empty on my pay. Why don't we ask it to drop you off at the Gellstrasse?"

"Kind of you," she said with a slight headshake. The white hand with the green ring resumed brushing, up and down. No other answer came and I did not solicit one.

"I'll arrange a little waiting time with the taxi, just in

case," I said, nodded, and left, supposedly to phone the cab from a booth.

The ceiling in my room had fourteen crosswise beams, eight lengthwise ones, all carved of oak. I remember the exact number. I lay fully dressed on the bed, smoking and counting; listening to the chapel bell strike away the quarter hours. The chestnut branches stirred against the window. A new drizzle streaked the panes, faded. The plumbing yammered faintly in the walls and the Five O'Clock Tea piano sounded like a far-off music box. When it stopped, my heartbeat took over; very softly, systematically, pulsing through the room. I remember that too. This was the only unsure phase of the plan. I knew that a direct offer of the limousine would have frightened her away. The taxi was much more convincingly spur-of-the-moment. I just wished it would arrive.

And then it did. The chapel bell struck six. More minutes passed, clocked by my heartbeat. The staircase sounded. A knock on the door: the green-aproned fellow with the cables. I took them and, as soon as the door closed, slung on my coat. The staircase sounded again with the man's descent. I was free to go down myself.

I ducked into a dripping pavilion. A good spot from which to observe the gate without being seen. She was nowhere. Yet. I prayed that the taxi was waiting it out; that KarlHeinz had been firm enough in his instructions. Then—those footfalls. Those light, long-striding steps, crunching over the wet gravel, clacking across flagstones, receding beyond the gate. I waited long, unbearably long, for the start of the taxi motor. It noised faint but definite

from the other side of the Venetian bridge. Rrrroommm.
Gone. With her inside.

My palms grew moist. It was really coming off.

I counted to two hundred and fifty before I ran out the
gate. The streets on the West Berlin side looked empty.
But just as I crossed the bridge the limousine came into
view.

"Everything is fine, suhr," said KarlHeinz.

We cruised for a few minutes. KarlHeinz whistled;
audibly, but not unpleasantly, a soft co-conspiratorial
waltz. I kept my eyes on my watch. At six thirty-five
sharp we entered the Gellstrasse, where the taxi was still
drawn up. I paid it off.

The back part of the pet shop was a veritable stew of
Afghan hounds. She sat on a stool in her raincoat, with
four pups bubbling about her, her white hand frisking
with them, probing their little mouths and feet.

"Hello," I said. "Couldn't resist seeing how you like
them."

On the instant she was sheathed in blandness.

"I haven't seen pups for years," she said.

She gathered up two little females; one tiny one and a
slightly bigger creature with a white spot above the right
eye like a white hat. The pups in her arms, she walked
past me to the proprietor. I said I hoped she would let
Dowle Hotels take care of the matter. She gave a small
irrefutable head shake. I desisted. She paid and took the
pedigree certificates. We were outside.

"What happened to the taxi?" she asked.

"Oh, I let it go," I said. "They just fixed up the
limousine, you know. That's how I got here."

For a moment she stood motionless. KarlHeinz leaned,
faintly smiling, against the limousine hood. Then she

discovered she couldn't look at her watch because her hands were full of dogs.

"It's about six forty," I said. It was six forty-seven.

"They close the gate at seven," she said, and got into the limousine.

The last phase was peculiar because I sat so treacherously close to her. I noticed the shell-ribbed stocking knee and the absence of perfume. But the dogs helped create a nice innocuousness. The tiny one kept licking the window. The spotted one—I called it Little White Riding Hood—protested and whimpered steadily until the car broke down.

"Oh, no," I said. "Not the battery again, KarlHeinz?"

"Yes, suhr," he said. He tried the starter. He tried and tried.

"But they just checked the car," I said. "It couldn't be anything big. Do you think you could fix it quick?"

"Yes, suhr," he said and busied himself persuasively behind the opened hood. All of a sudden, before I could say a word, she was out. She had seen through it.

"I'm getting a taxi," she said. But we were on an empty side street, it just so happened. And then, unplanned, Little White Riding Hood increased my margin by becoming car sick. She had to massage the poor thing while I, with much show of haste, loped to the corner to make vain "Taxi!" gestures at the deserted crossing.

Six fifty-seven, and she came up rapidly, wordless, white. She would have passed me as though I weren't there. But I took the bigger pup from her arms to help her make more speed. I was glad to; we'd never make it. Our footfalls rang together through the quiet streets of villas. When she began to run, I ran too. The white Venetian bridge came into view three blocks away, and a far-off sound fell across the twilight. The chapel clock had struck seven. In the distance two East German soldiers walked back from the locked gate to their sentry box, one slightly hunchbacked.

We had come to a halt. Silence all about us, except for the high breath pulsing in our mouths. She didn't look at me.

"Well," I said, "we won't be able to get back there tonight."

We stood next to each other, panting, stroking the live fur in our arms.

Done.

2

The first thing that happened was that she didn't say a word.

I had caught the unicorn, the glimpse between leaves, the footstep beyond the wall. Now she was a woman smelling slightly of dog, whose long smock stuck out way below her shorter raincoat. I couldn't see her face because it was bent over the pups. We were sitting in a cab that carried us toward the Kurfürstendamm. And she didn't say a word.

I had no immediate attitude or device. The little Afghans were all helplessness and whimper. She was all quiet solicitude. They kept each other busy. And I, author of the whole elaborate trap, felt like some goddamn fifth wheel. To give the pups some air, I rolled down the window. I began to talk angrily, uneasily about slipshod garage mechanics and limousine breakdowns and getting a room at the Grand Hotel for her night's lodging.

"My identity card is at Schatten," she said, covering the dogs with her coat. Apparently you couldn't register at a hotel without one.

I informed her brightly that that would be taken care of. She didn't seem to hear. She said something about the Zoo Station restaurant being open all night.

"A station restaurant!" I said. "We'll dine at the best place in town. It's the least I can do."

"In these clothes?"

The red of a traffic light fell on her smock and her heavy brogues. I found a spontaneous next step at last.

"Cabbie," I said, "are dress shops still open?"

"Closed, sir, seven o'clock sharp. But you'll still catch the Kaufhaus."

The Kaufhaus, an enormous bargain department store, shut down at eight thirty, which gave us an hour. The place crawled with fat Hausfraus fighting for staff attention and goggling at us—that is, at her. In her long Schatten-style smock, under the large-brimmed coif-hat, she looked like some famous actress costumed to play a World War I nurse. Silently she drifted alongside me, the stares bouncing off her like raindrops. She'd zippered herself up in self-possessed impassiveness. When the ladies' fitting department swallowed her, she handed me the pups. She'd developed a confounded way of suggesting a shrug without moving her shoulders.

I went to browse at the *Tierecke*, or animal corner, and bought two plastic pink leashes; also little plastic dog coats, spotted brown and white, to match Little White Riding Hood's color scheme. For a long time I looked for nonplastic dog tags, but finally had to resign myself to plastic ones. I went back and found her waiting.

It was a shock. She wore Kaufhaus clothes, all right: a modishly short skirt made of bright black stuff, a blue stiff nylon blouse, pumps and shiny nylon stockings. Yet by some trick she'd taken the curse off all the office-girl crassness. She'd converted it into something severely chic. Her blue-black raincoat held down and matched the other colors. A dark-mauve leather band—God knows where she could have got it in that plastic palace—belted the whole ensemble together. Somehow it had a nice simplicity fit for *Vogue*.

She looked altogether different and yet completely herself. Andy was right: a witch. She had, abruptly, assumed a twentieth-century body. Within the hour she had grown long lovely calfs and a well-defined bosom. The coif-hat was gone; her hair was piled high and proud. There was a touch of lipstick on her mouth, of shadow on her eyelids. The fluorescent light came down on the lofty cheekbones, the high forehead, on the fine bridge of her nose with the very pale, almost fawn freckles—and on the fact that she had passed her early thirties. Her gray eyes weren't so much large as long; the eyes had depths and the cheeks superb hollows not given to young girls. She was what I'd suspected all along: a classic beauty.

And she was still the good old Nun. Her mouth was still set with unyielding poise. One hand tapped slowly against a counter. She still carried Schatten around with her. Now she had a bit more physical presence, more obvious attractiveness to be laconic with. Now that she had been dragged out into the world, she used worldly colors as camouflage. Nothing had changed underneath. And yet: the very deftness and composure with which she defended herself betrayed familiarity with the idea of attack.

No real reaction from her on seeing the pups dressed up. "Thank you," she said, and took over the leash.

Paying for some very ordinary clothes for a woman in that woman's presence must be one of the most domestic acts in the entire behavior range of the human male. I'd never bought any of Nina's clothes with Nina. No one had ever called Nina and me the equivalent of *Herrschaften*, a conjugal term the Kaufhaus cashier used when he thanked "us" for the purchase. I couldn't resist that.

"I know a good restaurant half a mile down," I said. "Shall we *Herrschaften* walk or taxi?"

"The pups need some fresh air," she said. The tone indicated that she was not participating in the escapade. She was enduring it. I decided not to become coy with Her Highness again.

I took her arm by way of neutral guidance. We walked down the Paulanerstrasse toward Dinny's. Arm in arm, she airing two dogs, I carrying her wrapped Schatten clothes with a husbandly grip, a couple among couples in the strolling hour. By then I knew that I must not fight her silence but use it: that this couldn't be approached as an evening out with a new woman. Strenuous wit or strategic urbanities wouldn't help. I decided not to force anything for the present, but to enjoy myself.

Her mere presence at my side was a tremendous achievement. And a tremendous joke on Dr. Ahn's superior eyebrows, which by now must be raised sky-high at her absence. It was a joke, too, on the other men in the street. There was a great deal of staring. Actually it only amused me. They must all have been convinced that our silence implied an intimacy beyond conversation. So far I was intimate only with her elbow. I cradled it discreetly in my palm and found it rather experienced for a cloistral Schatten creature. With slight skillful pressure it signaled a slowdown when the pups stalled, an acceleration when they pulled ahead. We were seldom out of step; not bad for people who had never walked together before, never yet called each other by their names.

The air smelled verdant and vibrant as it always does in Berlin after rain. The wet pavements swam and shivered with headlights, street lights, neon signs. Our pups, very much revived, tumbled along. When we turned into the Ku-damm, the storefronts became all marble and mirror. She glanced at them quite often. I guessed it was her first window-shopping in years. Sometimes we caught something astounding on dark plate glass: our couple image. It would stop both of us for a moment. Her mouth would budge a bit. "Come on," she would say to the pups, and thus to me. And that's how we reached Dinny's.

It was a crowded posh evening at the Club. Perfume, midnight-blue dinner jackets, alligator-leather shoes. My Club key had gotten us past the astonished doorman. Dinny himself chanced to be sitting at the front bar. A fingersnap at a captain created a reservation for us. She let herself be bowed along to our table in regal unawareness of what the other women's gowns—and their eyes—did to her poor clothes. She waved aside the hatcheck girl's attempt to take her dog leashes along with my parcel and coat. She ordered soup and steak—shockingly simple things at Dinny's—agreed to Burgundy, and asked for a bit of milk for her pups.

There now appeared in her a nuance of amusement. She looked at home in the small sensation we created. A compact had established itself between us. She accepted the mad plot of the evening. And I accepted—for the time being—her aloofness.

I claimed one small victory. Something made me push my cigarettes toward her, though I'd never seen her smoke at Schatten. Her hand reached for one, and the next moment she seemed astonished by what she had touched. My match was already there, however; her first exhalation told me that I had reawakened an old habit. Fifteen:love—my service.

Milk for the pups arrived in a small silver dish. Little White Riding Hood made a minuscule mess, which rendered our table even more picturesque and brought me to my first move. I suggested that if we gave the pups names now they would, perhaps, behave with greater dignity.

"I'll think of names when we get back," she said.

"Better tell me by what name *you'd* like to be called," I said. Dinny was approaching. "I'll have to introduce you in a minute. Fräulein Ahn?"

"If you wish," she said.

Fräulein Ahn? The name threw Dinny into entrechats of delight. Dr. Ahn's daughter of *Schatten?* How wonderful. What? Such base Burgundy? Not seriously! A bottle with an astonishingly curlicued vintage label—I can't for the life of me remember what it said—was fingersnapped into existence. He personally filled our two glasses. But he wouldn't *dream* of giving them to us (he held the glasses theatrically away from us) unless we first promised to raise them to Prince Schatten's health and to a happy Schatten-Dowle collaboration (to which he, Dinny, tried to contribute a teeny bit), and unless we promised to sip the wine only after he had evaporated, when we were *mutterseelenallein*—i.e., utterly alone with each other—which was how old wine must be drunk for optimum effect. He retreated on gracefully suggestive tiptoe.

One of those performances he's famous for. The fact that he had selected our table invested it with yet more piquant interest. The evening's madness became real fun. I lifted my wine with a *mutterseelenallein* flourish. Her face, though noncommittal, had those faintly sucked-in cheeks which seemed to shelter a grin inside. The wine warmed headily. The soup turned out to be an excellent non sequitur. Livia, the Javanese he-lovely, tripped to the microphone, and with the voice of a cold-ridden castrato began to vonder vhy she sped the lodely night dreamig of a sog. A great number of Ruhr baronesses, ladies with German necks and French dresses, had themselves marched up and down the dance floor by their spouses. My table partner's mouth said nothing. Her eyes missed nothing. I asked her to dance.

She complied without a word, and she danced with perfection and reserve. Her hand lodged white and neutral in mine, her body in the damned raincoat responded objectively to my steering. She certainly knew how to follow—at a distance. Our feet resumed the common rhythm they had kept on the street, and on some turns I felt her breath, wine-spiced just like mine. When the orchestra paused between numbers, she could have led the way back to the table as some other women did. She stayed. It could have been inertia as easily as volition. I started to dance faster.

"Slower," she said at last softly to my shoulder.

Suddenly I felt cocky. By a providential connivance Livia launched into a brisk jazz tempo. I improvised a lindy hop. It jolted the breath out of my partner; her lips came open, the lower releasing the upper into a full heart shape, into a revelation of two slightly separated white teeth underneath. Round ripples came into her cheeks. It was the girl-smile of the album suspended against the mature madonna face. She saw that I saw and hid her face, the blond plumage-soft hair brushing my temple. I felt her rising to the surface of her skin. The whole marvelous woman warmed in my arms.

"Slower," she murmured. "I'm not used to high heels any more."

"That's your fault," I said, blithe, merciless, and went into a pirouette. It shook out of her a gasped protest— tinged with a laugh. Her hand became alive in mine. Her arm tightened behind my collar. I slowed down temporarily, experimentally, but her body remained committed to me. I turned her around, and as our thighs touched and brushed, the music died.

For two seconds, till the floor stopped swaying, we clasped arms. Her eyes remained half closed, but the smile had drained away. I felt as though set down on a hard new shore. She walked swiftly back to our table.

"Excuse me," she said and picked up her bag. She went toward the powder room. But she passed it. She paused just long enough in the vestibule to let the doorman swing the door open. And then she was gone.

I was left with two beefsteaks cooling on the table and two pups who had wound themselves around a chair leg.

At this awful point Dinny turned out to be a brick. He came up instantly, and as if with some bright new thought (not at all as if anything untoward had happened) ushered me into his office and straight out of his office into the street. The doorman already had a taxi with the motor running and pointed in the direction her cab had taken.

"You'll catch her," Dinny said. "Go on! I'll keep the pups. Dear, marvelous man, you got a *Schatten* person into my club! You'll get the Prince yet! Go on!"

I don't think her loss caught up with me until I stood in the Zoo Station restaurant. After all, she had mentioned the place; it lay exactly in the direction she had chosen. But she wasn't even in the ladies' room, which a slimy crone cased for me for two marks. I felt shiveringly cold when I returned to the taxi—I'd forgotten my coat at Dinny's. I was starved, having had only soup since lunch. I was lonely, because less than fifteen minutes ago we had still shared a table together. I felt ridiculously lonely and deprived, a damn fool for having started the mess at all, for not having talked with her, not having opened her up a little more while she still sat safely at my side. Round and round we circled the block—in vain. It remained intolerably empty of her. The thing was to hunt her down on foot, crevice by crevice. I swore to get her back.

How long the chase lasted I don't know. I started with a system. I tried to be cold and calculating about it. Without identification card she couldn't hole up in a hotel. Nor could she waste money on a taxi ride. The pups must have cost most of the cash she carried, and she had to be prepared to buy drinks till the Schatten gate opened at four a.m. Everything pointed to the cheaper bars.

In the Zoo Station neighborhood these turned out to be

sleepy suspicious affairs, staring strangers away. No Nun. I veered back to the Ku-damm area. There the mass consumption of night fun had started. Huge tourist buses sprayed people into the street. It makes me tired just to think of it. What followed was a hike through crazed and spastic brightness, a flicker of club portals, a twitching scream of invitations. At one point I came up flush against the Wall; it resembled a clumsy sideshow with its splashy warning signs and histrionic barbed wire. It looked like a stage prop which by accident was infinite and went around the world.

I turned back. No Nun. More buses washed up against the gutter like stranded whales. A thousand faces flowed through me, none of them hers, all doing Berlin, the Western midway set in the Eastern apocalypse. The surf cast me into a telephone restaurant, a monumental dance floor ringed around with hundreds of tables from each of which you could dial calls to all the others, all interconnected with pneumatic mail tubes. Flirtation thundered here like a heavy industry, hectic and deafening, a furnace of sexual play electronically amplified. Bells shrilled, teeth leered, messages thudded, lips laughed, trombones blasted, waiters pounced, fingers intertwined, corks flew, tongues moistened. She might have picked this as a hiding place. Nothing. No Nun.

She was nowhere. I found a cave that clapped masks on all guests and where anonymity and a hot piano boiled into glass-shattering giggles. I couldn't see the Kaufhaus skirt that would betray her. In a side street I stopped to smoke and think. The air stung with the smell of Prussian pines, of rubble, perfume, urine. The question was whether to give up or not.

As I stood there two things happened. Both hard,

well-defined events, quite separate from the rest of the delirium. First a procession of cars passed very slowly, escorted by a drunk—a police car, a truck and an empty precautionary ambulance. The drunk bawled in an ecstatic North German accent, *"Achtung!* Herr Russia, bomb-removal squad. *Achtung*, a beautiful World War II Yankee blockbuster, an Ami beauty, just discovered under a foundation. Twenty years old, still chipper, fuse intact, not a spot of rust on her. Not one blemish! Herr Russia, put that into your pipe!" He blared along like a circus barker, and tumbled into my arms. I pushed him away. I might have given up that moment. But then I saw the second thing. Her.

She stood against one of the ruins tinged with neon green. A group of tourists confused my line of vision. I could only see the blond pile of hair. I ran toward it. I was less than three feet away when she turned around. She extracted a paper flower whose wire stem had been stuck deep into her bosom and attached it to my lapel. A male flower-girl with two pincushions for breasts and a wrinkled, stubbled, hideously rouged smile. "Three marks, my sweet."

She got my elbow instead. I was trembling mad. I was going to find that bitch. And so the night and the search resumed.

What came afterwards seems to merge with what came before. Many drinks were put before me, none of them touched. I always ordered, paid, looked and looked about till I was sure, and left. No Nun. In one dive, women wrestling in a spotlighted cauldron of mud. Elsewhere, a harelipped Negress dancing around a python; substantial gentlemen rumbaing together, watchchain rubbing against watchchain. Cascades of faces, none of them right. A quick shower puckered the pavements, setting the night afloat in wet gleams, just as it once did when we walked down the Ku-damm together. I felt so homeless. Schatten began to seem like a fabulous haven. I cursed myself for abandoning it. I felt like a monk who'd jumped the wall only to drown in this boundless evil dusty nocturne. This endless useless inferno created by man to trick up his mortality. I thrashed about in a moonscape of unanswering roars and impervious plinths. No matter how many corners I rounded, on how many bars I left how many coins, the loneliness jangled and glittered on. No Nun.

Until suddenly it stopped.

It all stopped on the square before the spotlighted ruins of the Memorial Church. Weeks ago, on my first Berlin night, I'd looked for Uncle Julius here. A hundred young and rosy hookers cooed and clicked about me, just as they had then. Some smoked their off-duty cigarettes on a café terrace. One, sitting three rows back, had a blond upsweep and a short black skirt. I went closer.

The moment I was sure, there was no gladness left. Only anger. I approached very slowly, amidst giggles and proposals.

"Well," I said. "Hello."

"Hello," she said.

She spoke so softly she made me bend down. If at the start of the evening we had looked like man and wife, we must have resembled customer and prostitute now. The three hours had done something to her. Her eyes, which had disclosed nothing but the aloofness of Schatten—her eyes had changed. The city night had entered them.

They had reddened, fiercened, widened. In the pupils lived a phosphorescence. Her lips were no longer closed but faintly parted, faintly puffed. The cigarette kept traveling to her pale face, to a mouth fixed in an attitude of exhalation and derision.

Then I saw the white exposed skin of her collar bone, stippled with cold, The night had chilled. All she had on was the thin raincoat and the thin blouse. And no doubt she was just as starved as I.

"You're freezing," I said.

"You get used to it," said her open, contemptuous lips.

"You've chosen an interesting location."

"Yes."

"Why?" I said.

"I can't go to a good place alone," she said. "And every bad place is the territory of other ladies. So."

"You're not alone now," I said.

She looked at me. She got up without another word and walked ahead of me into the bar next door.

Actually it was less a bar than one of those flimsy modern pastel caverns where passers-by negotiated with ladyloves just chosen. A heap of teenagers twitched in front of a juke box. But the place was warm. We sat down, ordered pizza—that is, the entire menu. Her lips were violet with cold. She ate the pizza with a fork, with crisp withering speed. A blond wave had fallen down her temple; she never let go of her cigarette. It had been brutal for her too.

I ordered double brandies. But I hated her.

"You gave me an interesting three hours," I said.

"My pups seem to have gotten lost," she said.

"They're at the Club," I said. "Dinny is taking care of them."

"They've done their duty for you. Give them lots of sugar."

"Why did you run away?" I asked.

"Why did you start this whole game?"

"Let me think carefully now," I said. "If I say the wrong thing, you'll run off."

"No," she said, exhaling through curled lips. "Not that again."

"Good," I said. "Perhaps we can actually have a talk."

"Is that the object? All this ingenuity was exercised for talking?"

"At Schatten a lot of ingenuity was exercised in the opposite direction."

"I had the impression there was talk every day."

"Between us?" I said.

"You never missed a chance. You were very painstaking about that."

At least she was roiled. The night had ripped her open. And that was very satisfying.

"Fräulein Ahn," I said, "there were men with whom you chatted at much greater length."

"My husbands?"

"To mention some convenient examples, yes."

"Shall we have our talk about them?"

"They'd make a worthwhile topic, don't you think?"

"Perhaps you'd like to work them into your hotel pageant?"

"Yes," I said. "If the Prince doesn't get well enough in time, I might have to. We might use their effigies."

Suddenly she laughed—a sound low and hard. I had never heard her laugh before. It shook the blond lock down from her temple to her cheek. With her sharp, shapely brandy-moist mouth, with her high pale cheeks, those long lowering gray eyes and the blond sheaf all athwart, she looked like some fine mask which a blow had simultaneously bruised and ignited. Something inside her had been broken apart and it flickered out at me together with the cigarette smoke, full of acridness and perfume.

"My poor husbands," she said. "They're much too dull for your hotel. My second one's just a diabetic in France. My first one, the dead one, was a bore. Everything that happened from '33 to '45 was a bore, you know."

"That's why nobody mentions the boring years," I said.

"Yes!" she said. "Whereas now everything is so exciting!"

She drank up. Her body leaned forward a little, with a motion that was both parody and a subtle female deployment of arm and shoulder. She dabbed her lips and smoothed her hair back. That slight adjustment turned confrontation into flirtation—or rather into a lush sardonic caricature thereof. A curl still shaped her mouth, a direness stayed in her eyes.

"You're pretty amazing," I said.

The laugh came back, low, jagged, perhaps covering a shiver.

"Oh, yes, amazing," she said. "There's this amazing woman. She's lived quietly on an estate for years. For years, busy pruning her little hedges. Then a man moves in. He has to, because he's opening a hotel miles away. He pulls this woman outside. He puts her into the funniest clothes. He throws her among the street ladies. And then he calls *her* amazing!"

"She must be," I said, "to make him act like that."

"I see," she said. "Nobody else ever has?"

"No."

She drank up her second brandy. "Really," she said. "No one. No experience with women who are out of cigarettes?"

"Sorry," I said. I gave her one and lit it. She almost blew the smoke into my face. Whatever game she was now playing with me, I could play it too.

"All right," she said. "We might as well make it amusing, this whole ingenious plot of yours."

"It's a little late," I said. "But we can try."

"Let's get back my pups."

I looked at my watch. It was three fifteen. "God," I said, "they close at three thirty."

"We can always break in," she said.

"We will!" I said. "They're not going to keep the pups after all that trouble."

By then a tart heady wildness worked between us. I jumped up and paid and grabbed her hand. When we got back to the street, most bars were letting out and each taxi taken. We ran side by side as we had run before, scaring drunks and policemen, the only people left in the world. Suddenly I felt her stop, her small nails digging into my palm. She had broken a heel.

"You go on," she said.

"You'll be here when I come back," I said. "You're not going to vanish again?"

"I want my pups," she said.

I went on. Once I looked back, and there she really was, hobbling after me, a strange creature made of three a.m., a disabled beautiful witch. The Club was only a few blocks away, quite empty, with Dinny high, telling luscious jokes to a small circle of male bar ladies.

"Oh," he said, "the lovable little Afghans." He snapped a finger and they appeared, sleeping in a satin-bowed giant fruit basket.

"Afghans à la Dinny," he said. "You found her?"

"Yes," I said.

"Hallelujah," he said. "Next step, bed her. The only way to get the Prince for the opening. Bed her, you marvelous man."

"I'll try," I said. I took the fruit basket and the parcel with her Schatten clothes and rushed outside. She waited before the entrance, standing on one leg, blonde, pink and black, only half witch now and half flamingo. She stroked the sleeping pups, but didn't take them. My shoulder supported her as she changed to her Schatten shoes.

"I want to look," she said.

She was pointing at a fancy couturier shop across the street. The lit-up store windows on the Ku-damm were the only thing left of the night.

"Now?" I said.

"While I'm here. I haven't seen anything for years."

She ran across, in flashes of pink stockings and gold hair which I had no choice but to follow. She stared at the window mannikins. "Nothing but legs and leopard skin," she said. "All those bad German knees. I was one of the better-dressed women in that club of yours. They were all that dreadful."

And then she was off to the next window in dog-romping tempo, to a furrier and then a jeweler. Sometimes she glanced back and saw me follow across the desolate sidewalk, loaded with the pups' basket and the brown paper package of her Schatten clothes and the Kaufhaus pumps which wouldn't fit into the confounded parcel—and the bruised-mask smile glowed in the darkness.

"Back to mink mittens again," she said at another furrier's window. "They had them twenty years ago, in this very store. During the millennium. I used to shop just like this, you know. We went to bed at seven in the morning. By the time I got up again, the silly stores were closed. So we went past all the good windows at dawn like now, and I left a shopping list for the maid. People don't know how to live any more."

The window lights went out, suddenly. We stood in the darkness, deep in the recessed store façade.

I asked, "That was during the boring era?"

"Yes," she said slowly. "For a while I shopped like that. Only, the lights lasted longer then."

I didn't care whether she was taunting me or herself. The basket was already on the pavement. My arms rid themselves of the parcel and the shoes and closed around her. My mouth hunted hers. I felt neither resistance nor response. I didn't care about that either. I wanted to crush the queer wildness out of her, her cursed gay Hitler years. A sound escaped her almost like a laugh. She freed herself. Parted, wordless, we returned to the sidewalk. All the other store windows had lapsed. One by one the bright gods of the movie posters died above us.

"How intense of you," she said.

A moment later we sat in a taxi bound for Schatten. Her head lay back and her eyes were closed. Her lips, too, with that ironic curl intact. But I'd gotten more than irony out of her. The basket rested on her lap, and her hands stroked the pups in the same rhythm in which I heard her breathe. The city swerved past us like a gray dream. We passed the Dowle Hotel. The X's painted on the brand-new window panes ghosted white through the darkness. I didn't point it out to her. For a moment I thought I saw her hideous double selling flowers.

And she, as though suddenly shocked by it, sat up. She began to order her hair into her Schatten coiffure. She put her combs and hairpins on my knees. There must have been room on the seat, but she put them on my knee. I still remember the slight swift touch of her fingertips. Her hair was neat in time for our arrival. It was ten after four and the gate open. The two East German guards who had unlocked it stood smoking on the empty highway.

Schatten received us; a silent grotto, roofed with a dark-violet sky on the verge of dawn. The gravel tittered under our shoes. There was a breath of magnolia, and some insomniac bird cried out. As we crossed the bridge over the lake I saw a swan sleeping beneath. Poplar leaves were mumbling moonless. The manor was silent and dark. She gave me her arm to hold, for only she could find her way through the utter blackness. Once, on the stairs, she hissed to quiet the dogs. The gas lamps had been turned off in the corridor. We groped toward my door and she stepped in behind me.

"I don't want those Kaufhaus clothes in my room," she said.

She took the parcel and walked behind the Chinese screen. I heard her move behind it. I turned on the gas lamp, low. The baroque beams stretched across the ceiling as if nothing had happened, as though nothing would. There were still fourteen beams crosswise. I closed the window blinds. The bird in the garden fell silent the very moment her movements stopped. I walked behind the screen. She stood there, fully dressed in her usual Schatten clothes, immobile.

The same small sound escaped her as at the mink-mitten window. But now she didn't free herself. She consented and grinned into the kiss. Our embrace grew in the Schatten silence like some crazy carnivorous flower. I breathed in the warmth of her shoulders and her hair and, more than that, the whole fantastic, tortured opulence of the evening, the scent of Kaufhaus perfume and the wine from Dinny's, the tobacco of her cigarettes, the acrid neon frenzy, the lonesome night dust of the streets. She toyed with me even as she sighed, she seemed to grin through her kiss, she watched through her closed blond-lashed eyes, she withheld, relented, withheld again, and only slowly did she let my thighs bask themselves in hers, slowly her arms warmed and ripened against me, tangling upwards from the waist like vines, mouth lolling into mouth, and then suddenly we were like canoes torn loose from their moorings, and there was nothing, nothing but the river of her flesh.

She could not be possessed. All the small burning mishaps, the clumsy buttons, the obstinate zippers, the small humiliating details which are lust admitted, lust amok—it was I alone that suffered through them all. In that ultimate impact on the high bed she was smooth, white, inhuman lava. She poured out her white plenitude of breasts and thighs, imperiously and silently, smiling, as display, as goad, but nothing more. She used them to infuriate but not to surrender. I had been the seducer of the evening, but now she was the one who bent us both into a bow ready to burst—and at her pleasure, at the cruel virtuoso moment, she reached to turn down the light, and delivered us. I was set aglow, and puffed, and stubbed out like a cigarette. At her command I spent myself in the dark, toiling, voiceless, tired unto death.

She lay there quietly, eyes open. But she didn't look at me or speak. Nor would she come under the covers. Instead she dressed and returned to the bed. She sat next to me, combing herself, recreating her Schatten hairdress for the second time, escaping into her inward rhythm.

"Usually it's the man who's in a hurry," I said.

They were the first words between us.

"Forgive me," she said.

The dawn, sudden, ran through the blinds and onto her hair.

"You have a nice Viennese accent," she said.

"Thank you," I said.

"How did you get to be an American?"

"I was a racial bore in Vienna in the 'thirties," I said. "So I had to grow up elsewhere."

"You grew up into a determined man."

"Oh, I used to be different," I said. "I was a poet. But then I became a tough hack for Mr. Dowle. Which is useful because I'm meeting a lot of tough people."

"You are angry," she said.

"I?" I said. "Not a bit." And it was true, I had no reason to be. I had gotten what I wanted.

"History does repeat itself," she said.

"Lie down," I said.

She stopped combing and lay down next to me.

There seemed to be a sudden openness, a willingness to

talk which I suspected. It was really a bone she was throwing me, to make up for—what? Who had made whom around here? It was ludicrous, and, ludicrously, I snapped up the bone.

"Who am I repeating?" I asked.

"Oh, nothing really," she said, "just an old story."

"I like old stories," I said.

She took a deep breath. "When I was a girl," she said, "I mean a very young girl, I had one afternoon a week outside."

"Outside the estate?"

"My Tuesday ballet class in the city. Twenty-five years ago. Now it's another Tuesday."

"Was it the Prince's grandson?"

"Oh, yes," she said. "He came down on me just as I walked out of class. In his uniform." She paused. I waited. "The uniform was funny," she said. "I only knew about the estate, just riding and a lot of books and the gardens. And the Prince and my parents. Nothing from outside except some diplomats and him."

She stopped. I held out a pack of cigarettes, but she shook her head.

"Just horses and diplomats," she said.

"Go on," I said.

"It's very simple," she said. "He came down on me. He was good-looking and glamorous. Though his movies were disappointing, his parts were so small. Afterwards I had to see them all."

"We haven't reached afterwards yet," I said.

Something had happened to her voice. I couldn't help her. I lay next to her and waited.

"He came down on me. He made a very passionate speech," she said. "Not like you. And no pups. And he had this uniform to impress me, SS braid, boots and everything. I'd never seen him in it. The Prince wouldn't let him into Schatten like that. It looked perfectly silly on him."

A pause. I waited.

"I said to him, 'You look like a tin soldier.' He looked so hurt and sweet."

"Poor fellow," I said. "And?"

"And so I slept with him," she said. "Mostly because of the funny uniform. It's very simple."

"Look," I said, "there's no obligation to tell me anything."

"I was sixteen," she said. "I married him three months later."

"That's when you began to do your shopping at dawn?"

"For a while," she said. "Yes."

I said nothing.

"I was very good at the grand life," she said. "I was very good at it for a few years. And after the war I was very good at it again."

"Not lately," I said.

"No," she said. "Not lately."

"Your first name is Irene," I said.

"I can't call you anything," she said.

"Why not?"

"I must get back to my room."

Her mouth brushed against mine. She'd already gotten up.

"Wait!" I said. "Irene!"

She was gone before I could find my way to the door. I heard her in the corridor. She was a footfall beyond the wall again. More light clustered on the window slats.

There were some other birds now, robins and blue jays. The pups in the fruit basket were gone with her, and the Kaufhaus clothes hung from the Chinese screen, the shiny skirt glimmering in the grayness.

I went back to bed. I missed her. I missed her terribly, and the first cry of a peacock came from the gardens.

JOURNAL

October 6th

Once upon a time I dreamed that I had come back to the little street in Vienna where I was born. To the real cobbled little street, not the caricature with smooth asphalt which you see now. My real parents lived in it, those cruel cranky gods, not the polite shadows that write me from New York today. My real tutor was there in the dream, in his old familiar checkered jacket, waiting to teach me childhood again, teach me my real self, after my long and lying truancy as an adult.

Today I'm only good for sentimentality. Everything else seems caddish and dreary. The dream—I dreamed it long before last night—haunts me because that little cobbled street may be the central locus of my life, the source of heaven, nirvana and inferno, my anchor in eternity. The rest is shadows and chimera, tantalization and cheat and vanity. I ought to remember that today. Schatten, if it exists at all, is just a bit of vapor above the cobbles.

At fourteen I stood in a park next to a girl I knew, whose hair had caught the sun. Her beauty seized me, but instead of touching her I went to an ice-cream vendor two hundred yards away. When I brought the stick to her half melted, I was sick with desire and humiliation, with all the tortured indirections crawling inside me like fresh-spawned maggots. That very day they must have covered my little street with smooth asphalt. Maybe that day I began to learn the performances of courtship, ambition, success. All the grown-up's narcotic dances. Each day I'm sucked into them, willy-nilly, the moment the alarm rings and I rise from bed. And only sometimes something outrageously pure will wake me into truth and pain.

October 7th

Yesterday, as usual, the limousine brought me to the city at ten a.m. Two hours of sleep. A kind of romantic extravagant fatigue, not unenjoyable. I let myself go in the journal (see yesterday), then got Dowle work done. Remembered some strapping blond transvestites I'd run across in a place called the Kant Club during the Wild Night. Arranged through the Littel Partners to have a couple photographed as Valkyries on the unicorn. Amusing that no one, including Dave, will know the difference; also that this weird nocturne can be turned to some daytime account. It's reassuring, somehow. Wrote Nina a postcard in our code, special delivery, instead of calling. Did call Uncle Julius, pressed another day of bed rest on him.

Then I summoned KarlHeinz a bit earlier than usual, and got to the furrier—her furrier on the Ku-damm—just before he closed for lunch. The store looked strange in the daytime. The mink mittens were ninety marks. My fourteen-year-old's melted ice cream had been twenty groschen. Apparently one doesn't forget such prices.

At Schatten they were at lunch in the dining alcove. (Minus the doctor, who eats upstairs since the Prince's arrival.) Her I met in the first-floor corridor. There was no one else about. Her face, as usual bare of cosmetics, seemed pale, perhaps by contrast to the lipstick of the night before. She was dusting a figurine from a wall shelf, dusting with white fingers whose calm and arrogant deliberation I resented. They acted as if it didn't matter that I knew the arm to which the fingers were joined, knew the shoulder that moved the arm, knew the breasts below the shoulder. Since her "Good day" was neutral, mine was too. The pups were well, she reported in answer to my query. Yes, I could see them. When? At three, she said, polishing. I asked where.

"The floor above this," she said evenly, in beat with the motion of her hand. "Three doors to the left of the landing. The glass knob with the rose inside."

I couldn't be sure she was serious. The glass knob with the rose inside. But, as yet, I wasn't able to invent an appropriate new public stance with her. Sounds approached from below and I said fine.

The dogs were still there at the first-floor landing. When I left my room at the stroke of three, the dogs were gone. Slowly I climbed up along the scaled snake that is the railing of the banister. No sound except the groan of the steps. A special new silence flowed down from the top, a silence into which the Prince's presence was dissolved together with the events of the night before. At the top the snake has a fierce spitting head and a tongue whose mahogany tip is broken off. The corridor no different from the one on my floor, though smaller. A grandiose double-winged door opposite the landing, with unicorns as the inlaid pattern of the central panels. Highness' quarters, no doubt. The dogs sat before it, transplanted statuary. Snooty statuary that watched my passing with black porcelain eyes, jet tails flicking faintly.

The rose doorknob appeared—a ridiculousness to match my uncle's. It yielded to my touch.

Her room has the same heavy beams as mine. But it loomed larger and darker, possibly because the blinds were drawn. It isn't the least bit feminine, doorknob notwithstanding, though I seemed to smell the Kaufhaus scent of the night before. I put the box of mink mittens on the table, lid open, and went to where she pointed. Little White Riding Hood dozed in its basket, its friend's paw against its mouth, and didn't pay attention to my patting. I turned around. She stood before me. Her hands were covered with the soft fur of the mittens. They fit. I had known her size. I knew her hands and they knew me. In thought we had touched all day. Now the mink hands glided around my neck, tickled and caressed down my body, awakening delicious vile new nerves as they went. It was a diabolic jest. Her hands were still furred when we were both naked, they stroked my sex, my fury with a thousand teasing electric hairs. Again I couldn't snatch a moment's detachment—as with other women—to observe and enjoy her lust. I couldn't even loosen her hair as I'd wanted.

And then she changed. She is very good at switching gears. In the sudden aftercalm her hands shed their fur and took one of my cigarettes, and put a finger gently against my mouth because someone was walking in the corridor, and then her hands brought me, on proffering palms, all my clothes and helped me dress in a sad and gentle parody of the obedient oriental odalisque, a bantering in pantomime that was really a way of saying "Please hurry," and I walked away again, past a statuary of dogs, down the broken-tongued snake.

For half an hour I stood by the window in my room.

There was no sign of her in the garden; so it pulled me down to the hall. And she really sat at the Five O'Clock Tea table as always, between father and mother, her hair and her coif impeccably in place once more. Her father's wide-sleeved arm fell across her chair back. She returned my bow with exactly his inclination of the head.

I was glad to go on to the library, where a servant followed me with an enormous candle (the days are growing shorter) and where I could sit under the pretense of work. The door between us was slightly open. I could feel its very texture, the graining of its wood. I could feel it like the thinness of a glove separating two hands. I loved the slow waltz that dribbled in because it touched the inner whorls of both her ear and mine.

I sat there until she and all the others had gone and the music died. Then I dined and went to bed early, to make up for the loss of sleep.

October 9th

The day falls into a certain rhythm. I sleep well but wake up itching with puzzlement and impatience. From my breakfast table I've got a good view of the ceiling corner above which I know her bed to be. All night footsteps flowed from that corner into and out of my dreams. The dream shatters. But the footsteps have soft stubborn echoes. I take all Schatten with me to my Berlin desk. Dave's genius is not exactly traveling light these days. The whole confounded manor has absorbed itself into my body as one of its secret smoldering parts. A sort of spare groin when the working groin is making sufficient trouble.

In a way it's pleasant to duck out of that dubious sweet twilight into the office; into Ida's *oo*wonderful no-non-sense work-and-espresso empire. There's a pleasant glut of problems. Example: the purchase license for the Dowle Casino site at the estate cannot be granted unless the Prince permits inspection of the adjacent territory by the municipal bomb squad. It turns out that he hasn't permitted municipal inspection of any kind since the war's end. And the matter of this permission cannot even be broached until my first interview with Highness, now set for Thursday. So Dr. Ahn informs me. However, I've gotten Dr. Ahn's daughter without the Prince's imprimatur, and it's just possible that I'll get the Prince himself too.

Meantime I'm hip-deep in other legalities prerequisite to buying the Casino property. The Littel Partners twitter into the phone on my behalf the morning through. Uncle Julius turns up at the office, sufficiently recovered to conduct a silly but energetic tiff with me. I thrust and parry with Dave via cables. I perform phone calls to New York, and if love be measured by guilt, I love Ninepins more than ever. If love be measured by insecurity, man, I'm hung up on that Nun. When I shop in the Ku-damm stores—buying little gifts for her has become part of the day's ritual—my purchases are an act of jealousy, not gallantry. Maybe loving someone means choosing someone to be most jealous about.

By which I suppose I mean this: that my morning pose doesn't really work. I try to feel victorious, the trium-phant offhand Don Giovanni who turns to other matters during daylight hours. For a few hours at least, it should be enough that I've conquered her. But there is not enough sense of conquest. There's a suspicion that I've only been bribed by her, delectably bribed. The smug carnal memories on which the rogue male likes to coast, and on which I want to count at odd moments—they're curiously absent. It comes to me that the Nazi bitch has scanted and withheld in the very act of opulence; tossed me a small bone when by rights I ought to get a luscious haunch. She's made an Andy out of me.

Back at Schatten, during lunch, I feel the gathering of some splendid spangled resentment. It grows as I walk upstairs to the top floor. The house, so unfailingly sound-less and deserted, acts like an impassive accomplice, not necessarily well-intentioned. I don't give a damn. I walk past the snake's head, past the dogs, to the flower in the doorknob. Inside, the present is presented. It's always one of those small things she looked at in the Ku-damm windows.

"You see," I say, "with me you can also go shopping at four a.m." Or some such thing.

But she never takes me up on vexed allusions to the past. She fingers the gift; with simple ironic virtuosity she drapes it around herself or puts it on, depending on whether it is a hat, a scarf or a French satin stole. And then she asks me one of her tartly smiled questions: Is it like this that such things are worn nowadays by the great ladies of my acquaintance? Or like that? Or is she acting like an obsolete fashion vandal? And the shawl I brought yesterday—is it the ideal accessory to twist the twist with? The *comme-il-faut* thing to wear when being pushed into the swimming pool? Does it wet well? Will it be the last cry at my hotel-opening opera and other superb occasions? I must tell her about all the last cries she's been missing. I really must civilize her.

I try to answer suitably. We act as each other's provocation, as mutually delicious goads. There's an appetizing sharpness to these preambles. Our words grapple with each other, find warm traction and friction in our arms and limbs.

She keeps on the scarf or stole, even in bed. The woman has a demonic virtuosity in catering to the visual lust of the male. But she's also a connoisseur at having me minister to her. She guides my body with the back of her heel, she draws me through her, as a bow is drawn across a violin. And there's always a cunning impatience in those moments. She whips and romps me across lust; and the same curl shapes her mouth that I see from afar when she whips and romps her Afghans through the garden. Sometimes she seems on the point of contriving a pause, a delicious breather, of letting me simmer down, come to my senses on the lee side of desire—but no, she arches and tenses and launches both of us into new accelerations.

Afterwards it becomes different. She always seems to feel cold; she almost flees back into her clothes. For additional warmth she even brings Little White Riding Hood under our blanket. The pup lies there between us, licking one or the other. We are stretched side by side, we three—man, woman and small creature—in a sort of family pathos. We listen to feet downstairs, descending toward the Five O'Clock Tea. After this she will talk, very softly, but almost without sardonic undertow, she'll really talk if I touch on certain carefully limited things. Yesterday I asked her about the rose in the doorknob.

"That's many years back," she said. "I made it when I was sixteen. A nanny showed me how to make them out of lace."

"Will you make one for me?"

"I wanted to make one for each door in the manor. I

became so ambitious about it. A different color for each door."

"Where are the others?"

"I never made a second," she said.

She didn't explain and I didn't press it. Her sixteenth year was the year of her marriage. But sometimes I can't help pressing things. There's a small Saviour on her wall next to the window, crossless, simple and Gothic, like the one in the chapel. Yesterday it moved me to ask her whether she was Protestant.

"Lutheran," she said. "We all are. Like the Prince."

"What's the Prince like? At all human?"

"I hardly see him now. Father's so protective about him."

"You must have an impression."

"He's become very fragile. That's being very human, isn't it?"

"Do you like him?"

"You'll see when you talk to him. He gives meaning to this place."

"Irene," I said. "Is shutting yourself away here mean-ingful?"

She had become so damn diplomatic, so unapproach-able, it made me lash out. But a frontal attack is as futile as the most subtle flanking maneuver.

"Meaningful?" she said, easy. "It was restful until you came along."

I couldn't pursue it. She was up, getting my clothes. That happens whenever I try to steer the conversation toward any area involving the practically relevant. She turns glass-smooth and makes her escape.

It's already become a semi-comic tradition, this bring-ing of my clothes, this helping me on with my shirt, socks and shoes in the half-dark room, buttoning and lacing me like a child, with a kissless wordless tenderness, before the moment of parting. Meanwhile Little White Riding Hood, abruptly abandoned by the two big warmths at its side, fumbles dispirited about the sheets.

Then I walk down one flight of stairs to my room; and, after a few minutes, down the second flight to the hall, past the brave old Five O'Clock Tea, past the woman who sits so closely locked against her father, face hard and perfect under the coif: the woman who once was a girl wanting to plant a hundred roses inside a hundred glass knobs, and who an hour ago embraced me with her thighs; and I nod to her and receive my single nod back.

Then all I have in the candlelit library is the door slightly open between us, the music welling precariously through the fissure. And our affair seems so naked and needy, so un-dressed-up with the customary vows and plans, so limited to the frantic touching together of intimate skin and the brief strange tenderness which comes of that and which is so iridescent and treacherous with expectations. For there seems to be something in a man which makes him think that once he's pushed a nerve-ridden piece of his flesh against a similar piece in some special woman, physiology will turn into revelation and he into a young god forever. And then he wakes up with her left-over breath in his nostrils, mortal, sweaty, feckless as before.

I brood about it back in my room. Brood about it during dinner, and while I watch her shadow romp the dogs below. It's even in my heavy dream-colored sleep, until I wake into a view of the ceiling corner and into the day's impatience which swells and smolders and cannot rest until I've gone past the glass rose once more and feel her hair against my face.

October 10th

Why can't the rest of the world just go away?

In today's cable Dave complains that the Polaroid shot of the Prince's portrait is much too fuzzy for reproduction. It won't even do as the model for a drawing. COMMISSION SAME ARTIST TO DO NEW PRINCE PORTRAIT STOP OFFER EXACTLY SAME SUM CONSTABLE RECEIVED FOR PAINTING DUKE OF WELLINGTON.

Sweet publicity stuff. Not so sweet for me who has to work hard enough to get a single audience out of His ancient ornery Highness—let alone a series of sittings.

I did mention the idea to Ahn when I ran into him this noon. A rare encounter these days, because the old doctor is almost constantly closeted with the Prince.

"Another portrait?" he said on his hurried way to the chapel. "You just mention it to the Prince. Bring it up at your tea with him Thursday."

"It's already a crowded tea agenda," I said.

"Oh, you mention it. You'll get what you want." He stopped for a moment, smiled for a moment. His cane touched me lightly on the arm. "You're getting everything else these days, aren't you?"

No, the rest of the world will not go away. It hovers and grins and makes my ears burn like a schoolboy's. It's full of queer unsettling surprises. The rest of the world as exemplified by Ahn displays an uncharacteristic torn-off button on his smock and, more shocking, the friendly cynical consent of his smile. I'm surprised, not that he knows, but that he makes such an insidious show of his knowledge.

The rest of the world as exemplified by Uncle Julius gives no peace either. Yesterday morning the lawyer called, the one I put in charge of Julius' restitution. He's now sure he could get a sizable settlement (in the neighborhood of sixty thousand). I immediately fired off a messenger to Julius' hotel with the good news plus a list of supporting documents wanted by the lawyer.

Less than two hours later, who should come boiling into the office? Julius himself. Charged in, Littel Partners indignant at his heels because he hadn't even bothered to be announced.

"Good morning," he said formally, bitterly, and then didn't know what to make of the momentum of his entry and kept pressing back his glasses while trying to find his tongue.

"Hello, Uncle," I said. "You look better." I knew what was bothering this sensitive stubbly soul: my message had omitted any invitation to resume our Schatten sessions together. I could just imagine him dogging me as I went upstairs after lunch instead of going down to the library. Great talmudic commentaries pronounced over our copulation on the bed. Over my dead body.

"Isn't it great about your restitution," I said brightly. And explained that now he didn't have to travel all the way out to the estate any more; the lawyer would take care of the practical points of the Schatten petition and I'd enlist the Prince's moral support at my interview.

Julius opened a button of his overcoat and said nothing.

"All we need now are those documents," I said. "You

can bring them to the office any time."

No answer.

"I have an idea," I said. "Why don't we have lunch somewhere around here tomorrow?"

I realized how stiffly he was standing there. I'd forgotten to ask him to sit down. "Take a chair, Uncle," I said. "Tomorrow we'll celebrate the good tidings."

He didn't budge. "I see," he said. Suddenly he began to grub into his pockets. Not into his food pockets for a change, but into other kinds of pockets, for he had myriads of them, on the outside of his black overcoat and inside, jacket pockets at the breast and the hip, secret pockets near the armpit, untold trouser pockets and at least one inside his waistcoat. He produced a stream of canceled passports and expired vaccination certificates, tax receipts and visa applications, fragments of letters annotated at the margins, landing cards of extinct airlines, customs forms, birth certificates, affidavits, whole dossiers of his emigrations, no money whatsoever, and, along with this dusty heap, the documents needed, even down to the incorporation papers of his parents' defunct business.

"Here you are," he said tersely. "Thank you very much."

"It would have kept till tomorrow, Uncle."

"No, thank you very much. I don't have to disturb you again."

"Look, sit down—"

"I assume you won't need my assistance at the Schatten library either?"

"I'm really finished, Uncle. You were a great help—"

"Of course. Now, how much do I owe for the doctor you sent me?"

"The doctor?"

"He came twice. I have means now with this settlement. How much?"

"I'll have him send you a bill. Don't worry—"

"And the lawyer?"

"The lawyer will ask for his fee when the case is settled."

"In that case, his address, please. So I won't have to trouble you any further."

He stood there. The black rim of his hat trembled. I was really tired of his indignations. I'd brought him such good news, and here we went again. I guess there's no point bringing Jews good news. They don't know what to do with it. And I had other fish to fry.

"Uncle," I said. "What seems to be the trouble now?" He stood there, putting all the documents back into their various pockets. "The petition won't go to waste," I said. "I'll mention all the important points to the Prince. . . . Do sit down, will you?"

Not Julius. Suddenly he began to walk up and down. His coat brushed against Ida's bright tourist statistics, his sleeve almost upset her pencil mug, and in his grim absent-mindedness he prodded the lever of the espresso machine so that it gave a smart hiss and made Fräulein Lieselotte's head pop out frightened from behind the door. The noise also jolted Julius to a decision.

"I shall make one more attempt," he said. He stopped. He took a deep breath. "I would like to invite you."

"Invite?" I said.

"Yes, invite," he said angrily. "Before it's too late. I'd like to invite you to my Old Testament Community in Israel."

"Wait a minute—"

"You were a professor once, right? We will have a

college at the Community. You can organize it. I have means now—"

"One moment," I said. "That's lovely, but—"

"It's not far from Tel-Aviv, a metropolis. You won't be bored. And you will live in comfort—"

"Uncle," I said, "let's be realistic about the size of the settlement money—"

But it was impossible to connect with him. "I want you to get out of Schatten," he said, "before it's too late."

"But I have a lot of work at the estate—"

"You just said you were finished."

"Only with the library. Not with the Prince—"

"Ah, you see?" he said in black triumph, as though I were wriggling helplessly in the meshes of his cross-examination. "It's *them!* They know I'm on to them, the Spider and his daughter! That's why they asked you to get rid of me!"

"Oh, for God's sake!" I said.

"Do you want to get rid of me—yes or no?"

"Will you stop it now?" I said.

He went up close to me and said softly, tremulously, "She cast her wiles on you. I saw it the moment I came in. When she laughed at me."

Whereupon I got very sore at this dreary and absurd duenna. "Good-bye, Uncle," I said. "Have a cold beer and come to your senses. And then come back tomorrow afternoon."

"*You* come to your senses!"

His arm, stuck into some extra-special superpocket, uncoiled and thrust a piece of paper at me. Something crinkled and sweaty from being crushed in his palm. It unfolded into a magazine article, one of those glamorous nostalgic exposés of the Third Reich that go on endlessly in German illustrateds. This one was about Nazi drug addicts. It began with Goering, and among the small fry at the bottom of the reverse page, so heavily and furiously underlined that I could barely make out the print, there was a reference to the late Baron Helmut von Lausche, Assistant Secretary of the National Socialist Actors' Front, who had been fined for narcotics possession at eighteen, in 1932, the last year of the pre-Hitler regime. A small picture of him in uniform—the SS insignia touched up lovingly by the magazine—showed the very man of the wedding photograph, her Tin Soldier with the Schatten chin, the self-indulgent overly curved lip line, the same detestable man. The caption referred cutely to his wife, Frau Irene von Lausche, "hostess of a salon attracting everyone who was chic and Nazi." That was all. I didn't know where he had dug up the piece and I didn't care. I gave it back to him.

"I don't see all the excitement," I said.

"You don't see? She's corrupting the Prince! Just like she corrupted her husband. She'll corrupt you too!"

"Uncle," I said, "read the article. The man was caught with narcotics years before he even married her!"

He took the piece of paper, folded it with quivering fingers. "I understand," he said hoarsely. "You are defending her. Very good. I shall pay the doctor and the lawyer—"

"Uncle, let's try to be sane—"

"Very sane. Very sensible. I thank you for the good lawyer. My own nephew. I'm very easily gotten rid of. I thank you. Good-bye."

And he really walked out, folding the clipping—that futile last ace of his—folding it into smaller and smaller folds, folding and folding he walked through the anteroom, past the Littel Partners' dismayed and bewildered stares. Bang, the door.

He is such a pain. Yesterday morning and this morning too, I dedicated at least an hour each to my good uncle. First I asked the Littel Partners to get hold of him at his hotel. The answer was always, in a strange Balkan accent, that "Herr Spiegelglass is not available for the telephone." Considering this a vile piece of *chutzpah*, I then sat down and wrote him a cold note giving the doctor's and the lawyer's addresses and washing my hands of him and his wretched tantrums forever and saying so right out. And then I repented and tore up the sheet to draft something much more conciliatory, only to get mad at pampering him so and to tear up version number two. And to decide in the end not to do anything and let *him* get in touch with me.

No doubt I'll do the same tomorrow morning. The funny thing is that the day seems to unroll more easily once I've undergone my daily cycle of Julius indecisions. Some crazy incongruous nerve connects his bent glasses with her blond hair on the pillow. If she is some kind of transgression, he is some form of penance. Maybe I wear him as a hairshirt for an hour each day. Who knows, maybe atonement is the most intimate way of staying in touch with your sin.

October 11th

Poor Littel Partners. They bore the day's brunt. They and I. And it started out so well for them. Even

fairly amusing for me. Let's not skip bright beginnings.
Let's be amusing while we can.

Imagine Ida all in white, entering the office shortly
after my latest vain try to phone Julius. Ida in a white
tailored suit, with white gloves and especially small shoes.
KarlHeinz right behind her, dressed in—surprise!—civ-
vies, but holding his cap in hand. The Littel Partners,
smiling rigorously, bring up the rear.

Ida takes up position by her desk. Around her the
Littel Partners form an exact, portentous half-circle. The
Littel Partners have an enormous talent for forming
half-circles. It would take at least three well-drilled
American regiments to produce the same effect. Ida clears
her throat. A deep overture-like breath. She is very
happy! she commences, to give before her American
friend! (her tiny white hat bows toward me) an example
of the very fine American custom of advancement on the
basis of merit, respectless of race or religion! (another
bow toward me, this one to indicate that she has discovered, probably via Julius, that I am also her Jewish
friend), and respectless of past or previous background.
ooWhat is forgotten is forgotten. The new people of
Germany! believe that ooone should not be imprisoned
forever in ooone category of life. And so, to meet the
demands of a growing organization! and to reward this
very fine industrious man! she is most happy to announce
Herr KarlHeinz's appointment to: *Office Coordinator!!*

Her white-gloved hand takes from KarlHeinz's pious
paws the chauffeur's cap; with a fine flourish she casts it
into the wastebasket. The Littel Partners applaud and
laugh, mouths at attention. Ida shakes hands, deeply,
profoundly, with KarlHeinz. The Littel Partners trip up
at five-second intervals, give him one meticulous slap on

the back, call him *Du alter Kerl du,* and snap back into previous position and more applause. Throughout it all KarlHeinz simpers and whistles ever so softly through his teeth.

*oo*Wonderful.

Only the day doesn't stop there. In midmorning I must inspect the just completed interior of the Dowle Main Hall. Two nonobjective chandeliers and three Renaissance mobiles. The rubber mermaid already lies pregnant in the swimming pool, but the head plumber tells me it'll be a month at least before there will be water. Which is fine: let the plumbers' tardiness match the Prince's. The new chauffeur, a thin little creature who knows no English, surveys the Dowle domain and says, *"Herrlich! . . . Schön!"* The last positive comment of the morning.

It's quite obvious on my return to Ida's that evil has come upon the anteroom. Fräulein Ursula is typing with one hand only, the other dabbing her eyes. Fräulein Edeltraud and Fräulein Lieselotte support themselves on card files. All three have shaking shoulders, pink eyes and white handkerchiefs much resorted to. The poor things are beside themselves.

In the inner office, the newly civilian KarlHeinz sits by Ida's desk and drinks what strikes me as an excessively equal cup of coffee. Ida drinks too, but in hard tiny sips followed by napkin stabs at her mouth. She is much better at being beside herself.

She has a littel news. A littel info just forwarded. A littel tidbit about our friend, Prince Schatten. Three hours ago he appeared at the city registry. He renewed his hotel license. The invalid unhealthy old Prince. Interesting? A nice move, plotted certainly by our delicate

Fräulein Ahn. Essentially it doesn't matter. Except that once her, Ida's, office had a plan, a careful plan: a whole intelligence system with the special purpose of telling her about such a development in advance, so she could hold up the license renewal, to use it as pressure on Schatten. By itself it doesn't matter. I, Leon, can cope *oo*with the Prince *oo*without this. She, Ida, can cope *oo*without. It is just the unreliability of the German people. The monumental, incredible, horrible unreliability. This is the thing that spoils this day for her. The weakness and chaoticness of the German people! This made necessary the tyrant Hitler, otherwise they would have disintegrated altogether! . . . She, Ida, has labored for many years! She has tried everything with these three women. No, they are still incapable to relay a simple telephone call from the registry office in time. In-capable! She cannot dismiss civil-service employees. She has tried begging, tried force, tried every psychological device. Kindness, encouragement, fraternity, everything. No. No! Incapable! They cannot relay a simple message in time!

KarlHeinz stands up and says that, suhr, he will drive me to Schatten because the new man would take too long to find his way. Somehow this offer seems indescribably solacing to Ida. It makes up for so much. She cannot bear to escort me through the anteroom past those three archetypes of German chaoticness. But she has my hand to press, and KarlHeinz to smile and sigh at, and no doubt a whole box of chocolate squares waiting under the espresso machine.

And me?
What waited for me on my arrival in Schatten was Dr.

Ahn, on his way to the chapel, carrying books and frames and so peculiarly absorbed in the effort he damn near knocked me over. Which suited me just fine.

"I hoped I'd run into you," I said. "I see you've got almost as much energy as your invalid Prince."

It didn't stir him out of his abstraction. He just shifted a painting under his arm and said this was some of the art the Prince had brought back for the chapel.

"Your invalid Prince had a very active day in the city," I said.

"Oh, yes," he said, with a smile yet! "That's really in honor of your opening."

"How mysterious," I said. "Just exactly what do you mean?"

He groaned faintly but frankly. If it was an appeal to help him carry his chapel art, he had another groan coming. I waited. And he explained, bumping into me as he labored forward with his load, explained innocently that the Prince's license renewal was due immediately after the hotel opening and that the Prince, afraid he'd be too tired from his pageant exertions, had decided to get rid of the renewal first.

"Since he is so well," I said, "can I talk to him today?"

And now hold onto your hat.

"Oh, yes, your talk," my good abstracted Dr. Ahn said. "The Prince will be happy to meet you any time after next week."

"After next week!" I couldn't believe it. "You mean now it's going to be even later?!"

"The license business was a bit too much too soon," he said. "A little patience with our decrepitude. Pick any day after next week and he'll be delighted to have you for tea."

What threw me was the look he gave me; it had such an unexpectedly fraternal air. During my first days at Schatten he would have enjoyed springing a surprise like this on me. It would have been another display of courtly malice. But now, no more virtuoso sparring, no more extended-arm maneuvers, no more fine-honed conversational hostilities. And the button on his smock was still missing. He didn't even shave today, and the white dust on his chin was somehow a confiding negligence. He panted along at my side, his feet in step with mine. I think the inward side of his eyeballs, that watch those exclusive spectacles inside his head, just glimpsed *me* there for the first time. Irene—this crucial but unmentioned factor—seems to have become the premise of some crazy camaraderie. It's almost as if I heard him say, "Oh yes, I suppose now you're really one of us."

Of course the old gent may be off his rocker—or off it further than during my early weeks at the estate. Now he seems to assume some vast complicity between us; some difficult but rewarding enterprise into which he has gained me admission, which I don't comprehend as yet, nor am expected to, but where I've nonetheless been elected as participant. The son of a bitch. It's probably the biggest trick of all.

"Dr. Ahn," I said, "this is still another postponement—"

"Will you be a friend?" he smiled. "Help an old man at the end of his tether? Take those two books? I'm not what I used to be."

He breathed hard and his chin jerked at the volumes he meant. I took them from under his armpits. They were huge beautiful illustrated volumes of the Old Testament and didn't look like new imports of the Prince's. They looked like family Bibles which I seem to have seen somewhere in the hall before. He vanished, with his picture frames, into the chapel, then came back for the two volumes. The cunning bastard.

"Thank you," he said. "Tea, Tuesday, the nineteenth?"

"Dr. Ahn, I just ought to tell you that I can't indefinitely—"

"Oh, don't mope," he said, almost gently. "What's a few days to a young man?"

And then I was at liberty to go up and enjoy my lunch, which, like dinner, is almost always some form of beef stew. Frankly, I'm getting tired of that too.

Incidentally: had kind of an eerie dream, though while it lasted it wasn't eerie at all. It was quite stately and baroque. The Prince was sitting with his whole court on an enormously long willow branch above the lake, with scepter and crown just like a king, and the Nun at his side as princess, in a long flowing gown. And all the great guests from the great era were reclining against leaves, the Prince of Wales expansive in a lovely tintype-colored vest, and Byron with flowing hair, and archdukes in morning coats, all chatting in the lovely weather and the sun looking like a Louis Quatorze clock, radiating fluted rays made of antique gold—until suddenly the Nun saw me and gasped, "There he is!" And the Prince took her hand, with a casual smile, quite superior and amused. "Ah," he said, "I suppose he'll say we're illegal." He signaled with his hand, the entire assembly leaped off the branch into the lake and vanished without so much as a ripple. And I threw pebbles into the dark merciless water, furious and desolate and scared.

Now that I'm awake, it occurs to me that the water looked like beef stew.

October 12th

I've just made a few decisions. Number one, I've just worked out a new schedule allowing at least a week's delay even beyond the newly postponed Prince interview next Tuesday. We can still open fairly soon after construction ends. And if His Highness, better named His Sickness, yet further prolongs his indisposition, I'll have an alternative plan ready for a Schatten pageant that includes a salute to the Prince without the Prince's presence.

And if Dave objects—enter decision number two: if Dave objects, I'll just object to Dave. I'll quit. So long, Dave Dowle. Let Dave be Teddy Roosevelt without me. I won't even bother with Stockholm. It's been a cushy big-money job, and the only gadfly in the ointment, Dave, will get nicely swatted with this sudden exit. That final, unsafe cable will be a pleasure to draft. I've got a most desirable and, incidentally, talented woman waiting for me with whom monogamy should be quite painless. I'm healthy, tolerably young, with a nice little bundle in savings and stocks, not counting Nina's more sizable sock. Behold that clockwork gem, my life; poise and counterpoise crafted with dazzling exactitude. Behold the mathematical proof of my happiness. With those new decisions, career as well as love life are solved equations.

Seriously, not even the routine sex of marriage fazes me. That I've got licked too. I'm stocking up against it with my best affair yet, the crowning trophy of bachelorhood, over which I intend to gloat for years to come. I ought to stop being a gentleman sometime and put down the words that bring us to bed in the afternoon; her opening sallies (centered around the little gifts I bring) which have become much hotter and sharper; my answering moves which already touch her nipples and loins; the motion with which her buttocks flash out from under her smock, white and insidiously female and somehow sardonic in the tiny lingerie I bought her, her legs clasping and heaving me down to the lush death on the unicorn-embroidered sheets. It's an experience that ought to hold me for a while. My theory is that no woman is totally possessed by a man until she turns into a memory-fantasy he can freely manipulate in his mind, an ecstasy idealized and canonized. (Credit for some of these meta-erotica goes to Andy.) And I'm collecting images for a rich recollection: from the tiny tooth gap against which her tongue strains at the ripe point, down to her thighs which keep fluttering slightly, like a butterfly's wings, with the soft excited vulnerable furriness in the middle— fluttering when I withdraw and suddenly get up just to watch it flutter.

And afterwards, when she has dressed, she talks much more than she used to. This is also a satisfaction, another trophy. She talks about yew, of all things. The maze of yew hedge by the gate which she prunes with such passion. There's a secret about the pattern which she pointed out the other day from her window. These

hedges aren't just a formal French garden. They consti-
tute her "house." Honestly, her house. She's created out
of yew leaves the various architectural features of the
manor; each separately, and scattered across the lawn into
an entire little park; on one end she's clipped the pagoda
tower into existence; on the other, the arched entrance; in
between, the baroque roof; and now she's working on a
likeness of the chapel. All these forms are barely suggested, almost coded hieroglyphs of the things they
signify, and yet, now that she's given me the key, quite
discernible. That is, they are recognizable only from the
distance of her window. To me the "house" reveals itself
only from far away. When I'm near, it disintegrates into
odd configurations of clipped green.

But for her the damn "house" exists very exactly.
Often I find her working to the steady rhythm of the
pruning shears, her coifed head inclined sidewards in
appraisal, like a happy matron absorbed in the preening of
a happy home. In bed she can talk about it endlessly, with
a vibrant voice. To participate in the excitement somehow, my hand gathers up her skirt, and this reundressing
after she has redressed herself is more of a conquest than
our wildness earlier. I'm getting a whole course in evergreen gardening. She talks about the techniques of fighting nature into shape (shows me the shears' callus on her
thumb and has it bitten by me); talks about how the yew
must always be clipped a shade wider at the base—i.e.,
wider than is called for by the shape of the "house" part,
in order to give the base leaves sufficient sunlight. She
becomes animated, adorably illustrative, one hand being
the yew shape, the other wielding imaginary shears, her
tongue peeking out for a second in vicarious effort.

In all my time with her, even the most intimate phases,

this is perhaps the only time when her guard is down. She talks of how she's nursed the "house" along for years, protected its blossoms against hungry peacocks, the young leaves against her trampling dogs; and that she used to curse me silently during my first week for the cavalier way in which I used to walk on the low shoots. She'd actually been tempted to turn the water sprinklers on me.

We both laugh. Her cheeks grow hollow, lovely, with the sucked-in smile. My hand rests on the lambs' wool of her loin. But it might as well not be there. In the end her outpourings about the "house" always veer off into some remote inaccessible emotion. I try to get at it.

"All this excitement about hedge-cutting?" I say.

"Don't you know?" she says, raising her guard again lithely, casually. "Spinsters like to play house."

It's really of a piece with Ahn's self-absorption, this yew business, with Schatten's mystic ironic contemplation of its own mirror image. And you can't budge her from this inward surrealism into something relevant and concrete. Let me try to bring up, for example, the Prince's surprise visit to the city and the five days' delay it had cost me. Instantly she sweeps my hand away and begins to stroke Little White Riding Hood.

"Why," she says lightly, "you should have trapped the Prince while he was out there in the city. In your usual manner."

"Would you recommend the experience to him?"

"Oh, yes," she says. "It's priceless."

The infernal thing is that facetiousness becomes a wall around her which both invites and defies attack.

"Tell me," I say, "about your first husband, the first trapper."

She raises her S-curved eyebrows at me; the sucked-in smile flashes hard and cool. "Good God, it's all so ordinary," she says like a sardonic, superior nanny telling the same fairy tale for the thousandth time. "There's this mixed-up sixteen-year-old girl who knows nothing about the great world outside the gate. So she marries this—this appealing city man in the uniform and gets to know everybody and everything in the great world outside, and has everything and everybody until she can't stand it. And then she gets divorced. And then she finds out she's a mixed-up eighteen-year-old in the middle of a war. That's all. It happens all the time."

Said in a fashion that makes ridiculous any further, more detailed inquisition.

"And your Frenchman?" I say.

"Here." She sits up and gives me a card that has lain on her night table all along. A picture postcard from Beaulieu-sur-Mer, written in French in a slightly tremulous but fine large hand that can be read even in the uncertain light. It says the doctors have grown so optimistic about the undersigned, it looks as if he'll die a healthy man. Meanwhile, when will she ever collect the Mediterranean suntan waiting for her? And will she please shock him by answering within a year? . . . Poor man. Reduced to the same kind of facetiousness.

"Sounds like a nice fellow," I say.

"He's lovely," she says. "He saved the estate from the Russians."

"Was there anything else to your two? I mean, beyond knowing the great world and keeping out the Russians?"

"Such as?" she asks, smiling and stroking.

"Such as—what do they call it—love?"

She smiles. She leaves off stroking. For an answer, her head with all her long unfurled mane falls against my shoulder; my mouth feeds for minutes on the thick silk of her eyebrows with the extra little curve by the temple, and on her lips which continue to smile as they kiss. I bathe my face in her breath. I thrive on this silent declaration she seems to have made me. I live on it while she brings me my clothes, while I dress and am dressed, and walk down the snake-carved stairs into the afternoon's solitude.

But I can't live on it forever. Soon her thoughts oppress me. I mean the thoughts, silent, invisible, self-possessed, which move inside that lovely skull just a few millimeters below my kisses and which keep on moving imperturbably whether I'm close by or not. I can sense them glide past like fantastic clouds, like yew shapes more bizarre than she could ever sculpt. And when I'm many rooms away from her, I can feel those damn thoughts of hers move out of her skull and pursue me through the distance, still soundless, fantastic and laconic.

I think what bothers me most is that she's so damn offhand about the upshot of it all. She never even says "till tomorrow" or any less corny equivalent of such a phrase. With other women there was always a very carefully articulated assumption about the future. You might almost say that the woman gives the man her present in exchange for getting his future. Sometimes the bargain consists only of a vow or a promise, or only of some vague understanding, only the old "I'll see you again . . ." played by sweetly mendacious, basically just courteous violins. But it's always *something*. The pretense to a more permanent relationship is one of the amenities by which man civilizes lust; one of those tactful treacheries necessary between two animals who are able to talk and look into each other's eyes while their hips forge an ultimately impersonal ecstasy together. This pose of permanence constitutes the basic convention of the love affair, and in my experience it's always the woman who has invoked it. The woman, so goes the story, wants to own her partner, while the man is happier just borrowing his. And I hate her for not being like the story, for not having the slightest element of Nina or any of the others in her.

In fact, I've tried to use Nina against her, in retaliation. At the same Ku-damm store where I buy her little presents, I began to pick out more expensive items—to be sent to Nina. And then it came to me that by this I was trying to betray a strange woman called Irene, an intense, yew-pruning but incidental lay, with the woman I'm going to marry. Which is ridiculous.

I talk to her at length about my career strategy. That I intend to open the Berlin and Stockholm Dowles as the grand finale of my hotel career. How my real-estate agent meanwhile has combed the New York suburban area for a nightclub site and found and secured one for me. How I would foil boss Dave; that I wouldn't spend my life as a would-be great poet subsidized by and indentured to Dowle Inc.; that I'd taken a hardheaded inventory of my capabilities and decided to make the most of what is not a major talent but really a major flair; how I'd exploit it for my own benefit henceforth; how I needed Dave only for accumulating enough savings and enough reputation. That, in brief, I'd put an end to the arty stance Dave has constructed for me, a stance that let him milk me conveniently. That from now on I'd be my own Dave.

In all this fine coming clean—I also expound on the nightclub racket, and self-honesty concerning one's gifts, and the psychopathic climate of New York—in this frank parading of my plans, only the detail called Nina is missing. The career of Leon Spey stands as a solitary enterprise, with no indication that anyone else, any woman, might be crucial in it. Which omission is the point of the whole thing. That's the part I relish. It's my revenge on her. On *her* stubborn silence about several subjects, particularly about how this fling of ours is going to end. On all her withdrawals and withholdings. The days are ticking away.

And she, she lies on the bed next to me, Little White Riding Hood between us. She listens to me go on; sometimes she strokes the hair from my eyes, as one does perhaps with a little boy who gets needlessly upset. But I'm not upset. I couldn't be. I am, as I've demonstrated earlier, a happy man.

I should be such a happy man.

October 13th

Had a night out in Berlin. Honest and no kidding.

It's an odd chain of events, which started just as I was about to leave her room yesterday afternoon. She gave a small start and ran to the window. I hadn't noticed a thing, but she has antennae I couldn't even begin to grow. "Oh, no!" she said. I looked out the window and noticed, beyond the gate, the glass roof of a huge bus. I looked back at her—and she was already out the door.

I wanted to go with her, but still feel funny about being seen with her out there in the sunshine right after a tryst. So I waited in my room for a couple of minutes to give her a start. Then I went to the gate—or, rather, not to the gate itself, but behind a hedge right next to it.

Well, she and my old tray bringer (summoned God knows how) were defending the estate. It was two against a mob. The mob milled out of the bus, American sightseeing females with rhinestone-rimmed glasses and flowered hats, fierce alligator-clad cameras and wan guidebook-bearing husbands. Irene opposed them on the threshold of the half-opened gate. Every time a couple tried to come near, the old retainer staved them off by thrusting a picture postcard of the manor at them.

She said—a cool courtesy in her voice that was very much Papa Ahn—she said that she appreciated the interest of the ladies and gentlemen, but this happened to be the rest period of the inmates at Schatten estate, which could not be disturbed even by such exciting visitors from the United States, the doctor's orders. However, she hoped the postcards would be nice as souvenirs, and she was happy to point out a few interesting facts—and went into the same quick spiel about the gardens and the architecture which I got a few weeks ago.

Now I know that she'd glimpsed me behind the hedge and that bit about the exciting visitors from the United States was meant for me. But something else was for me, too. And just because she wasn't aware of it, it was entirely adorable. She spoke English, you see, the first time I've ever heard her speak English. Her vowels are very classy, testifying to some Oxonian nanny, but she has charming difficulties with consonants, which she tries to overcome by working those S-shaped eyebrows up and down, and by gesturing with her arms more than usual. There was an extra flourish of her tiny-nailed forefinger for every difficult *r*.

I thought she was exquisite. But our bus vandals didn't. They didn't appreciate her. Their cameras clicked right through her speech. Impatiently they fanned themselves with the picture postcards. One midwestern spokeswoman said they'd be so quiet, couldn't they sneak one look inside? "How about on tiptoe?" said another. "We'll take our shoes off!" And already there was a good deal of bending down and unbuckling till it was too much for me.

I wasn't going to let that horde come into our estate. I don't know exactly why, but suddenly I was out from behind the hedge, in front of them all.

"Excuse me, nurse," I said, combining vaudeville German with Dr. Kildare. "Emergency in the quarantine ward." (Working my own eyebrows up and down.) That in itself straightened up a good many shoe-unbuckling ladies.

She fell right in with me, gave me one of her famous sucked-in smiles. "You mean, what we have been fearing so much?"

I nodded. To avoid laughter, I whipped out my handkerchief, coughed into it, helpless, examined the result and rolled my eyes at it in the direst Uncle Julius fashion. Then I stepped backwards prophylactically from the crowd, which made the crowd retreat in turn, shoes tripping over shoes. It was a backward movement that gained momentum. Three minutes later we were left with nothing except a small litter of abandoned postcards.

She released her sucked-in smile. "Never mind you," she said. "I could have managed all myself."

She was still speaking English, perhaps because of the retainer who was picking up the postcards.

"Any time you want to be rescued again," I said, "just let me know."

"Actually?" she said. "All right, I shall cable you even to New York."

"Do," I said. And then, the retainer gone, I pulled her behind the hedge and we fell laughing into each other's arms.

"Tell you what," I said. "A victory celebration. We'll have dinner out."

She shook her head.

"Why not?"

The tiny-nailed finger pointed back to the manor. "I eat here."

"A great big victory dish like beef stew?"

"*Natürlich*," she said, relapsing into German. And all of a sudden I realized that she was escaping again, after having been especially close before.

"Look," I said. "Tell you what we'll do. We'll zip out for champagne and caviar in the city. At least, let's have victory hors d'oeuvre before your goddamn inevitable beef stew."

But she had retreated into hard diplomatic glitter. "Ah," she said, "you don't like beef stew any more? But I thought it was for beef stew that you crashed Schatten? Wasn't it for beef stew that you upset everything and everybody here? No? It isn't beef stew you're protecting from those bus people? Are you sure?" Her long gray eyes flashed with mock astonishment. "You mean you don't care for beef stew any more? You'll forget all about it in New York? You're ready to move on to something else? You see, beef stew always suffers in the end."

She'll launch so swiftly into her sardonic fantasies, she paralyzes any attempt at repartee. "Last chance," I said.

"Champagne and caviar."

"I'm sorry," she said.

"I'll have to have it all by myself then," I said.

She sucked in a cool smile and left the hedge.

"*Bon appetit*," she said.

Well, I did have it all by myself. That's how I had a night out in Berlin, all alone. I decided on that soon afterward in the library. Call it childish, but I felt quite distinctly that she'd treated me as though I were a bus vandal myself. I dropped everything, got my shaving gear from upstairs, taxied into town. It was the sudden aggravating feeling of not getting anywhere, not even beyond beef stew.

In town I took a luxurious room at the Hilton, lolled in the hot tub, enjoyed the most voluptuous champagne-caviar-lobster-crêpes-suzettes dinner at Dinny's, and no need to talk to Dinny for he was in Hamburg. I danced with one of the shepherdesses behind the bar, who turned out to be all woman and gave me unmistakable evidence thereof. I decided not to follow through, for sweet comfort's sake. Ended up with brandy, one of my rare cigars, and a delicious feeling of playing hookey.

I slept very well. There was a moment of panic when I woke up and discovered a sleek ceiling instead of the beams in my Schatten room. But my brain focused and I realized I'd be back at the estate by noon. Funny, it seemed hard to get used to shaving with running water again. And my poor driver goggled when he found me at Ida's office just as he was setting off to pick me up at Schatten.

The real pay-off came this afternoon, in her room. I

noticed her looking at me several times in ways she doesn't usually look at me. Not a word out of me about my brief sabbatical.

Finally, by the door, she said, "Was it nice, celebrating victory last night?"

"Very," I said. "Real Beluga caviar."

"Good for you," she said. "Of course one can see you didn't sleep here."

"How?" I said, surprised.

Her forefinger made a stab at my cheek where I had nicked myself slightly.

"You didn't shave here," she said. "So you hurt yourself."

And then she pushed me out playfully, but strong.

In my room I saw that the shaving nick had started bleeding again. She had stabbed that hard. And I got terribly gay. For the scratch itself is no clue at all to my whereabouts last night. I've often cut myself here at Schatten. No, she knows that I shaved elsewhere simply because she went to my room to check and saw my razor missing. She actually must have gone to my room last night after she found out—maybe from the dinner bringer—that I wasn't here. There's no other explanation. She really did, perhaps on her way up after romping the dogs. I'd have loved to see her tiptoe in.

If you add that to my good lobster, my night out is a smash hit. Who knows? Maybe I ought to be grateful to the bus mob.

October 14th

It promised to be such a lark. Little White Riding

Hood and friend should get a medal for being unwell.
Because the pups are so listless, I could offer to drive them
to a vet with her.

"No, they just need to be taken out a bit," she said. "I
can't walk the little creatures here. My big boys get so
jealous."

"All right, let's take them out for some gourmet shopping," I said. I was still mad at her beef stew. "Maybe you
could cook us up some fancy seafood for a change."

"Oh?" she said. "Just so you can jilt our beef stew?"

But she agreed! Even when I insisted that lunch be part
of the venture. That was at the gate this morning as I was
leaving. I had to work fast. First, bought her a discreet
dress (since she didn't have any "civilian" daytime
things), bought it at one of those plush hush-hush-car-
peted places off the Kurfürstendamm; the kind that's full
of the ulterior smiles salesgirls uncurl if you're a lone male
buying a dress whose size you're not sure about. I picked
a full-cut gray thing that would fit a tallish yew nymph.
It was so discreet it cost two hundred marks. Raced to
Schatten and gave it to her. Zoomed back into town, to
the office, to dust off some letters and get advice from the
Littel Partners on the right food market and the right
restaurant.

She was wearing the gray dress when I picked her up at
the gate shortly after noon. She too had prepared herself.
A dotted veil down to the bridge of her nose, falling from
a little round hat that was really rather Ida. Her hair was
rolled into a bun at the back of her neck. I think she tried
to match the townishness of the dress. Evidently she's
kept the Kaufhaus cosmetics, because there was powder
and lipstick on her face. Her face was hiding behind
them. She wears powder and lipstick as other women

might wear a domino mask to a costume party. And round the pups she had put the plastic coats.

It was all like the first time we sat in a car together. But now the occasion promised much less tension, much more fun. She was gay.

"Well," she said. "Where's the trap this time?"

It was a hot lovely day. Little White Riding Hood didn't even get car sick. And yet—so quickly bright things came to confusion.

I dropped her off at an enormous store near the Potsdamer Platz. It's called the Freedom Supermarket, being right by the Wall. According to the Littel Partners, it has the largest selection of gourmet foods in the city. I went on to a stationer's next door to select our local Dowle letterheads.

When I came out twenty minutes later we were already in some trouble. The area was jammed with cars sightseeing the Wall, and my limousine had been told to move on, official license plate notwithstanding. Karl-Heinz would never have let that happen; but the new driver, a trembling-nosed schlepp, quakes at the sight of a cop. I ordered him to double-park before the food store. I thought I'd be out with her in a minute.

Ha.

The jinx was on, the moment I entered the Freedom Market. The Freedom Market is an antarctic of seven thousand different frozen fruit juices, frozen ducks, nearly everything in the animal and vegetable kingdom killed, cut up and frozen, the fractured carcasses arranged into a whole landscape, illuminated by frozen fluorescent lights and reflected by hundreds of chill mirrors. This snowy continent is organized in traffic centers, with crossings and one-way lanes along which upper-class

Prussians march like performing penguins behind shopping carts. Everywhere the chill fog of a loudspeaker voice announcing the special of the day, which happened to be frozen salmon, detailing in precise Berlinese not only the price but the entire biological profile of the species, *piscus salmonicus* or whatever, its habitats, mating and emigration cycles, all of which apparently contribute to its eating and freezing qualities.

In this droning, traffic-rule-observing icescape I picked her out immediately. You really couldn't miss her. Her dress was too large. I'd gotten her the wrong size. At Schatten she looms taller than she really is. The Kaufhaus pumps, whose heel she claimed she'd fixed, made her limp slightly. Being a virgin to supermarkets, she was quite innocent of shopping carts. In one arm she'd gathered up a dozen cans, the other was busy with the pups. She stood out much more than she ever had at Dinny's that evening. In a night club she blended better, if only because it was dark and one of her essential ingredients is night. But now, in this daytime frigidity, this consumers' concentration camp, she looked like a childlike savage, ill-fitted into a grown-up's dress, her tongue feeling the unaccustomed lipstick, frolicking with the little dogs.

"*Alors*," she said. She always speaks French to dogs. "*Cherchez-là!*"

"What's going on?" I said.

"I want to make pike in beer sauce for my father," she said. "He hasn't had it for years."

"That's what we are here for," I said. "To get away from beef stew."

"But you can't find anything in this mad place."

I was thinking what the people in this mad place would say about Schatten.

"Did you try the information phone?"

"Where?"

The Freedom Market has prominent black telephones all over, with an operator to give you the exact longitude and latitude of each item. She hadn't even seen the phones. She hadn't noticed the shopping carts. I wonder if she ever tried shopping before 4 a.m. There was no contact between her and the reality here.

Instead she stood by a huge revolving rack of cereals. One of her gloves was hung on a narrow package at the bottom; she'd rotate the rack with a push, and the pups would start chasing after it with a tiny yap and catch the glove triumphantly as the rack slowed down. Once they're outside Schatten, the pups really seem to revive.

"*Cherchez!*" she said happily, while the penguin Prussians goggled all around.

"Christ," I said. I got her a shopping cart, phoned for the location of the items she wanted, begged her to hop to it and rushed out. Outside, the limousine had been told to move on again, as I'd feared. I had to wait till it came around the block and instructed it to keep circling.

By the time I came back, her cart was full of cans and packages, the pups crouched on top of the heap.

"Carts are fun," she said as she sped past me. She romped with the shopping cart the way she romps with her big dogs at night. Penguins scattered left and right before such imperious velocity, the figurehead pups parting them like waves. She raced up a one-way lane the wrong way, headed for the *Below 50 Marks* check-out counter though her load was plainly beyond that amount, and, as a nice topper, zoomed past all the waiting customers right to the head of the line.

Such a thing probably never happened before in modern German history. The counterman opened his mouth at her. He got a casually devastating glance.

"*Couchez!*" she said to the pups, who promptly jumped off the cart. Within two seconds she had established a kind of diplomatic immunity, an immunity from all Freedom Market rules. "All right," she said to the counterman, who closed his mouth. To everybody's astonishment, including no doubt his own, he began to check out her purchases. The flouted line of penguins didn't mutiny, just sighed.

Me too. The more I know her, the less I get used to her; to those leaps into grave radical play of which she is constantly capable. You never know what sudden but dead-serious game those long gray eyes will spring on you—the sixteen-year-old wanting to put a hundred roses into a hundred doorknobs, or the child bride throwing herself into swastika glamor up to a 4 a.m. extreme, or an older bride assuming French seigneurdom, or playing the most mysterious game of all at Schatten with her yew shears. She has such a way of being irresistibly, sternly willful. The shaky heel didn't keep her from limping masterfully out the supermarket door.

But it wasn't my day or hers.

The Littel Partners had organized a portable icebox in which we stored the stuff in the car. Which is how we discovered that the pike she particularly wanted, all six pounds of it, had disappeared in the shuffle. The counterman must have revenged himself on behalf of all the lined-up penguins. The lined-up penguins always will be revenged in the end. And we couldn't get back to the market because it closes on Wednesday afternoons. And Little White Riding Hood looked very fatigued.

I promised to retrieve the pike tomorrow. We drove on to lunch. At least the restaurant seemed to be all the Littel Partners had promised. It overlooked Lake Wannsee, an expanse of fluted light-blue water, rimmed with pines and full of that rustic Scandinavian grace which sometimes surprises you in Berlin. The weather was unseasonably warm. For the first twenty seconds everything seemed perfect.

But at the entrance we met a woman with a very stylish blond turret of hair.

"Irene!" she said. She was quite handsome, in a sexy white beach robe and very white high heels. "Why, Irene," she said. "We were talking about you, just the other month. Someone said you'd gone back to Schatten. I said it couldn't be, you were still in France. You live in Cannes, don't you, that marvelous place?"

"I live in Schatten," Irene said.

Then the other woman saw me and, I suppose, the black limousine.

"Such a nice surprise, my dear!" she said and went up and briskly delivered on my Nun's cheek a methodical American cocktail buss. Rather a mistake, because I noticed from close up the many tiny burst veins under her make-up; and the robe split and revealed a two-piece bathing suit much too small for a well-fed flabby figure. The kiss was also a mistake, because Irene not only didn't introduce me but began to walk right on.

The other woman was surprised but also impressed. "Lovely to have met you!" she called after us, and walked toward a huge white car with a driver standing by the door. "Herbert!" she shouted to make sure we saw what *she* had. "Herbert, are you ready?"

I thought it was quite amusing.

"Someone from your French era?"

"No," she said. "That's what she'd like you to think. No, that's one of the great social queens from the 'thirties here."

Then a waiter took us down to the dining-and-sun terrace by the shore. The place is obviously quite fashionable. It would have been pleasant except for "the college people," as the waiter called them. The college people— young smooth-skinned editions of Irene's flabby friend, all white bikinis and white high heels—hung across chairs and tables in desperate contortions to catch the October angles of the sun. They swamped the terrace with askew feet, navels, bosoms, shaved armpits, limbs so densely mingled they seemed communal, not personal property. Each blond-turreted head had a transistor radio pressed against it, each set giving forth the same cacophonic Schönberg symphony. To a chorus of electronic keening the college people chewed gum, adjusted halters, oiled backs, sipped vodka and lit cigarettes with fingers borrowed from the communal pool of hands.

We sat wedged between them at the one free table left. I cursed the sun and hated the Littel Partners. It was worse than the Freedom Market. And the hot sun made us too inert to leave, particularly since our orders had already been taken.

"That cheek-kissing," she said suddenly. "It's the thing now, isn't it?"

"Oh, yes," I said.

"My friend does it well," she said. "She does everything well in its time."

She stroked Little White Riding Hood and asked for a cigarette.

"Everybody is having such fun," she said. She blew smoke at the white bikinis. She was in a sulfurous mood. The whole excursion had gone sour, and I didn't know what to say. To the consternation of the waiter she threw the barely lit cigarette into the lake. "These sunburned darlings here," she said, "they're having such fun too. They'll never get tired. That was the trouble with me. Fun got me so damn tired in the end."

She leaned her head against my shoulder. A parody of both exhaustion and devotion. She gets these acid half-tones into her gestures. But I also have a hunch that she hid her face against my shoulder because she didn't want me to see it.

Sitting in the blatant sunlight, among such blatant youth, she looked what she was: almost middle-aged. The schoolmarm hair bun accented it, and the deep vertical line in the forehead which frowned under the brightness, and that much-too-long dress which was my fault. Here she couldn't run or romp, fall into the élan that can still fling her into beauty. Her tongue kept scraping the lipstick off her lips.

"You know that big white car of hers?" she said. "It looked like an ice-cream truck!"

Our trout arrived at long last, with a much too salty sauce and miniature Austrian flags stuck into their gills. Evidently the management spotted us as foreign tourists because of my Viennese accent and my companion's unfamiliar get-up. The management himself appeared, and as a special favor to us visitors from the Danube began to tell us—against a background of Schönberg dissonances and bronzing crotches—that the very place

where we now ate oversalted trout had once been Dr.
Goebbels' personal (wink) hideaway. Confident that this
tidbit would thrill and please no end, he began to amplify.
The seductions of the demon *Doktor* were detailed with
the same precision as the mating cycle of salmon at the
Freedom Market. When I got the bill I realized that Dr.
Goebbels' past titillations contributed much to the present level of prices, at least as far as Austrian tourists were
concerned.

The management, to show that its services continued
beyond the passing of money, escorted us as we got up; it
then began to launch into the frolics of a Goering visit. I
saw that she had picked up the miniature Austrian flag
from her trout and that her jaw twitched perilously. But I
found no way to stop the flow of managerial anecdote.
She lifted the emblem and suddenly stuck it into the
nearest bikini bottom. She did it with the same offhand
casual effrontery that used to paralyze me. It paralyzed
the management. We left it standing aghast before the
deed. No one else had noticed, being too absorbed in sun
and Schönberg. The stuck girl apparently was what she
seemed; namely, brown foam rubber. In the absence of
flesh or nerve, she just scratched herself vaguely in the
neighborhood of the flag-planting and turned up the
screech volume by her ear. The last I saw, the Austrian
colors still waved proudly from the buttock.

It may seem funny now. It didn't occur to us to laugh.
Little White Riding Hood got sick as soon as the car
started. She massaged the pup. Suddenly, in the last five
minutes of the ride, she tore off the wrapping of some
gum she'd dug up God knows where, began to chew it

and, chewing, put her head against my shoulder once more. She put it there with such noncommittal abandon, in full view of the rear-view mirror, in cold sardonic imitation of the college people; it didn't warm, it froze my heart. I didn't know what to do, especially before the driver's furtive and puzzled eyes.

She didn't withdraw her head when the car stopped in front of Schatten, not even when the driver came around to open the door. She chewed; her soft hair kept pushing rhythmically against my shoulder. She kept sitting there as though she didn't want to get up and return to the estate. I'm not sure of that, of course; just as I'm not sure whether, when she got up at last, there wasn't swimming in each of her eyes a very bitter drop.

Maybe it's just me and the aftertaste of that oversalted sauce and my whole rotten mood.

October 15th

Helmut, Jacques and Leon. Tom, Dick and Harry. Kraut, Frog and Semi-Yank. No. 1, No. 2, No. 3, me. In less than a month it'll be all over. I'll be in Sweden. That'll be the last of her No. 3. Unreal, in a way. But maybe the unreal thing is the prejudice we have against endings. A typical prejudice of the romantic Western individualist. We always want to begin—nothing else. The rest is so unpleasant. And we forget that every beginning is the continuation of an ending.

And even if we don't forget, it doesn't do any good.

Anyway, today I did it. I'd meant to keep in reserve this drug thing of her No. 1. But it slipped out just the same. She was talking about her gardening problems, and I asked why she didn't go back to her Frenchman on the Riviera, away from all that toil.

Those gray eyes can become very cool and impervious and amused.

"You mean," she said, "back to a lot of young white bikinis?"

And resumed talking about the garden, particularly about the chapel shape she was pruning into the yew, talked so blithely past and through me that I sprung it on her, about her SS husband's dope conviction. Just to make her come to.

"Oh," she said, stopped in her tracks for the second time, but amiably. "When did you get wind of that?"

"Someone showed me a clipping."

"You look upset." Suddenly she laughed. "My Frenchman was relieved when he found out."

"Relieved?" I said. Apparently the surprise was on me.

"It's how I discovered my Frenchman is a diabetic," she said. "I always thought he took no sugar to stay slim. So when I told him about Helmut's problem he said, 'Ah, that was very interesting of your husband. The men that need the needle cannot be dull. He had the heroin. I have the insulin. You should only have husbands like that.' That was his proposal!" She laughed.

"I couldn't even propose," I said. "No heroin. No insulin. I don't even qualify."

When she laughs, low and slow, the vertical furrow in her forehead shows. A strange, frowning laugh. And when she kisses or copulates, does what is for other women serious, there is a faint grin on her lips. She has a built-in contradiction; that is, a built-in distance, which I can't ever seem to overcome.

I asked: "Was No. 2 ever jealous of No. 1?"

"Jacques? He doesn't care about dead rivals. He's very Gallic about it."

"I'm not so sure I am," I said.

"All right," she said. "I'll do to you what I did to my two others."

She stabbed her forefinger, hypodermic-like, at my thigh. And laughed once more.

After which we took up again the matter of pruning yew.

The ornery thing is that this isn't the first time she has referred with such crisp contempt to the white bikinis and all the other ridiculousnesses of our outing the other day. As if it proved conclusively the folly of the outer world.

But to me the trip now tastes sweet in retrospect, quite apart from the fact that the Freedom Market contributed to the meal variety here. When you think of all the disasters that day, it becomes unreasonably delightful when I look back on it now. Perhaps the delight was in the juxtaposition of contrasts—her, and the ordinary non-Schatten daylight world. Perhaps I should arrange the juxtaposition again and again, until the novelty and therefore the charm wears off. Perhaps that's how this thing is going to end. Perhaps I should whisk her away with me to Stockholm and expose her daily to common daylight until the juxtaposition and therefore she become as ordinary and boring as—as her pruning of that everlasting yew.

October 16th

It's damn white of Schatten to let the clothes worn on the estate become dirty with time, just as clothes do at more ordinary places. It's reasonable that these clothes, coming back torn from some machine laundry, must be mended and that Irene is the only woman in the place young enough to put thread through a needle. But must these clothes be mended on my time? They must. Madame has excused herself for today. No tryst. And I said okay. The trouble with me is that I'm too proud to beg, but not too proud to boil. Does Madame intend to become difficult at the very end? I think all good breeding in a woman can be summed up in a simple injunction: You don't have to say yes. But if you do, don't welch. Fuck.

Not every blasted entry has to be about her. There are other women in my life, right here in Berlin. Her mother, for instance. Old Frau Dr. Ahn has taken to staring at me lately. Eyes steeped in some deep watery plea. When I return the glance, she drops hers about eight inches to my collarbone and slowly walks away. This afternoon she even showed up in the library after lunch. I found her before the Prince's portrait, giving his Highness the same beseeching glance.

For all I know, she beseeches any old thing that comes along. But her focus on the picture reminded me of *Edw. v. Priske '57*, the painter's signature in the corner. Dave's cables have been yapping for a new *Edw. v. Priske* portrait of the Prince, Constable's fee for the Duke of

Wellington and all that. The Littel Partners, it so happens, dug up *Edw. v. Priske* in the current Berlin phone book, but found his number busy all morning. To make a long story short, I went to see *Edw. v. Priske* about five seconds after Frau Doktor turned around in the library and began to supplicate my collarbone.

I just didn't feel like mooning around with the old lady while her daughter did her super-important unpostponable mending. I didn't care to be in Schatten at all during those needlework hours. It was too galling. I wanted to get away.

I got away all right. You would expect an old-fashioned Prussian society painter to live in some sort of small version of Schatten. Well, *Edw. v. Priske*'s phone-book address turned out to be a smooth pink Miami Beach hotel façade, with the lobby inside full of mosaic-tiled pillars. Switch one. Switch two: it wasn't a Miami Beach hotel but an old-age home. An old-age home that thinks real young. Another case of our good friends, the Germans, taking a carefree American trend and making a fine upstanding obsession out of it. Switch three: *Edw. v. Priske* doesn't exist any more. Only his widow of five years' standing does, but she insists on listing her husband's name in the phone book and the home as her private address. The gum-chewing person conveying this intelligence lounged behind a switchboard full of busy signals and made a slight head motion implying, "Don't even try her, brother."

I did, just the same. It was early. Rather than mope around the blasted mother-mending estate, I thought I might as well get an additional angle on our elusive Prince.

Poor Frau v. Priske, my second other woman of today.

She sat in her room, in a contemporary nightmare of a pink pastel cubicle, rinsed with tinny "Tea for Two" music by some hidden and unrelenting loudspeaker. She sat on a kind of sling chair and with the sleeve of her shapeless black dress polished a ring on her finger. There was something in her motion which made me think that she had polished all day for the last five hundred days. When she became aware of my entrance, she got up and with no change of expression extended her arm. Her hand rose, showing that it still retained the automatic expectation of being kissed. Her face registered nothing when this didn't happen, and nothing when I introduced myself and asked about her husband's experience with the Prince. She was deaf. I had to repeat myself several times. I had to shout. Suddenly her wrinkles panicked. It was the damnedest thing. It was as though she'd just realized that *Edw. v. Priske* had, by sheer inadvertence, kicked me in the balls years ago and then died without setting the matter straight; and that the delicate and urgent task of apologizing was now left to her.

"Oh! . . ." she said. "That! . . . Yes, you see, you must understand, my poor husband . . . after the war . . . there was nothing. So when he got the Schatten commission . . . you see? . . ." She spoke with a fine lisp which must have been a social asset fifty years ago, and she cupped my elbow in her palm faintly, unconsciously, to make me understand whatever phantom thing she was trying to elucidate. "You see? . . . And they paid double for it at Schatten. . . . They were so lovely to him. . . . He was already sick and they took care of him. . . . And before he died he told me, 'It wasn't a wrong thing. It was a special thing.' . . . That's all. It was a special thing."

I was caught by her tone. I tried to get her to explain that special thing. But I couldn't get through. She forged ahead deafly, blindly, cupping my elbow. "You see? . . . That's why he did it. And then they paid up in this . . . this modern institution here for our lifetime. . . . Such lovely people. . . . You see? . . . It was a special thing."

A squat squalid nurse appeared with a face saying, "Go." I went. The old lady came out of the sling chair, still talking beneath the loudspeaker drizzling "Tea for Two." To bring the interview to some sort of close, I took her hand after all and raised it to my lips. It smelled faintly of pine soap.

After all of which no one is wiser, only a little more uncomfortable. A trend summing up the progress of civilization.

Down with mending and with manners. What's a love affair without a scene? I should have made one with my inamorata. It was an awful afternoon without her. I should have made a great big broiling scene that would have ended in fornication, the best reconciliation there is. We should have stood in bed. And so should humanity.

October 17th

There's something unkosher about Schatten Sundays. No office to go to. No regular weekday charades to be watched from my window. They all hide in the chapel or in their chambers. I pace in my room.

Today was a champion Sunday. You simply can't get any more unkosher than today. Its over-all premise was rain. Slow rain, slimy rain, wretched rain, dabbling everywhere against walls and leaves. The kind of rain that brings restlessness to a perfect pitch.

Impossible to stroll in the garden; or to go up to her before three. I cruised the stairs and the corridor several times. No life visible, except the guardian dogs lying curled on the upper steps. I worked on a cost estimate for the Casino, combining Andy's Norman façade with Dinny's exotic ideas for interior decor. To put it more precisely: I *tried* to work. It's not that I ache for her every second. It's just that I know her weekday routine pretty well by now (it gives me peace to know *where* she is) but her Sundays aren't nearly so well charted.

All of a sudden, KarlHeinz. Like on that other Sunday. Walking on the main path, right through my view from the window. His clothes announce his new stature: gray belted raincoat, a sharply brimmed fedora with a hatband as blond as his little beard; leather gloves. A walk suggesting whip and riding breeches. A whole new Karl-Heinz walk which took him straight to the manor entrance.

I went down. Don't ask me why. His Sunday cemetery visits were familiar. And it was natural, his coming into the house to wait out the downpour. He looked satisfyingly drenched even in that regimental raincoat. His company was still no great treat. But I guess at that moment he was a welcome disturbance of my solitude. Any diversion would do.

When I reached the hall, he seemed to have left again. I looked into the kitchen corridor to make sure he hadn't ducked into the service entrance. Everything was lifeless there. When I came out again I found him.

He stood in an alcove next to her. Yes, next to her, though I hadn't heard her descend. She examined a fountain pen which seemed to have just run out of ink. His hands were thrust into the trenchcoat pockets. He took them out to greet me.

"Good morning," I said. "Looking for me?"

"Oh, no, suhr," he said. "I would not bother you Sunday. It's just about my uncle's grave."

"He wants to plant a flower border," she said, putting down the pen. "We've got to forward the request through our little bureaucracy here."

"A flower border," I said, in exactly her easy tone. "That's very nice and pious of him."

He took his hat off the table and with a small bearded smirk shook a few raindrops to the floor. "All the other graves have it, suhr," he said. "Before, I couldn't afford it."

"Our friend here has been promoted," I said to her. "Did you congratulate him?"

"Yes," she said. "Yes, I did."

"Good-bye, suhr. Good afternoon," he said. And I stood my ground until he had put on his hat again, and walked to the door, and vanished just as the others returned from Sunday chapel under black clouds of umbrellas.

I know their lives never touch except, possibly, transiently during these Sunday visits. It's the only time he enters the estate, and she, of course, never goes into the city. There's no possible meaningful connection. But all through lunch I was persecuted by the image of those two side by side, her slender aloof figure and, next to her, the belted dripping creature abruptly materialized like a monster out of a well. My brain probed that image as the tongue probes an abcessed tooth. Each touch fanned the inflammation. Each time the two faced me with a little more of that extra braced motionlessness of people who have just conducted secret business together.

My watch said three at last, and let me go upstairs. The image clung; not even our meeting could erase it. On most days I catch my first close-up sight of her when I walk into her room. The encounter in the alcove had poisoned that magic. Little White Riding Hood wasn't in good shape either; it lay on a pillow with a troubled little belly and in a tragicomic yawpy manner tried to bark like a grown-up dog. Our laughter wasn't quite right. We retreated into passion.

Afterwards I didn't let her get the pup. I took her arm and laid it across my eyes. The image still persisted: she holding the fountain pen in the alcove, he a bare two feet away, dripping. I was sick of all these weeks of prevarication.

"I've got another three weeks here," I said. "Then Sweden."

There was a pause. Her arm tensed just slightly. "How interesting for you," she said. "All this traveling."

"After that I'll be in Berlin only for the opening, for two days, that's all."

"Doesn't give you much time, does it?" she said in that maddeningly neutral manner she can assume.

"I have to be in Stockholm the second week in November," I said.

"Oh, yes," she said. "You've got your new palace there."

"Will you come with me to Stockholm?"

There was a pause. Her arm tried to remove itself from my face. I didn't let it. I had finally touched on the forbidden.

"Are you giving me a vacation?" she said, perhaps not as lightly as she wished.

"We'd have another six weeks in Sweden," I said. "We could see how it goes. We could take it from there."

She gave a gray, derisive, toneless chuckle.

"You could stay with me," I said. "But it has to be planned now. I want to count on it."

"Come to Stockholm," she said in the same horrible tonelessness, "the Venice of the North."

"Irene—"

"One glides in the canals."

"You aren't answering me."

"One trails through the waters. And opens other palaces. There's no end to the pleasures of the great outside."

"If you don't want to discuss it," I said, "tell me."

"There must be gondoliers in Stockholm. Blond viking gondoliers—"

"Listen to me," I said. I didn't let her withdraw her arm.

"Come to Stockholm —"

"I am going to take you there," I said.

"My arm hurts," she said. "Please."

"I want a real answer."

Her arm tried to escape. I clamped it down against my face, and she tried again, and then again, and underneath her skin I felt a fury mounting. Good, I thought. I wanted to provoke her more. Her and myself. I didn't let go.

"I want you to come," I said. "I want you to get away from here. And I'd like an answer, please. Now."

"Now!" The word was catapulted at me sardonically, the loudest I'd ever heard her say. "*Now!*" Her arm no longer pulled away, but suddenly tightened; her other arm became a sudden vicious constriction around me. Like a rush of pythons, her legs coiled around me. Her mouth pulled at mine—and suddenly she gave me what I've always wanted but never have been able to tap in her, not till now: a flinging away of all control and caution, a liberating panic which let me drill and crush blood-red dreams out of her, all the brute treasures finally quarried from the flesh. We had no mercy; destroyed and re-created each other. And she didn't grin.

Little White Riding Hood had fled with the other pup into a corner and whined at us in fright. On the other side of the room the crossless Saviour floated by the window sill, his arms reddening with sunset.

She had moved out of bed for her clothes. The room took a long time falling into place, into echoes of the afternoon tea music. My wristwatch said, amazingly, ten minutes after five. It was a full hour beyond my usual time.

I slipped into my clothes. This time, no oriental odalisque for my dressing ceremony. I felt strange in the room which is so very much the opposite of a boudoir. The collection of old riding whips on one wall, and on the other nothing but a huge calendar that showed etchings of Afghan hounds; by the window the crossless Jesus, and near it a huge mottled mirror framed in birchwood, and the carved beamed ceiling brooding over all. It looks like the chamber of some eccentric, melancholy young sport. I remember feeling for her that moment not only new desire but an enormous and strangely wistful fondness.

She came back from the bathroom. Her eyes were still wet. She dressed herself. The subsiding sighs shook her and sounded in her throat. They diminished but continued when she went to the mirror. She disdained to suppress them as she stood straight, her arms raised, combing her hair, pyramiding it and fixing her coif with precision, shaken now and then almost proudly by a sobbing breath.

I found it hard to break through the silence. As I rolled down my sleeves I found on my right arm, above the wrist, a round dark blemish, something like a tattoo.

"Yes," she said suddenly. "Here." She led me to the gas lamp. The blemish was not only a tooth print; it was a suck mark of terrific force which hadn't broken the skin but caused a respectable little hemorrhage.

"That'll last over a month," she said.

"Irene—"

"All the nice canal weeks in Stockholm."

"Will you come?"

"It's late. Go down."

"Think it over—"

"You'll have to keep it covered, my dear," she said, harsh and smiling, and pulled my sleeve down hard to the wrist. And opened the door, and let herself be shaken slightly, disdainfully, by another sound in her throat, and smiled, and pushed me out.

And, as though nothing had happened, it's still raining the same lazy rain.

HINDSIGHT

My brain keeps harping on those final twenty-four hours, even today. There's a good reason for the magnetism of the past: the past is so beautifully irretrievable, so comfortably beyond challenge, so nicely tucked away beyond the reach of volition or alteration. I think it's the past's certainty we are so nostalgic for—that is, for its very deadness. It's such a safe thing to be thrilled about.

The journal has nothing to say the next day, the last day. I think I know why. I awoke confused, scared, with an immense new commitment brewing. I stayed away from the journal because I wanted to stay away from her, at least from conscious focus on her. I was wary of introspection, of touching the commitment that waited inside me, enormous but unarticulated, unborn. Making a decision can be murder. Sometimes it's worse still to face a decision already made. Her suck mark tingled on my wrist.

Actually the uproar into which I walked at Ida's made it easy for me. To begin with, it was so diverting. The whole office ran a rousing temperature. KarlHeinz was the only calm person; whistling faintly, he was fixing up a desk of his own behind the espresso machine. The Littel Partners' print dresses were at their brightest and most jittery, couldn't be calmed no matter how often they smoothed them down. Dinny was present—a rare treat—huddling with Ida and italicizing with SOS intensity some *mar*velous fact about Frederick the Great's palace in Old Berlin.

At my entrance they all froze.

"My dear Leon," said Ida from behind a faintly trembling cigarette holder. And then she told me the news. That the Prince had just matched our bid for the Casino site, the very site he had sold to the city years ago. That he was bound to get it, since municipal law gave preference to German citizens and Mr. Dowle was non-German; and that this was too much, we were too good for such shabby games, it was not *oo*worth it any more.

To stall for time I asked how she knew.

"Oh, my littel intelligence service. The same as with the hotel-license renewal. The same as never getting an interview—"

"The interview is now set for this Tuesday—"

"My dear Leon, there will be nothing Tuesday! There will never be anything, no Casino, no hotel opening— that *oo*woman there destroys everything. No, we don't put up with this—"

And Dinny, interrupting, wouldn't either, not for another *mo*ment. No, it had to be Frederick the Great. Switch the opening theme to Frederick's court, the golden age of Berlin culture. *The* thing. Frederick's reception of Voltaire. Mr. Dowle as Frederick. Or Mr. Dowle as Voltaire—

I didn't hear the end because I was on the phone, putting through a top-urgent long-distance call to Dave's real-estate vice president, Abe Vierer, in New York, and a local one to our lawyer in Berlin. I didn't dream of giving up Schatten. Everything had exploded so beautifully into the open. In the explosion the commitment to her had been born. I'd go off with her, for good.

Our lawyer was a doll. He instantly proposed to file a new Casino-site bid on behalf of the one Dowle corporation (there are three Dowle companies in Germany) having German citizenship, promised to pull some fast strings within the day. Then long distance cut in with Abe Vierer.

It was five thirty a.m. at Beekman Place and Abe dead with sleepiness when I came down on him with my life-or-death urgency to up-the-Casino-bid-or-kill-the-whole-Berlin-operation-and-no-time-to-cable-Dave-old-boy. The sonofabitch had enough presence of mind to switch on his phone tape-recorder, beep, beep. I had to repeat the whole statement together with a few additions dictated by Abe. Only then did I get my authorization for an additional sixty thousand dollars and was called old boy in return by Abe. Such is the stuff Dowle vice presidents are made of. I got back to our lawyer with the newly raised bid, and when I finally hung up— there stood Uncle Julius in front of me. He must have burst in through the unguarded anteroom minutes ago.

Not that a single soul took notice. Every iota of shock the office could summon was collectively leveled at my head. They all stared at me, at the ogre who instead of stopping the Schatten madness had now continued and compounded it. The Littel Partners clutched their curls. Ida bumped her gloved fist against the espresso machine.

And Dinny gave away that those red bangs of his were toupee after all. He produced a wonderfully scented handkerchief and in mopping his hairline dislocated it slightly. Uncle Julius watched, and sniffed his eau de cologne, astounded.

"What? . . . Who is that?" he asked me, pointing.

Poor Julius. Some two thousand of Ida's sharpest little teeth spat at him. "Mr. Spey is in a business conference! Thank you for immediately! waiting outside!"

Poor Julius turned white, pressed his glasses back and retreated, still sniffing helplessly the strange handkerchief smell. His nephew loved him. Not, I'm afraid, for any humanistic reason, but because he was such a godsend of an escape ladder.

"Excuse me," I said to the office. "A family matter. I'll call you." And before indignation could collect itself and strike, I walked out with my dear old uncle.

Andy may be right in calling me a cold fish. But I bet warm fish never experience the thrill of the thaw to which my kind are privileged. Having it out with Ahn or the Prince had become quite minor next to going off with her for good. Repeat: for good. Not just Stockholm. For good. The genius eloping. That's what the commitment amounted to. It was ridiculous, banal and intoxicating. The naked heedlessness of the prospect rubbed so strange and new against the grain of my experience. It wasn't just running away with her, but letting an impulse run away with *me*, which seemed incredible and exhilarating. Irene and I on a plane together, her long hair furled against the cloud window—image after image brushed along my spine with vertiginous sweetness. The

advantage of being a cold fish is that you can be de-
flowered again and again by emotion and particularly by
rank sentiment. Sentiment remains a rare foreigner who
brutalizes, puzzles and delights each time as if it were the
first. That afternoon I rode the crest of a golden shock. I
warmed toward all the welcome wild leaps in the world.

Naturally I had no office limousine. It took us half an
hour to flag down a taxi in the midday rush. Nothing
bothered me. Not even my inevitable uncle. I couldn't
just dump him after making use of him at Ida's. And
though he clung, he was more quiet than usual. Several
times during the cab ride he turned to me, only to pull
back from some dark edge of utterance, to content
himself with a cough and violent adjustment of his
glasses. I loved him. He was my mascot, the mascot of a
regiment that goes off singing into battle.

Arrived, we walked through the green silent gardens at
Schatten. In the manor, in my room, no lunch was
waiting for me. An unprecedented negligence. Nothing
bothered me. But Julius was disturbed by the absence of
food. He began to dredge his pockets murmurously. A
sardine can surfaced, and a rusty can opener. The opener
broke at his first try, the can clattering to the floor.

"It's . . . it's a sign," he said suddenly. "It should be
taken from me."

"How's that?"

"My project. It should be taken from me. I'm not
equipped to be the leader."

He rubbed his broken opener with a kind of glowering
helplessness.

"I thought about it. All by myself it would never

work. I'm too clumsy. Too rude—"

"Not a bit, Uncle—"

"I insulted your friend with the strange smell—"

"He's not my friend—"

"And I insulted you—that time. I always have fights."

"Don't worry about it, Uncle. Today you did me a favor."

"No, I always make a spectacle of myself. People get angry. All these wonderful projects, and I destroy them with a spectacle. I thought about it. You're so excellent with people. I should make you co-chairman in charge of—of Relations."

"That's very sweet. But as you know—"

"And the Prince could be there too, at the Old Testament Community. Honorary chairman. Or Emeritus—"

"The Prince!"

I took a deep breath and told myself that since I was going off with her, Julius wasn't half as absurd as I.

"Uncle," I said, "the Prince—"

"He can live like in Schatten. I've thought about it. I mean, away from the world and from wickedness, but without the Spider around him. It doesn't matter he's a Christian. It shows we are tolerant. And he's good for prestige—"

"But, Uncle," I said, "the Prince is old and very hard to get hold of, very difficult. That's what the commotion at the office was about."

"You could explain to him. It would be like Schatten, only better. I mean, even the Pope went to Israel. You could wind him around your little finger. You've got this—this glamorous way. We have the means now—"

"Uncle Julius," I said. "Remember our argument last time? The whole thing is financially unrealistic—"

He bent down for the dropped sardine can, but mid-way in the motion fell into a chair. Only then—pretty late in the day—I noticed. He was white, ashen-white. His stubble looked about two thousand years old. There'd been none of the usual business with nuts or shells or apples.

"My God," I said. "You idiot, did you have another ulcer attack?"

"No," he said. "Days ago. Ridiculous."

"That's why you didn't show up again!"

"It's nothing. Just the electricity broke—"

"What electricity?"

"At the hotel. So the hotplate—"

"Oh, for Christ's sake!" I said. After his attacks the moron lived off his hotplate on boiled milk and milk-soaked bread; and since the hotplate didn't work, he was simply starving to death, right before my eyes.

"Now don't you make a move," I said. "You're such a goddamn child! You stay put till I come back!"

The kitchen, like the rest of the house, seemed entirely lifeless. I'd never been in it before. It had a dim high ceiling which further emptied an emptiness, a gas lighter which looked like a praying mantis, a glum-looking black gas stove which when lit howled like a dervish set afire. The pantry yielded milk and lots of stale bread, thank God, and nothing else except an enormous dead ant.

Nothing bothered me. I strode through a grotto filled with laughing gas. She and I were going off for good. Even being stuck with Julius was all right. He made my lone room a family apartment, a whole cozy warren of annoyances and solicitudes; a homey base from which to make my final sally and carry her off. I swept the hot milk pan off the dervish stove and ran upstairs.

And Julius ate away, all the milk with bread soaked into it. He sat up, strengthened.

"Where does the Prince live?"

"Upstairs," I said. "Better finish the bread."

"Let's go up now," he said. "Tell him my idea."

"First get back your strength."

He did, too. No longer feeble, he was no longer crestfallen. He began to modify his new approach. The idea now was to convert the Prince to Judaism at the Old Testament Community. A coup! We would map out a campaign, theological and philosophical approaches. . . . Stomach full, he became very happy and somewhat drowsy. . . . We would conceive a whole new strategy tomorrow. . . . He nodded at me with his eyes content and heavy. . . . We would not be rash this time . . . we would sleep on it, consider all the avenues. . . . And he began to consider them, and then, slowly, really to sleep on it.

His hand was still clamped argumentatively around my wrist, just below her suck mark. Not a move out of me. I wanted his sleep to deepen before removing his fingers and then going upstairs to her. Before making my definitive, conclusive ascent. I stayed by the window, in my chair, uncle-sitting, waiting and watching, and saw, as if in a dream, Ahn. He walked down there, through the twilight, cane in one hand, the other throwing up and catching a few coins. He must have just paid off a taxi, coming from town, dressed in a long overcoat and a homburg hat, no doubt fresh from some damn Casino-bidding exploit. And, no doubt, he knew by now that he couldn't stop us. He walked in this peculiar trance, tossing up coins, catching, losing a few heedlessly. At one of the marble benches near the manor he stopped. He took off his overcoat and threw it on the bench. It missed and fell on the wet grass. He stared at it. He let it lie there. He stepped on it and past it, strode slowly off toward the chapel.

The abandoned coat on the ground looked so strange that, unconsciously, I looked to see whether the sight had awakened Julius. He slept. His hand was still around my wrist; his body leaned forward slightly to my shoulder, with a touching confidence, as if he could sleep on only with my continued help; his mouth was relaxed into softness and just slightly, naïvely, even youthfully open. There was a sweet eagerness in my uncle's black-coated slump, an ability to rest in restlessness that only small boys or nomads have. Every time I moved, he sighed. His perennial tireless tiredness seeped from his fingers into my wrist. I waited for Ahn to return because I had decided it'd be a mangy showdown without the doctor. I wanted old Ahn to see me bear his daughter away. For good. I even wanted the Prince to see that; to show him, when we met at last, that there were a few surprises up *my* sleeve too.

I strained my eyes for the doctor's coat on the grass, but it had become too dark; too dark for the Chinese fishermen grinning from the silk screen, too dark even to distinguish the wrinkles on Julius' forehead underneath the hat. His breath came a little stronger now and merged with the hiss of chestnut leaves outside the window. I knew she'd come with me if I made it for good. I felt calm and sure after a series of exhausting days. My uncle breathed and the twigs outside sailed through the dark. They grew into my room. They enveloped Julius and me into their foliage, and slowly, very slowly—I don't remember fighting against it—slowly I myself became a branch that swayed together with my uncle in the night and joined the other branches at her magic suck mark on my wrist.

That night Julius ushered me into and out of sleep.

I was awakened by his hat which beat against my elbow, and by his voice which was breathing something about hellhounds in the water closet.

"After a—call of nature," he was now whispering, "on the way back—you didn't hear?—they tried to bite me!"

The next moment I heard it. A sharp thud on the floor above. My watch hand pointed to a phosphorescent four a.m. I tried hard to figure out why. The room floundered in darkness and daze. On the silk screen the Chinese fishermen bowed impassive in the flare of Julius' match. Thud. Someone was trying to kick in something upstairs.

"You see? They're killing the Prince!"

So far only my reflexes were awake. I ran because Julius was running. At the landing the dogs, seeing me along, didn't bite, only snarled. And then we were on the second floor.

That moment exists in my brain as a permanent, objective, three-dimensional fact. It's like a detail from the Chinese screen, sturdily stitched, yet delicate and stylized, mysteriously profound. In the background is the black lightless corridor stretching away into the dregs of night. In the foreground, under a gas lamp, by the rose doorknob, two figures stand face to face. Two men with their hands on each other's shoulders, mutually inclined as if about to dance. One, Ahn, in his tweed suit, minus the overcoat lying on the garden grass, grave and serene. The other, dressed in loose gray pajamas; his face, as construed by the gas lamp, is bulky with the imperious nose of Prince Schatten, his craggy chin, his half-closed heavy eyes.

But the eyes open fully and one leg moves forward. That motion is fatal. It always destroys the scene, pushes it into the maelstrom of life. The eyes widen, the leg twitches into a kick aimed at the rose doorknob. Abruptly, a misproportion warps the Prince's face: the cheeks too drawn and yet too young; the hair too thin and yet not white enough; in the pupils a terrible dilation. Ahn turns out to be not holding but choking him. The Prince's whole visage swells weirdly into rejuvenation. His cheeks puff and grow ruddy with uprushing blood. His lips tumesce into red lushness, his hair shakes youthful down his temple, the whole face brims with sensuality.

And it rises toward the lamp as the bridegroom of the wedding photograph, her Tin Soldier, Schatten's miserable grandson—and then, before the leg can really kick in his wife's door, he falls away unconscious to the floor.

"*Him!*" said my uncle. "Police! . . ." And was gone, past the dogs' riot on the stairs.

Silence.

"Will you help carry?" Ahn said, lightly somehow through his fast breathing. And I, still acting by reflex, helped. I picked up that waxen, sweating effigy. All I

remember of my thoughts at that point is an empty
rotation: *The end of the fable—withdrawal symptoms.
Withdrawal symptoms—the end of the fable.*

Together we carried him into the huge room, the
Prince's room, the innermost room of the manor. It had a
pyramided chandelier, sconces, carved pillars, the great
escutcheon on the mantelpiece. And for furniture, two
cots, a pile of smudged magazines, an overturned chair
and a low table also overturned, with cups and saucers
scattered on the parquet floor. The lovely chandelier
hung over a junky's pad.

Ahn didn't seem at all bothered. We set down our
burden on a cot, and almost immediately he sank something professional and elegant into that scraggly arm and
then threw the thing into the fireplace the way you do an
empty bottle.

"The last of the wine," he said, smiling slightly
through his strained breath. Exhausted, but with ironic
formality, he sat down on a footstool and gathered
together the dishes from the overturned table. Cups and
saucers, all whole. All lovely, flowered, unbreakable
asylum dishes.

"We've lost our wine waiter, you know. You've made
it too risky for him. He's gone on to much better
things."

I must have stared into that ancient sardonic smile for a
whole minute. It took me that long to comprehend.

"KarlHeinz," I said. Ye olde drug pusher. And I'd
never smelled him out. I stood there, dazed, and watched
Ahn. He was tucking a unicorn-emblazoned eiderdown
around the princely effigy; he stroked a forelock out of
the effigy's face; an old man playing tenderly with a life-
size doll.

"Well," he said quite lightly, quite as if he were his old self, "I told you you'd have your appointment with His Highness." I saw that he was really quite proud of this "Highness" who was, after all, his personal work of art. He walked about with briskness, righting chairs, assembling all the props for The Appointment.

Suddenly I was awake. Feeling flooded back; sheer tearing anger. There was my friend Ahn, moving with such crystalline grace, and here I, a dumb emotional mess. Nothing had changed, even now.

I think I started shouting at him. Of all people that night, I was the one to get hysterical. I felt so painfully, intolerably trapped. I shouted into that horrible room, tried to shout it down. What maddened me most was that Ahn could have spared me all this by lying to me just a little differently at the start. He could have said his fake Prince was away for a year instead of a week. I'd have gone away happily, I'd have switched to the Volksrocket, the whole excruciating mess would have been spared me. I shouted all that at him.

He squatted on the floor, ordering the pile of magazines, but could still look at me with his familiar affable snootiness. "Oh, we did send him away for a few weeks," he said. "Because of you. But he had to come back for the license renewal. He wanted to, anyway. He wanted his home. He's our Prince, you know."

"Yes," I said. "Congratulations!"

"He's alive for only a few hours a day," Ahn said. "And he doesn't wean easily now that he's lost his wine." The tea service was being reassembled on the righted table cup by cup for some preposterous four a.m. tea. "But he's our Prince. You see, I warned the old one not to die. I told him I'd have to get another. Would you be good enough? The saucer on the floor there? Right by your foot?"

I tossed it to him and he caught it. "Very kind," he said. "The funny thing is, this one was always so proud of his grandfather, despite his frightful Party. So I made him the grandfather. Lately we needn't even whiten the hair. D'you think we should?" He smoothed the effigy's fore-lock. "Occasionally I have to take him out for something official, and he's very sweet once he's had his wine. Only at first he had too many curlicues in the signature. It's perfect now, as long as his hand is steady. This one's *my* Prince, you know. As a last favor, that spoon under the cot?"

"You're a very smooth fraud," I said—and caught myself using, ludicrously, the intonation of an intimate family quarrel.

He smiled. "I ought to tell you," he said, "I knew you'd outbid me on the three-acre site. I knew you'd make a fight for it. You really got involved here. I liked that from the start. Remember some of the arguments we had together? The feeding walk we took?" He chuckled and deliberated how to place a vase as centerpiece. "I always wondered," he said, "who we'd have to end this with. One of these bureaucrat vultures from the outside, that would have been dreadful. But you're not even from the outside any more—not quite, are you? Otherwise you wouldn't have gotten my daughter." He smiled at the door and I saw her standing there, since God knows when. Then he smiled at my shock of seeing her. "You know," he said, "I *would* appreciate that spoon under the cot. My back won't take much more bending."

I bent down and got the spoon for him.

"Thank you," he said. "I was thinking, if we could go

on after you, maybe I'd almost miss you." He chuckled
again and gave the vase a final adjustment. "You're a very
nice ending."

"You mean," I said, "I've got the privilege of telling the
authorities—"

"Oh, I'm sure that friend of yours—" his gesture
indicated Julius—"he's taken care of that already."

I asked, "And what is left for me?"

He looked at the tea service which was now so perfectly, absurdly assembled. He went to the door and put
his arm around Irene's shoulder. "Oh," he said, "a little
more time, I should think." He let go of her shoulder and
she made a move to follow him out to the corridor, but he
gentled her back into the room again, almost pointed her
at me.

"Good night," he said with an air easy and proprie-
tary, sardonic and nostalgic all at once, and don't ask me
how, but I remember that "Good night" so well. "Good
night," he said and walked out.

Before, I hadn't been able to stop shouting. Now I
couldn't get out a word. And so the most ruinous moment, which came next, came in silence.

She stood with her hands hooked in her smock, eyes
smoky, burned-out like the gas lamp, staring past me at the
window. Beyond the window the gardens lay, purplish-
black, nightmare-gray in the false dawn, a phantasma-
goric blight of ashen leaves from which the first birds
cried to be released. I was alone with her and that
calamitous window and the vain chandelier and the tea
service ornamenting the table with such eerie uselessness
and her bridegroom's effigy gulping air on the couch with
its mouth open.

"Since when?" I said, pointing at the effigy.

"Nine years ago," she said. "If it interests you. Just before the Prince died. Back from a Russian prison camp. Does it matter?"

She spoke quite lightly, like her father. Obviously she intended to be just as airy and untouchable. But both her hands clung to her smock.

"Very convenient," I said.

"Not really," she said. "It would have been convenient the open way. Maybe his record might have kept him from getting Schatten. But they would have denazified him. They would have cured him too. He wasn't always so far gone. By now he would be a nice rich car dealer, like all his friends."

I think that to hate a person enormously you have to love that person first. I could have gladly killed her. But I was determined not to lose control again.

"Sure," I said. "In the end you would have been proud of your bridegroom."

"It would have been a working marriage," she said. "I'd have put on a white bikini. Perhaps you would have met me at the lake restaurant."

"Instead you're a saint," I said. "You gave it all up for the estate."

"My dear," she said. "Have you a better illusion?"

"Better," I said. "Anything is better than this moment."

Suddenly it cracked, her infernal veneer. Her hands crushed the smock material. She wasn't as hard as Ahn.

"Tell me," I said. "What was more fun? Betraying him with me? Or me with him? Tell me about it."

My only relief was punishing her. All I could use was the technique of my rare fights with Nina. Ridiculous, yet it worked. Her eyes had grown dire and moist. But she was still trying the light tone.

"With your permission," she said. "We wanted to keep Schatten. We couldn't, without continuing the Prince. Do you mind very much? That my father got a little bit of a reprieve that way?"

"And that you got the thrill of *him* meanwhile?"

A laugh broke out of her face, from under those dire eyes. "Thrill," she said. "This place becomes perfect only after there are no more thrills. I've been waiting for that. I've been praying for middle age. And just when it comes, you kill it off. Your timing is good."

"Obviously I didn't kill your idyll with him," I said.

She took a deep breath. "I had one brilliant year with him," she said, "twenty years ago. And two years with Jacques after the war. And even with you, one dawn and twelve afternoons. They all thrilled me. They all pass. You are passing now."

"Yes, I'm passing now," I said.

"My father is right," she said. "There is nothing outside."

"No," I said, "nothing and no one. So you needn't be faithful to anyone outside. Thank you for the logic."

She fumbled in her bag. "I need a cigarette," she said.

I found one, from a pack in my pocket. But as I gave it to her, our fingers touched. I couldn't harden any more than she.

"We can still go," I said. "To Stockholm."

We looked at each other.

"Little White Riding Hood died," she said.

"When?"

"This afternoon. I buried her."

She coughed. She had inhaled badly. Her full blond hair was shaking. And my arms laid themselves, helplessly, around her shoulders.

There's one small gesture two human beings have against death, infinity and loneliness, against all the intrinsic hopelessness of man. They can put their arms around each other. I put my arms around her. And the warmth of our bodies, the rough trembling texture of her warm smock, at last unfroze my soul. And then it poured out of me.

I told her it could still be managed. There was no reason in the world why not. We could still go, better than ever now that everything was clear and open to me. I could get *him*—I could only point to the thing on the cot—to a hospital where he'd be taken care of. She needn't concern herself any more. She was rid of that responsibility. And I'd have our lawyers take care of her father. Because of his age and good record, nothing would happen to him. And I'd cable Dave the shift to Frederick the Great, and to give the Frederick pageant time to develop we'd open Stockholm first. That way I could leave for Sweden. We really could go to Stockholm now, and that only as a beginning. We really could fly off together.

For several seconds she was a lovely bitter icicle, stiff inside the crooks of my elbows. Then she didn't melt. She broke. She shattered into small hard cries against my chest.

"Yes?" I asked into her ear.

She nodded. I remember the motion of her hair, her face and shoulders against mine. I held her. We walked together into the corridor, down the snake-head balustrade, past the jumping dogs, across the rigid empty hall into the grounds. Sunrise already greened the leaves in the gray gardens, and more birds stirred. Some young light had just leaped onto the treetops, the lake rippled pink, and the world was full of dew and jasmine and twitter and hope. I picked up her father's hat and coat which had lain the night through on the ground. The chapel door was open, meaning that he had retreated there. The coat was scented with clover and wet grass and I put it on a bench. I felt her shudder against me. We walked together with the crude rapture of a brand-new couple, my hand around her waist, her fingers curled through my button-hole, and I hoped Ahn saw us from the chapel.

Beyond the lake the mossy flagstones pushed soft against our stride, and I still feel the touch of wild wet yew against my shoulder, next to her hand. We stopped to rehearse again the future's practicalities: the cables and the flight reservations which were my chore; the packing she'd have to do meanwhile; and the cab with which I'd return at ten a.m. sharp to take her away.

We kissed at the gate. She took a leaf, a lovely rust-colored leaf, and put it through my buttonhole her finger had to relinquish, and I began to hunt, with furious heart-pounding happiness, for a taxi.

My impulse is to rush straight to the end. But there is no end without the golden little café just before it. The golden little café existed, believe it or not, for ten minutes or even more. I found it opposite Julius' hotel, where incidentally he had not yet arrived. The café terrace abutted on one of those green lots which in Berlin can be either a small overgrown park or a big overgrown ruin. The golden little café looms with great clarity in my recollection, considering how giddy I was with a radical new future, with bewildered triumph, with visions and confusions. I settled into a terrace chair; roused a dreamy table-dusting waiter into the promise of breakfast, and tried to distill from all the excitement the phrasing of a number of revolutionary cables.

The sky had that impossible, ingenue early-morning blue. The last of the milk wagons bumped along like four-wheeled sleepwalkers. One cyclist pedaled past, brightly wound up. One green-capped policeman jaunted, made of the very best of tin. Otherwise the street stretched in repose, no Julius in sight, which made me smile, for he was hardly the type to make a taxi stop for him at dawn. Oh, I enjoyed that golden little café.

Only, the phrases for my cables wouldn't crystallize. The waiter refused to appear with my breakfast. I went after him, into the inside of the café, and didn't see him. I did see a telephone booth and called Ida's office to tell her to withdraw our Casino-site bid and cancel our Schatten project. No one answered, of course. It was too early. My watch said half past seven.

I went back to my table. The sun had climbed the roofs. Brimming black with workers, the first buses rolled. My cables failed to resolve themselves into words. Behind me, in the bosky lot, a pneumatic drill began to volley. The little café was not golden any more.

It had nothing to do with the cable messages that had such a difficult birth; nor with the still more difficult call to Nina I'd have to devise before long; nor my impatience for Julius, my irritation with the waiter who withheld my coffee, nor my sudden hunger and fatigue.

No, it was the city. It was just that I could see the city more clearly, the street and its relentless waking into day. All about me the smoothness and sleek glints welled up which I remembered from my first day in Berlin. A shashlik stand which had fed the roamers of the night folded abruptly into spic-and-span aluminum boards; napkins stained with whores' lipstick vanished under a lustrously clean ashcan lid. A thin man walked away. On the very spot a fat man opened a flower kiosk trimmed with leaves which he watered against the waxing sun. A garage door opened to pour forth a huge shining stream of limousines. Shopgirls rolled up window shutters with crisp clangs. They unwrapped a brand-new street, lavish with displays of electric toothbrushes and minked mannikins and television sets on special sale for five hundred marks. A baby elephant of a sanitation truck sprinkled the sidewalks, and the sidewalks sprouted patent pumps, silk knees, poodles, pigskin valises, a carousel of polished car chrome wheeling past the curb. All around me the tables filled with business gentry who bit off cigar ends, and ordered two eggs, and opened their paper with crackling good Cold War news, and leaned back to enjoy the sun.

And I was filled with terror. The city day had just driven across our vows. It had plowed right through our future together. She would never come. It took me that long to realize it. These people here, clacking past on their prim murderous stiletto heels, each owned a white bikini. And she'd never join them. She could never skate so glibly from night into day with me, from Schatten to Stockholm. It was a hollow futuristic Stockholm around me, a cold-creamed smooth-shaven oblivion, a darkness across which had been smeared ten thousand shiny marked-down television sets. She could never romp those Afghans at her ease here. She would not come. Not to this.

And if not to this, where could I take her? Where,

after Dave? To some sour faculty apartment, me struggling with freshman themes and rejection slips, she a middle-aged faculty wife with a smirked-at accent, smelling of beef stew? All our visions melted before the clanging sun; shrank into a dead iridescence, some four a.m. foolishness already long past. Only Nina prevailed against the daylight with powerful familiarity, with conquering affection.

I couldn't face that. To get away from that, from the hunger and fatigue that wouldn't let me fight the city day, I shouted for breakfast. But breakfast wouldn't come. Nor would the cables that were supposed to flesh out four a.m., that were supposed to help me fight the city day. Did she sense the helplessness of my pencil above the empty cable forms?

It lifted me to my feet. I had to tell her that she had to come right now, even before the obstinate cables. The only reason I couldn't write them was that she didn't sit by my side. Suddenly I became so afraid for her, for her fine curved eyebrows, the lovely large white forehead. I was panicking. I waved for the waiter, gave up, left a ten-mark bill.

And I sat in a taxi, up in front, next to the driver to guide and goad him better toward Schatten. Double fare for going top speed. We swiveled, we screeched through the long litany of streets familiar to me from so many shuttlings back and forth. But this morning the turns, the crossings, the traffic lights seemed endless, each a distinct and painful delay, a new separation from her. Each block had become longer. And as we finally came close and passed the pet shop, not only the final streets appeared to multiply, but the people on them. People came out of their houses in incredible numbers; they swarmed in front of us and with us toward Schatten, they barely let us bully and horn our way through them—they all wanted to keep me from her.

But then we did reach the Venetian bridge. I got out, rammed my way right through some men protesting on the bridge. And the city which I'd watched grow out of dawn into whirring enormity, the city which had expanded as we drove—the city would not stop that day. Not even the iron gate of Schatten could withstand it.

Like a floodtide the city had boiled up and broken through. It had breached the fence from East and West. It had spilled into the gardens. City dust grayed into the misty green, rimmed leaves, lawns, hedges. Deep into the park the city had penetrated with the hard unmerciful contours of ambulances painted white and red, with crimson fire engines, with the clinical shapes of fire hose and oxygen tanks. The city was there with the crisp gray uniforms of East German guards and the metal helmets of West German policemen. Together they had overrun the manor.

The whole front of the house stood unscathed, had only an ominous cast in one eye. A single window was cracked. The poplars were intact, hissing with the same motionlessness to the same breeze. Very small parts of the pagoda tower had come off, bits of roof floating like ducks in the lake. But the back of the manor lay partly ripped open, and the chapel was disemboweled. Of one wall nothing was left except the very heavy and mullioned stained-glass window; Jesus hovered in the air, perforated, with the stained-glass sun exploding under him.

Most of the old crew—no, all of them, since I saw all nine—huddled by the big pergola, harried by the ambulance men and the press at once. They were all right; I knew that just as I knew she was not, neither she nor the Ahns. And as I pressed forward madly to find her, I thought of the bomb that had been there all along, underneath, waiting, waiting ever since the God-forsaken chapel had been built, waiting till Ahn was ready.

But now that it had happened, it looked as though it had happened years ago. With its combination of old death and new hustle, the estate had become another suburb of Berlin. It was no longer Schatten but new Berlin surrounding me here, coming down on me with busy greedy voices, the babel of a dozen reporters mingled with the snorty organ of a police officer who poised a big ballpoint pen.

My name? Occupation? True Marlene Dietrich once sang here in the 'twenties? How long resident at Schatten? Pose before the dead peacock? Age? Ever been to the chapel under which the old Ami bomb exploded? Any idea why they never let the police cart it off? So they could blow the place up one day? And who put the brand-new fuse on? Insurance angle there? Ready to identify the bodies of the Prince and of the doctor's family? Any idea why the four of them went to the chapel just before the blast? Inside exclusive as surviving Schatten resident? Any dope why the daughter's body found away from the others? Way over by the entrance? True she was beautiful? Got some sexy candids? Citizenship? Pose against the Schatten crest, please?

I stood there as it came down on me. I stood there while fine particles of debris still sifted through the branches onto the grass. I saw with odd surprise that a few

Schatten trees had begun to turn, as ordinary trees do in ordinary autumns in ordinary gardens. Yet her yew house with its pruned little spires remained stubbornly and glitteringly green. I didn't even know where she lay now, whether her hair was loose or drenched in rubble or untouched. The poplars hissed in the breeze. Two blue jays, exhilarated by all the commotion, pursued each other down the lake. And the sun shone, as golden and indifferent as ever.

I stood there. Julius emerged from behind the crowd. He looked almost like a darkroom negative, his black hat squashed awry against the left temple, his face beneath white and pinched. He couldn't get to me because of all the people between us. So he raised himself on tiptoe, raised his arm at me, pressed his glasses back, his eyes swelling black into focus with the imminence of some irate and terrible message.

That moment the photographers discovered him. A pictorial bonanza. There was a turning around, a stampede, and the last I saw of him was his black coattails pursued by flashbulbs.

He delivered me. Everything eased. A new police official supplanted the ballpoint pen. He had a lot of rank on his collar and a blond-downy hand which shook mine. With a single gesture he cleared a path for us. Utterly relieved to see me safe. Frau Dr. Holze would be so utterly relieved also. And I could walk away with him.

He offered a limousine, a long gray car with footrests and blinds and even a telephone which could communicate utter relief to Ida's office. When I looked through the blinds, the streets were basking in the midmorning sun. Quite innocuously. A dozen blocks away, and the city had already forgotten all. I remember glimpsing a man bent down to tie his shoelaces. A child stroked a large cat. We drove slowly, and I thought how everything runs down, evens out, smooths away. Only death is sure; and in the light of death, life consists of nice irrelevant children stroking large pointless cats.

Just then the car rolled over my uncle. Not him, of course, just the shadow of a tall dark pedestrian. And she flicked into my brain, and Little White Riding Hood, and her long stride across the flagstones, and her face half-shadowed in the Five O'Clock Tea, and her, and her, and her.

I wondered, as I have done countless times since, whether she hadn't changed her mind at the last moment, hadn't been on her way to me after all when the bomb caught her—whether that was the reason she was found by the door. She became present within me with such tearing, useless pain. I wanted to wrench the wheel out of the driver's hands and head back to that moment in the dawn where she stood by the gate, her finger in my buttonhole. I wanted to pull her away with me, away from this righteous unforgivable Teutonic self-obliteration of hers, away from the black fact that she'd never stand next to me again and suck her cheeks into a smile. I tried to find relief by hating her father and his murderous insanity. But, abominably enough, he wouldn't let himself be hated, not while the limousine purred through these sunny fat streets. All I could summon against his madness was the corruption everywhere around me. I couldn't hate him with any satisfying effectiveness, because I felt myself so safely and gracefully corrupt, managing to make conversation with the police official right through my most lacerating thoughts.

And since I couldn't come to terms with the thing in

any way as yet, I retreated from it. Suddenly I realized that the Stockholm Dowle must indeed be opened first, before Berlin; not only to give us time for Frederick the Great, but also to dissipate whatever macabre overtones the disaster might bring on our local Oyster. Suddenly the cables poured from my head onto my note pad. For Dave it would be no tragedy. It did get him off the hook. Frederick the Great would be much more fun, much kookier even than playing Teddy Roosevelt. Maybe it was just as well that Nina might hear a news report of the explosion before getting my own message. It would make her so unquestioningly glad of my survival.

As I jotted down the cables, sheltering myself in triviality, the relief could no longer be denied. A bitter, horrible, but inescapable relief which had been there all along. It pushed itself into the foreground now, together with the realization that I hadn't eaten since lunchtime of the day before. The Ku-damm swung into view and with it the first big terrace café, cake trays shimmering in the sun. I knew I'd have to come to grips with the thing later, but to have strength for it I asked the driver to stop.

They had what I had hoped for, yeast buns.

FREDERIC MORTON

Frederic Morton was born in Vienna, Austria, in 1924. With the advent of the Nazis in 1938, he and his family escaped to London, where he became a baker's apprentice. In 1940 they arrived in New York, and Mr. Morton completed his education at City College and the New School. At the age of 22 he wrote his first novel, *The Hound*, for which he was awarded Dodd, Mead's 1947 Intercollegiate Literary Prize. Subsequently he received a Breadloaf Writers' Conference fellowship and Yaddo residence fellowships; he became a Columbia University Fellow in 1955. In addition to *The Hound* he has published three other novels: *The Darkness Below* (1949), *Asphalt and Desire* (1952) and *The Witching Ship* (1960). His first nonfiction book, *The Rothschilds*, was published in 1962 and was the number-one best-seller for many months that year. Mr. Morton has written essays and articles for *The Nation* and *The Reporter* and he is a regular contributor to *Holiday*. His short stories have appeared in *Playboy*, *Esquire*, *The Atlantic Monthly* and the *Hudson Review*. Mr. Morton and his wife divide their time between Europe and New York City.